HARUM SCARUM

FELICITY YOUNG

Felicity Young was born in Hanover, Germany, in 1960 and went to boarding school in the United Kingdom while her parents were posted around the world with the British Army. When her father retired from the army in 1976 the family settled in Perth. Felicity married at nineteen while she was still doing her nursing training and on completion of training had three children in quick succession. Not surprisingly, an arts degree at the University of Western Australia took ten years to complete. In 1990 Felicity and her family moved from the city and established a Suffolk sheep stud on a small farm in Gidgegannup where she studied music, reared orphan kangaroos and started writing.

Having a brother-in-law who is a retired police superintendent, it was almost inevitable she would turn to crime writing.

Her first novel, *A Certain Malice*, was published in Britain by Crème de la Crime in 2005, and her second, *An Easeful Death* — the first Stevie Hooper crime novel — was published in 2007 by Fremantle Press.

To Mick with love

Glossary

The following is a list of Internet slang, abbreviations and symbols used in this novel.

;) :	wink
2moro:	tomorrow
F2F:	face to face
Gr8:	great
LOL:	laugh out loud
OMG:	Oh my God
PIR:	parent in room
ROFLMAO:	rolling on floor laughing my arse off
SME:	send me email
Squeeeeeee:	expression of glee
TDTM:	talk dirty to me
Rock spider:	prison slang for paedophile
Fan fiction:	stories written by fans about book and TV characters

For other useful abbreviations, please refer to:
http://www.noslang.com/top20.php

Prologue

Night. On the highway a car breaks away from the line of crawling headlights, turns down one side street and then another until it comes to a halt in wasteland near the river's edge. Under the full moon the river gleams soft as polished silver. Three figures get out of the car; they seem to be men, though they appear as no more than silhouettes. One is tall, one is of solid build and the other is small and as slight as the bamboo that grows in clumps along the river's edge, and trembles almost as much.

If the small man is frightened, the tall man is clearly terrified, standing hunched against the car as if he is cold. It is not hard to imagine the stink of his fear, fetid as the drying pools near the river. The solid man yanks the tall man away from the car and shoves him stumbling towards the water's edge. The small man follows, head lowered, hands rammed deep in his pockets.

The water laps at the shore. Mosquitoes drill the air.

The heavy man shouts and shoves the tall figure to the ground, then kicks him in his side. The small man turns his back, as if he cannot bear to watch. Heavy man barks an order. Small man shakes his head and looks with what must be longing back to the parked car. Tall man screams like a woman and the small man's gaze is drawn to the sound as if to a train wreck. If this were a film the camera would follow his gaze back to the solid man squatting over the tall man, his weight pinning him down, a blade flashing in his hand.

Then a burst of flame slices the blackness and the man with the blade topples over with a cry. His quarry eases out from under him and slowly pushes himself to his feet. He makes a sound that is part sob, part groan. He looks around him, but the sound of the shot has been absorbed into the silence. He puts his hand to the neck of the man he has shot and leaves it there a moment. Then he plucks the knife from the limp hand.

'Help me,' he pleads to the small man who cowers shaking but otherwise motionless.

The small man shakes his head, takes a few steps back on the rocky ground.

'God help me,' the tall man mutters again. He takes the knife and begins to slice at the dead man's face. He is no longer panicking; there is now a sense of calm purpose about him. After a while he looks up and says to the small man, 'I know who you are.' He stares at him for a moment then turns back to the gruesome task of carving and slicing, hand gloved with blood and glistening in the moonlight.

'And I know you too,' the small man shouts in a high-pitched cry as he turns his back and runs.

Monday

1

Excerpt from chat room transcript 080207
TIMTAM: thnx for the pic. Ur 1 hot chick
ANGEL12: wt about u?
TIMTAM: a bit like the drummer in the SMs ;)
ANGEL12: squeeeeeeee!!!
TIMTAM: ive got the stuff u wanted – wanna meet F2F?

Detective Sergeant Stephanie 'Stevie' Hooper wiped her sweaty palms against the legs of her jeans before checking her oversized watch. 'Not long now,' she said softly into her collar mike.

'These creeps are never late,' came Tash's response through her earpiece.

Stevie looked across the grass to a ragged patch of bush similar to the one where she hid.

'See anything?' Stevie kept her voice low.

'Not yet.'

Stevie scanned the adventure playground, deserted cafe area and car parking bays beyond. On the lawn nearby a young couple organised a picnic breakfast, spreading out the blanket and unpacking their basket. She noted with appreciation how the mother's gaze never strayed for more than a few seconds from the two small boys tussling in the sand beneath the slide. It was still early morning, there were few others about.

'Hey,' Tash whispered. 'A white panel van's just pulled into one of the parking bays across the road. A guy's getting out.'

Stevie peered towards the car park. 'Description?'

'Trilby hat, grey boardies, white T-shirt — he's coming down the path near the lake, heading towards you. It's Mason, it has to be.'

The man entered Stevie's line of vision, keeping to the shadows of the path and looking about this way and that.

'Yup, got him now,' she said, watching the man as he sat down on a bench beside a park signpost, looked at his watch.

'You ready?'

'Tash,' Stevie smiled, 'I was born ready.'

She took a breath and stepped from the shelter of the scrub and casually approached the man on the park bench, hands in the back pockets of her jeans, bubble soled trainers springing across the spongy grass. She adjusted the collar of her shirt so that the microphone was well hidden.

The man tensed when she sat next to him, and wriggled as far to the end of the bench as he could go. A fly floated through the sunshine and settled on his nose. He gave it an angry swipe and stood as if to leave.

Now or never, Stevie thought, taking a breath. 'Hey,' she called out. The man turned and she said, 'Cool hat.'

'Yeah.' He was younger than she'd expected, late twenties at the most. He had the name of a local rock band printed on his T-shirt.

'It's like the hat the drummer of the Stoned Mullets wears, isn't it? I love that band, one of my faves.'

The man grunted and turned away. She got to her feet and stopped him with a tap on the shoulder.

'Where did you get it? The hat I mean, I'd really like a hat like that.'

'Piss off, lady.'

His irritation proved irresistible to Stevie. She followed him to the lake, sticking as close as an annoying puppy.

Jeez, I love my job.

The water level of the lake had dropped and the air was tainted with the dank earthy smell of mud.

Stevie prattled on. 'If you're a fan of the band, you should check out their website, they have a chat room and ...' she broke off when he stopped mid stride and turned to face her. Feigning deep thought, she slid her fingers through her blond ponytail and looked him up and down. 'Come to think of it, you wouldn't happen to be Robert ...'

The guy reacted faster than she'd anticipated. Stevie swerved in time to miss the impact of the punch, but not enough to prevent the man's ring from catching her cheek and splitting the skin. She swore and called out to Tash for assistance.

He must have guessed they would try to cut him off from his car because he changed direction with a sharp swerve, taking off at a run towards the grassy Broadwalk. He hurdled the family's picnic basket, the trilby flying off his head and landing in their fruit salad. The adults sprang to their feet and watched the chase unfold with mouths agape. The little boys panicked and ran from the sandpit towards their parents, forcing Stevie to dodge left then right to avoid bowling them over.

Mason was already sprinting up the steep gradient of the Broadwalk towards the DNA tower — 1.3 k, the sign said. Stevie wondered how she was ever going to catch him. Her chest already burned. Give up the smokes, give up the smokes, gotta give up the smokes, she chanted in her head to the rhythm of her pounding feet. Her legs screamed, must get back, must get back, must get back to the gym. But she kept running, despite the widening gap between them. She'd rather suffer a heart attack than let the creep escape.

He came to where the road cut across the grassy sward,

confident enough now to slow to a fast walk. Stevie gained a little ground. If I were him I'd head down one of the bush tracks, she thought. Or make a sharp turn at the road and highjack one of the cars meandering through the park at funereal speed. I can't continue this chase on foot — Tash, where the hell are you?

Her silent curses were answered by the scream of Tash's trail bike from somewhere in the scrub at the side.

Mason had reached the double helix of the DNA tower and was leaning against a metal strut to catch his breath when Tash emerged from the bush on foot. 'Hold it right there!' she shouted, knees bent, arms and weapon extended. The man seemed even more stunned at the sight of the gun than Stevie, and stared back bug-eyed at the small, dark-haired woman in the tight black jeans and T-shirt. Tash approached to within a few metres of him, her Glock never wavering from his head.

Stevie caught up with them, bent at the waist, gulping air like a fire-eater.

'Shit, Tash, I didn't know you were going to be armed,' she gasped.

'Yeah, well, it pays to be a step ahead. There's no one around, no witnesses, so what?'

'W-what are you talking about?' Mason stammered, edging as far back into the tower as he could go.

'What I'm saying, shit head,' Tash answered through clenched teeth, 'is that we don't have to go by the rules with creeps like you.'

Stevie's spine tingled uneasily. What the hell was Tash playing at? This was not in the script, but she couldn't say anything in front of Mason. If he realised how out of order this was, the case would never stand up in court. She moved over to where the man stood, the sweat already turning cold upon her body. But she knew it was neither the cold sweat nor the exhaustion that made her fumble with the cuffs on her belt, dropping them once before managing to pin the man's hands behind his back. When I turn back around, she told herself, Tash will have put away the gun and I can pretend I've never seen it.

Wrong.

Tash stepped closer to their prisoner, waving the gun in his face. 'Robert Mason, you have been soliciting children over the Internet, pretending you're something you're not in order to have sex and do God knows what else to them.' She pressed her face within inches of the quaking man's. 'That's true isn't it?'

Mason shook his head violently, sweat flying from his short spiky hair. Tash took a step back and wiped her face.

Stevie pinched her partner's elbow and indicated for her to drop the gun. 'Tash ...' she warned.

'You can have it when this guy admits what he was doing,' Tash muttered. She drew the slide and Stevie held her breath.

Mason gasped. 'Oh fuck, okay, okay. Yes, I thought I was meeting a kid, yes, I was after sex, but it would've been consensual ...'

'Angel12 thought she was meeting a boy a similar age to herself. You knew she was a fan of the Stoned Mullets and you conned her, promising to give her posters and CDs if she met up with you,' Tash said.

'I didn't —'

'And if you hadn't started talking dirty, you might have got away with it — you just couldn't help yourself could you?'

'No!'

Stevie intervened, 'Robert Mason, I'm arresting you ...'

Aghast, Stevie watched as Tash pulled the trigger and Robert Mason staggered back as a stream of water hit him between the eyes. He fell, cracking his head against one of the metal struts of the DNA tower before crumpling in a heap.

'Tash, get away from him — right now!' Stevie pushed the words through the side of her mouth, hoping Mason wouldn't hear.

Tash was laughing so much she seemed incapable of action. Stevie snatched the gun from her and rolled the man over.

'Who the hell are you?' he stammered, blinking up at her.

Stevie clenched her jaw and snapped the plastic barrel across her knee before tossing the pieces into a nearby bin. 'You can call me Angel12 if you like.'

They handed Mason over to the custody sergeant. Tash suggested a cuppa in the canteen but Stevie guided her towards the nearest interview room and kicked the door shut behind them.

Her anger was at last free to boil over. 'What the hell do you think you were you playing at there in the park — Dirty Harry?'

'Jesus, you don't have to blow a gasket. This acting officer in charge crap has really gone to your head, hasn't it? It's totally wiped away your sense of humour.' Tash folded her arms and set her mouth in a tight line.

Stevie pointed to a chair. 'Sit down.'

Tash remained standing, one leg tucked back against the wall. 'Welcome to the real world,' she said coldly.

'Excuse me?'

'You're new to Sex Crimes, this is how we work.'

'Bullshit.'

'Yeah, well, just wait — it won't take long before it starts getting you down too. Day in day out, dealing with the scum of the earth — Mason got off lucky.'

'Oh c'mon, there's more to it than that,' Stevie said. 'What about the bust we did where that rock-spider dressed himself in drag to try and catch the kid? You didn't lose it with him.

Something's wrong, I know you, remember? You're going to have to give me some kind of explanation for all this if you don't want me taking this further.'

Tash looked away. 'It's the job, I told you that; these animals who use and abuse for their own sick pleasure, never caring about the consequences to the kid, the physical trauma, the lifetime of emotional pain —'

'If it's getting to you that much, maybe you shouldn't be doing it any more, maybe you should apply to a different unit.'

Tash screwed her eyes tight for a moment. 'You going to tell Dolly, have me put in for a transfer?'

'I won't if you give can me a more credible explanation for your behaviour. And if you can't talk to me then I think you need to speak to one of the counsellors about this.'

Tash pushed away from the wall and dragged the chair from the table with a nerve-grating scrape. Taking her change in position as a begrudging sign of truce, Stevie pulled up a chair and sat down too.

Tash inspected her chewed nails. 'Robert Mason reminded me of someone I used to know, that's all,' she mumbled.

'Who?' Stevie and Tash had been friends since they were squad mates at the police academy and knew a lot of the same people.

'No one you know. Someone from a long time ago, one of Terry's teachers, young, cocky and good looking in a creepy kind of way. I was only a kid, but I remember thinking when I first met him that he had gravy eyes.' She finally looked up. 'Robert Mason has gravy eyes.'

Stevie sighed. Terry was Tash's brother — her disabled brother — who had been in her care since their parents had been killed several years ago in a car accident. Gravy eyes — what the hell was that supposed to mean? Was that really the trigger that had set her off?

'Can't say I noticed his eyes,' she said. 'And neither had you when you decided to pull that stupid toy gun on him. But go on.'

Tash took a deep breath. 'Terry had finally been accepted into our local high. It was a huge achievement, he'd spent most of his life at a special school and we were all so excited for him. I was still at primary school, but I remember how proud he was. And he settled in well, most of the kids were really nice to him. Then the maths teacher said he was showing potential, and offered to give Terry tuition without charge, said with some extra coaching, he might even be able to reach TEE standard.'

Stevie knew exactly where this was going.

'Every week Mum dropped him off for his tutoring and every week his behaviour got worse. He started getting into trouble at school, knocked a kid's tooth out in the playground, started wetting his bed, having tantrums. In the end we had to send him back to the special school. The sexual abuse from the maths teacher was revealed during a counselling session.'

'Was he prosecuted?'

'Oh yeah, he got five years. But Terry still gets violent mood swings, terrible nightmares — Mum blamed herself. He was a gorgeous placid kid.'

'And you blamed yourself too I bet.'

'As a kid I did, yeah, even though I was younger than him, I always saw myself as his protector.'

Stevie shook her head. And you still do blame yourself don't you? You've picked up your mother's mantle.

'Look,' Tash said. 'Don't tell anyone about this, will you? If anyone else in the unit got to hear about this I'd be under a microscope. It would colour everything I did.'

Maybe it already has, Stevie thought as she searched her friend's face. If this story had been revealed during the interviews and psychological screening that went with the job application, she would never have been accepted into Sex Crimes, Cyber Predator Unit. Christ, it was a serious breach just to withold that sort of information.

Just then the door swung open and a uniformed officer entered. He did a double take when he saw them sitting in what he'd assumed to be a vacant interview room.

With a slight curl of his lip he said, 'Oh, sorry ladies, didn't mean to disturb the mothers' meeting.'

Stevie rolled her eyes at him then said to Tash, 'Yeah, all this gossip's made me thirsty, how about a cuppa, Tash?'

As they slipped past the officer Tash nudged Stevie in the ribs. 'You swear?' she mouthed.

2

Excerpt from chat room transcript 110207
HARUM SCARUM: U goin 2 park 2 meet boy?
BETTYBO: yup. 2morow
HARUM SCARUM: omg plz dont
BETTYBO: Ynot?
HARUM SCARUM: sme

In another park not too far away, Bianca Webster ran. She felt light and fluttery, as if her heart wanted to fly from her mouth, as if her thongs had turned into giant, bouncy springs.

'Yay!' she screamed at the top of her lungs as she raced across the grass, barely feeling the weight of the laptop bag as it thumped upon her back. I'm Katy Enigma; my computer bag has become my jet-propelled backpack. Any minute now I will press the button and bounce from my springs into the air and stay there, swooping high and low over the park like a hawk, hunting out mystery and adventure, saving lives and righting wrongs.

But as she rounded the grassy corner she was forced to skid to a sudden halt. The springs buckled and crumbled to rust; the breath flew from her body.

She wasn't alone.

Ahead of her, two boys played on a seesaw. Bianca dropped to her knees and crept behind a bush to watch them. Her nose began to run but she didn't dare sniff. She turned her head and wiped it on her bare arm.

For a moment the boys seemed perfectly balanced, but then the heavier boy bounced on his end, making it sink. He was about nine, Bianca guessed, and he was really quite fat. The other one scowled, swearing, because he'd been stranded in the air. She saw it coming: all of a sudden the fat kid rolled off the seat and his mate came crashing down, landing hard on his bum. The fat kid laughed and the skinny kid began to blub, then took off with the fat kid chasing after him yelling, 'Slow down, slow down, arsehole!

Bianca didn't mind being invisible to the boys; most boys were dickheads, anyway, except for Daniel of course. But even though she didn't care about the boys, she found she'd lost that light airy feeling from before. Maybe it was a sign; maybe she shouldn't be doing this. Maybe she should turn around and go home. It felt as if she was the one sitting on the seesaw now.

Daniel said it was good to take risks because taking risks makes us feel alive, like she felt when she was running down the hill playing at being Katy Enigma. Katy might be pretend, but Daniel was real and cool and mega smart. More than anything else, Bianca wanted to be cool and smart like Daniel. She also wanted to show that snobby Zoë Carmichael that she could get a boyfriend who was clever and popular too, that she didn't need any of those teasing dickheads from school.

There wasn't anyone on the swings. The heat shimmered from the ground and made the chains wiggle like spaghetti. She should have worn shorts. Her heavy jeans rubbed as she walked, making her legs feel hot and sore.

There wasn't anyone else in the park at all now. She was early. She looked around and identified the meeting spot, a closed up ice cream kiosk. Too bad it was closed, she thought, it would've been good to have an ice cream while she waited.

She tugged her jeans further down her hips and hoisted her boob tube up to expose her tummy. The belly button ring sparkled in the sun like a real jewel. She must remember to keep her belly sucked in. Not that Daniel would mind that she wasn't size zero, he wasn't that kind of guy. He always said it was the person inside that counts.

The cuffs of her jeans scooped up dirt as she walked. Her mum would chuck a psycho when she saw half the playground dragged into the kitchen. What should she tell her if she asked her where she'd been? What if the school rangs to say she'd wagged again? She did have a cold, she decided, so she could say she was sick. Her mum was on double shift anyway, so with any luck she'd miss the call.

She stopped again. A shadow from behind the kiosk made the breath catch in her chest. A man stepped into the sunlight. He wore shorts and one of those T-shirts with a collar and a tiny crocodile on them and his nose was small and red. She giggled, it was just like the fake noses you buy at the deli for the dead babies.

He wasn't what Bianca had expected, and he certainly wasn't Daniel. She took a step back.

'Hi,' the man said, not moving any closer. 'You come to meet Daniel?'

She nodded and nibbled at her bottom lip. The sun was hot and bright and she had to screw up her eyes to see him properly. Sweat ran like tears down the sides of his face and sparkled on his round red nose.

'Well, he's kinda shy, y'know? He's waiting for you in the car. I'm his dad.'

'Uh huh.' Daniel said he was shy with girls. He lived alone with his dad, just like she lived alone with her mum. He said that's what made them soul mates.

'You got your laptop in there?' The man asked. He talked a

bit funny, some kind of accent, Bianca noticed.

She nodded, the computer bag suddenly feeling like a sack of bricks on her back.

'Good, Dan'll be pleased. He's got a heap of really cool games to show you. And he's just downloaded another Katy Enigma story, he said you like them.' He put his hand out as if he wanted to hold hers, but she didn't take it. She was remembering Zoe's horrible words at school: You're ugly, you're stupid and you'll never get a boyfriend. And then she thought of Katy Enigma, girl detective, always ready for adventure, flying golden hair, long legs — would Katy go with this man?

'Look, if you're not okay with this,' the man said, 'Dan'll understand. To be honest, he's scared about meeting you.'

The man smiled. He had soft brown eyes and despite the strange nose and his peculiar voice, his face looked kind.

Bianca placed her hand in his and felt him shiver.

She didn't know why, it wasn't cold at all.

Wednesday

3

Excerpt from chat room transcript 020207
TIMTAM: send me pic?
ANGEL12: ok
TIMTAM: do u have webcam?
ANGEL12: no ... I wish
TIMTAM: tdtm

'Only on Monday,' Stevie spoke to the gathered year sixes and sevens in the classroom. 'My partner and I caught a man who had tricked a young girl into meeting him in Kings Park.'

A girl with pigtails put up her hand. 'But why would the girl want to meet him in the park anyway?'

'He knew she was a big fan of a local rock band,' Stevie said. 'The man had been talking to her in an Internet chat room, pretending to be a boy her own age. He promised to give her CDs and posters; even a hat like one of the band members wears. You see, these people pretend to be whatever the child wants them to be in order to entrap them.'

Entrap, was that too big a word for these kids? Stevie looked at the faces before her, searching for signs of confusion. She detected boredom in some, giggles in a few, but on the whole most of the children gazed back at her in rapt attention.

At first she'd been slightly anxious when she'd learned that one of her roles in the newly formed Cyber Predator Team was public speaking, but to her surprise she found she was beginning to enjoy it. In fact, educating children about the dangers of the Internet was the most rewarding experience she'd had in her fifteen years with the police.

A girl with round glasses and a thick mane of dark messy hair put up her hand. Her face seemed vaguely familiar. 'But how did you know the man was planning on doing this?'

'Our operations room in Central Police headquarters is filled with computers. We take it in turns to watch the kinds of Internet websites we think Perth children might be interested in. I logged into a chat room devoted to a local rock band and called myself Angel12. Pretty soon I began talking to a boy who began asking me all sorts of personal questions.' Stevie didn't go into the lurid details. 'And I got the feeling he wasn't the boy he was pretending to be. We arranged to meet and it was then that I discovered that he was an older man.'

One of the boys laughed and whispered to the boy sitting next to him. Donna, the school councillor, wagged her finger and shut him up.

The girl with the glasses put up her hand again. She had a pixie face, the tips of her ears visible through her hair. 'Anyone who gives themselves a name like Angel12 is looking for trouble. The name just calls out, "Hey, I'm a cute girl and I'm only twelve." No one should give themselves a nickname like that, a predator would know straight away how easily someone like that could be manipulated.'

The boy sitting next to her rolled his eyes, but Stevie was impressed with the girl's command of language, her confidence and her insight. She nodded. 'Yes, very good.' Where the hell had she seen that girl before?

Another boy put up his hand. 'Yeah, but it's only girls they're interested in, yeah?'

'No, not at all, quite a lot of these men go for boys.'

There was a chorus of gross, yuck and pervert from the group of boys in the back row.

'But all this doesn't mean you can't have fun on the Internet too or use it as a valuable learning tool.' Stevie nodded to Donna who turned to face the whiteboard. 'I'm going to give you a list of do's and don'ts and Miss French is going to write them down for you to copy.' She had leaflets she could give them, but if they wrote it themselves there was a better chance they'd remember it.

The children rippled like the sea as they sought their writing equipment.

'First, when you're on the Internet, don't ever think you know who you are talking to, no matter what someone might tell you about themselves — people will often lie. Never give out personal information, and never agree to meet anyone unless you can bring a trusted adult with you.

'Often the predator will try to build up to a trusting relationship with you. He might start in chat rooms, then private chat rooms. Instant messaging and emails would be next because it gives both of you the freedom of not having to be always logged onto the Internet. The more confident predator might even attempt to telephone you. When you hear a voice on the end of the phone, it's easy for you to think you're talking to a friend …'

Stevie knew the talk by heart and had to remind herself to slow down. Heads bobbed up and down as the children copied the notes and Donna's careful printing squeaked upon the whiteboard.

'Another fine performance, Stevie, thanks for coming.' Stevie and Donna made their way down the tiled corridor to the staffroom.

'No worries, all part of the service; I think the message is getting across don't you? It would be better if we could get more parents involved. I want to talk about the dangers of kids having web cams in their rooms. There are things the parents need to know that aren't suitable for the kids to hear.'

'I put a note in last week's newsletter for the parents' night you proposed, but so far we've only had three responses.'

Stevie sighed. What was it with these people? Child molestation directly resulting from Internet contact was rising daily, but it was a problem many parents seemed happy to ignore. Were they just ignorant of the dangers, or too busy with their own lives? It's never going to happen to any of my children, she'd heard over and over again. No wonder she wrapped her own child in cotton wool.

In the staffroom Stevie settled into Donna's cubicle with its window onto the oval. She had twenty minutes to relax before picking up six year-old Izzy from the school car park — luxury. She leant back in the chair and brushed her fingers across the bandaid on her cheek, teasing the minor wound underneath. The itch was a satisfying reminder of Monday's successful apprehension of Robert Mason.

Donna came in with two mugs of coffee. 'The kids loved your story about catching that guy in the park,' she said. 'One more chalked up to the good guys. I hope they lock him up and throw away the key.'

Stevie pulled a face and dived into her bag. 'Probably not. From what we can tell so far, the attempted abduction of Angel12 was a first offence — he has no prior convictions of interfering with children. We found kiddie porn on his hard drive and that's about it. We'll be lucky if he does two years.' She pulled out a packet of cigarettes. 'This is between us, all right? I shouldn't be telling you this sort of thing, but hey, there's no names … Can I smoke in here?'

'No, but I won't tell if you don't.' Donna slid the window

open and the sweet fragrance of the newly mown oval wafted in.

Stevie blew out an angry jet of smoke.

'It must be frustrating for you,' Donna sympathised.

Stevie tried to shrug it off. 'Most police work is frustrating, one way or another, whether it's directing traffic or a cold case murder investigation.'

'I imagine dinner conversations at your place must be quite lively at times.'

'They can be,' she said. 'But the good thing about not officially living together is that if one of us is in a foul mood or pissed off, we simply stay out of the other's way. Monty stays in his flat and I wall myself up with Izzy at my place until we feel like talking again.'

The staffroom door opened. 'Quick, put it out,' Donna said like a naughty schoolgirl. The half smoked cigarette plopped with a brief fizz into Stevie's coffee as Donna went and dealt with the person at the door.

Stevie twisted the ring on her finger as she waited for Donna to return. Monty was cooking at his place tonight: curry, she suspected. His taste for spicy foods, his rust red hair and skin that turned fire engine red with ten minutes of full sun — everything about Monty McGuire radiated heat. It was no wonder he lived near the sea. With all the stresses of his heavy workload lately, she thought the only thing that saved him from spontaneously combusting was the chance of a quick dip in the Indian Ocean.

She found herself worrying for Monty. The pressures of the job had been weighing him down more than usual and he'd been having trouble sleeping. He said she wouldn't be who she was if she wasn't worrying about something or other. If it wasn't Monty it was Izzy, and if she wasn't worrying about their daughter, it was someone else's child. Her mother always claimed that worry and guilt were a woman's lot. Reluctant as she was to pay much heed to her mother's pearls of wisdom, she had to concede that on this occasion, Dot was probably right.

Donna's voice brought her back. 'Sorry, that's the problem with being new to the job — so many files to catch up on, and my predecessor was hardly an organised type.' Donna paused. 'I suppose you'll have to leave to pick up Izzy. You're lucky your hours are flexible enough to accommodate school pick-ups.'

'Not always, sometimes Monty picks her up, often my mother —' This train of thought lead to another. Now she remembered where she'd seen the girl with the messy dark hair.

'What was the name of the girl sitting in the front row, the one asking the sensible questions?'

'Emma Breightling, why?'

'I'm sure I've seen her before; I think she baby-sits for one of my neighbours. My mother's away on holiday, Monty's stretched thin and I'm desperate for someone as back up for after-school care. What's she like, is she old enough do you think?'

'Some thirteen year olds wouldn't be, but I don't think Emma would give you cause to worry. As you've seen for yourself she's very mature for her age, comes from a good home, her father's a doctor, her mother's some kind of professional. Other than that I don't know much about her, which is good, really.' Donna patted the pile of files on her desk, 'I only get to know the problem kids.'

4

EXCERPT FROM CHAT TRANSCRIPT 150107
DANTHEMAN: tell me what u look like
BETTYBO: noooooooo!
DANTHEMAN: go on
BETTYBO: ule think Im ugle
DANTHEMAN: no I won't. u sound sooooo cute!
BETTYBO: I hav shot hair and im fat
DANTHEMAN: still sound cute to me!

Stevie carefully prised the fat from the chunk of curried meat and pushed it to the side of her plate. Her father used to say she had the metabolism of a greyhound, that the calories were burned up by nervous energy alone despite the arduous outdoor activities of her youth. But time had proved him wrong. The bull riding, rock climbing and orienteering had long given way to a demanding career and motherhood. The nervous energy was still there, but no longer seemed to have the same effect upon her body. If her metabolism continued to slow at this rate she thought, remembering the struggle to do up the button of her jeans that morning, the greyhound might soon be turning into a golden lab.

She finished a second glass of wine.

Then ate the scraps of fat from her plate.

She thought about telling Monty about Tash's behaviour in

the park, that she was worried her friend might be cracking up, but changed her mind. He was too high-ranking — his code of ethics wouldn't let the matter slide. Life would be a lot easier if one of them worked as a pen pusher for the local council, she thought with a sigh, leaning back in her chair to look at him.

The pale face and violet circles under his eyes spoke of sleepless nights, and the crinkles around his eyes had more recently been used for frowns, not laughter. This evening he'd been unusually quiet as if he too was absorbed by his own thoughts. As head of the Serious Crime Squad he was in charge of several ongoing investigations. The case that was losing him the most sleep recently was the discovery of a body some three weeks ago in the Swan River.

'How's the floater going?' Stevie asked him.

Monty put his fork down and pushed away his plate. 'He's Asian, had a couple of Triad-type tattoos on his arms. That's about all we know so far.'

'Did Angus Wong have anything to say about the tatts?'

'Angus said he'd seen something similar from Hong Kong, a dragon around one bicep, a white tiger on the other. But in our guy, the colours are different. He thinks the guy might have been from mainland China.

'The single bullet to the head, the mutilated face, the severed fingertips — all smacks of organised crime if you ask me.'

'Maybe, but not by an Asian gang; I think his murderer might be a westerner.'

'Why's that?' Stevie asked.

'If the murderer was Asian, especially an Asian gang member, he would have known about the tattoos and cut them out along with the face and the fingertips. The body was found in the river fully clothed, wearing a long-sleeved shirt. The murderer would have no idea about the tatts. He's probably be feeling pretty cocky, thinking he's done a good job at disguising his vic's identity.'

Stevie smiled, 'But not good enough to fool you, eh, Sherlock?'

Monty held up his finger. 'None of your sarcasm,' he said with the flicker of a smile. 'I've had people scouring China Town, Northbridge and East Perth, but nothing so far. It's hard when they don't have a picture to show around. He was probably an illegal.' He took several gulps of beer. 'And now I have a child missing under mysterious circumstances.'

She should have realised it would take more than a floater in the river to keep Monty McGuire silent. 'Shit. Is this going to be a combo job?'

'Afraid so. Unless she turns up unharmed within the next few hours we might find ourselves in this together.'

The Cyber Predator Team was under the umbrella of the Sex Crimes Division and joined forces with Monty's Serious Crime Squad in cases of overlap, such as child murder and abduction.

'Does she have a computer, have they checked her hard drive?' Stevie asked.

'She does have a laptop and it's missing. It's the first thing I asked when the file appeared on my desk. See,' he shot her a smile, 'despite what you think, I do listen to you. Sometimes.'

Stevie twisted the ring on her finger. It had been a while since they'd worked together. Not since she'd transferred from the SCS, when their engagement had become official. She wondered how she'd cope if technically he was her boss again. Before it had been easy, she'd enjoyed working with him — but now? Maybe he would finally see why she was still so insistent about keeping their lives separate. She squinted hard at the single diamond, as if she might see their future in it. Out of the corner of her eye she saw him looking at her over his beer glass and could tell he knew what she was thinking.

'We can't go on living apart when we're married, Stevie, no matter how much our job paths might cross,' he said.

'Can't we?' she said flippantly, knowing the look of hurt she'd see in his eyes if she chose to lift her head to meet them. It didn't help that, from one of those dark places deep inside her, she knew it wasn't only their careers that were the problem. 'Why change when everything's working so well ...'

She got up and started clearing away the clean dishes from the draining board. Monty's kitchen accoutrements were made up of a hotch-potch of odds and ends, the remnants of a former life and a former marriage. Nothing matched, but everything was stored in an orderly fashion, lined in rows of regimental precision in cupboards that would have made Martha Gardener proud. At her place she couldn't open a cupboard door without something falling out.

Monty remained at the table. 'Izzy needs more stability. She doesn't even have her own bedroom here. If you can't bring yourself to set a date for the wedding, we could at least live together.'

He was persistent, she had to give him that — it was one of the things that made him such a good detective. She looked to their sleeping daughter as she carried their dirty dishes to the sink. 'She loves it here, she loves sleeping on your couch.'

'She won't always, I'm going to have to find a bigger place.'

'But you won't be able to afford anywhere bigger and stay this close to the beach.'

'I can compromise.' Monty rose from the table, reached out and pulled her away from the sink. It wasn't hard, surrendering to his embrace, and she wondered, not for the first time, what was wrong with her. He was all she'd ever wanted. Hell, she'd been in love with him since she was ten years old, when her older brother had brought him home to the family station. Still, this didn't stop her feeling like a marathon runner at the end of the last gruelling race of her career, stopping just before the finish line to look behind her. She glanced at her ring. She loved the autonomy of the single cut stone in its simple no-frills setting, but there were times when she felt another ring next to it would spoil its effect, that two rings upon the same finger would be nothing but an encumbrance. It was a stupid thought and she knew she shouldn't have it; Monty was everything to her.

He nuzzled her neck. 'Things are different now, time to write a new script.'

His breath on her skin made her back arch with anticipation. 'You been watching Oprah again?' she managed. He undid her ponytail and ran his fingers through her hair, sending a wave of pleasure up her neck and into her scalp.

'My mother was on the phone again yesterday, wanting some idea of a date. If you don't want to commit to one just yet, fine, we can tell her that, but we can't just leave her in the air about this.' Monty's mother lived in Scotland. 'She's old, she's not well, a trip here is a major military operation for her. She needs plenty of time to organise herself.'

Stevie moved over to the fridge with the magnetised calendar on its door, twirled around in one spot until she was dizzy and stabbed her finger at a random date. 'Okay, next year: July 14.'

There, she'd set a date, no promises of living together yet, but at least she'd shown that she could compromise too.

He rumbled a deep belly laugh, the first she'd heard from him in days. 'You want us to get married on Bastille Day?'

Shit, talk about the power of the subconscious. She went through the twirling routine again. 'There, March 15th.'

'The Ides of March? I'd rather take Bastille Day, release you from your prison.'

'Oh, you assume it's you who does the rescuing? Maybe I

should be the one releasing you from *your* prison?' she said with as much sass as she could muster.

'Fine. I'm more than happy to be rescued. My only worry is that you won't be able to pick me up and throw me over the saddle of your white charger.'

She patted him on the stomach. 'Better do something about this then.' There wasn't much fat there, he was solid as a brick dunny, but teasing him made her feel better.

Monty refilled their glasses but the phone interrupted them before they could seal the date with a toast. He listened for a moment then swore. Stevie deduced from the conversation that a girl's body matching the description of the missing schoolgirl had been found. Barry was on his way to pick up Monty; in fact he was pulling in to the apartment car park as he spoke.

Monty was in the bedroom changing into a suit when Barry pounded on the door. 'Hey stranger, long time no see,' he beamed at Stevie when she opened it, bringing a salty tang into the flat and the rumbling sound of breakers.

'Never long enough,' she said, having no trouble keeping her face straight.

'How's everything in the chick squad?'

'If you mean the Cyber Predator Team, everything's fine.'

'Bloody discriminatory if you ask me, a female only squad.'

'It's not a female only squad, that would be ridiculous. Often boys are more comfortable talking to males than females; we've just not had that many guys apply for the job.'

'Well,' he puffed himself up like a rooster. 'What do you reckon on my chances?'

Stevie pinched her thumb and forefinger into a zero.

Barry didn't skip a beat. 'That partner of yours, Tash, is she available?'

She hid her smile. 'Fancy her do you?' He certainly wouldn't be the first.

Barry didn't respond straight away. He looked at Stevie and then stepped back as if he'd just discovered she'd been in contact with a contagious disease. 'She's not gay is she?'

Stevie flicked him a shrug. 'She's never tried to crack on to me.'

Barry relaxed, rubbed his hands together. 'Good. So here's hoping we combine forces on this case, then. Where's the boss?' He moved over to the closed bedroom door, was about to thump on it when Stevie grabbed him by the arm and pointed to Izzy, putting her finger to her lips.

'Sorry,' Barry said in a stage whisper, plonking himself on the other end of the couch. She looked at his face as he regarded the child and sensed a crack peeping through the brash schoolboy veneer.

'Barry, is it really bad?' she asked softly.

He nodded, smoothed his shaved scalp, dashed her a smile and turned back to face Izzy before she could read it. 'One of those times when I wonder how we do this,' he said in a voice barely audible.

Monty emerged from his room and Barry sprang to his feet. 'Ready boss?' he boomed. Izzy stirred on the couch and mumbled in her sleep. Stevie shot him another scowl.

Monty kissed her goodbye. As he opened the door to leave the distant breakers greeted her like the sound of giant guns pounding the shore.

5

Excerpt from chat room transcript 200107
BETTYBO: Danil says Im sexy and cute
HARUM SCARUM: did u send photo?
BETTYBO: no im not that dum!
HARUM SCARUM: then how does he know?
BETTYBO: Ooo ... ur jelos!
HARUM SCARUM has left the room.

Barry pulled up alongside the several police cars parked on the perimeter of the floodlit building site, jumping from the car before the blue light on the unmarked stopped whizzing. Monty stayed where he was for a moment, closed his eyes and counted to ten. He should be used to this, but he wasn't. He'd lost count of the body dumpsites he'd been to, men, women and kids, their bodies hidden in ways that made the desecration even more monstrous, one more stab of the knife into the flesh of those grieving their loved ones.

The scene could have been a movie set and he the director, summoned now the props and the actors were in place. Portable lights shone from newly erected scaffolds, the rubbish skip centre stage, like a World War One tank stuck in the mud. Monty changed his mind. This wasn't like a film set at all, this was a battleground. He donned overalls, took another deep breath and stepped into the fray.

A police photographer circled the skip, let off a few flashes and retreated to make room for the scene of crime officers. One man was dusting the bin for prints. When he'd finished with one side of the bin, another hauled himself into it and began clambering around. He pointed out the protruding limb to Monty, as if he could have missed it. The leg emerged from the rubble like a spindly tree from a barren hillside, twisted, small and naked.

Her head was also exposed. Someone had already wiped away much of the dust and debris from the small waxy face. He mentally compared the features with the file photo of ten year old Bianca Webster: hamster cheeks, badly dyed hair. Just a runaway he'd hoped, until he'd been told about the missing computer. It was still early, they might find her yet, he had thought at the time. Jesus, his own optimism surprised him sometimes.

The mortuary chief, Henry Grebe, arrived in his white van. Funny, Monty thought, child abductors had a propensity for white vans too. The rings on Grebe's fingers flashed under the lights as he rubbed his hands, addressing his band of body snatchers who rattled the gurney along the rough ground beside him. His voice carried to Monty across no man's land. 'Come on lads, chop, chop. If we get rid of this one good and fast we might still catch the end of the test.'

Monty caught the eye of the pathologist, Melissa Hurst. She beckoned him over. 'I thought you were supposed to be doing something about that odious man.' She'd pulled the hood of her overalls off and powdered cement covered her short wavy hair, making it appear greyer than it was.

'That's just what I was about to say to you,' Monty said.

'He's been at the mortuary twenty years, it's easier said than done.'

'Can we take it now?' the object of their dislike called out.

Monty clenched his fists. 'No,' he snapped. 'Doctor Hurst

and I aren't finished. Go back to the van and wait till you're called.' To the doctor he said, 'C'mon, I'm sure you've got something to show me, let's stretch this out.'

The doctor spoke from the side of her mouth. 'A grebe is a bird that under certain circumstances will eat its own young — did you know that?'

For a moment Monty forgot his misery and smiled. 'You going David Attenborough on me?'

Someone had fashioned some loose bricks into a crude set of steps for the doctor to stand on, but Monty was tall enough to view the body without aids. He forced himself to follow Doctor Hurst's gloved fingers as she manipulated the jaw like the star of one of those American forensic shows. 'She's not been dead long, no signs of rigor yet. And look at the eyes,' she pointed.

Monty recognised in them the glaze of the newly dead.

'At a rough guess, I'd say she's been dead no more than a couple of hours. I'll be able to tell you more when I examine her at the mortuary.'

'Any idea of the cause?' Monty asked.

'Nothing confirmed, but it looks like the preliminary cause could be asphyxiation.' She extracted a paintbrush from her overall pocket, flicked away more dust and shone the beam of a penlight up the child's nose. 'Look at her nose, can you see the congestion?'

Monty put on his glasses, held his breath and peered as closely as his position allowed, not seeing a thing, not wanting to see a thing; he'd take the doctor's word for it.

'The poor kid had a bad cold, lethal when combined with a duct-tape gag.' Doctor Hurst circled a finger above the child's mouth. 'There are sticky marks around her mouth from the glue, see how the brick dust has adhered to it? And look at the petechial haemorrhage in the whites of the eyes — a sure sign of asphyxiation. At this stage I'd hazard a guess that murder might not have been intentional.'

Small comfort, as if that would make it easier for the wretched mother, Monty thought. 'That'll do for now, get the ball rolling,' he said, holding his hand out to her and helping her down from the wobbly brick steps, something he would never have dared do for Stevie. Then again, Stevie wasn't sixty years old and five feet tall. He beckoned to the men from the mortuary van and told them they could collect the body.

Standing well back from the taped area, he lit a cigarette. He turned his back on the body snatchers and took a deep drag as if it might mask the odour of every crime scene he'd ever attended. And this wasn't even bad; he'd detected nothing but the smell of brick dust from the skip. Imagination can be a powerful thing.

'I thought you'd given up,' the doctor said.

'I have.'

'I'll spare you the lecture then. Did you get my fax? I'm afraid I didn't send it till late.'

'Don't tell me the blood tests on the floater have finally come back?'

'No, not the blood, better than blood, it's the tissue tests.'

'Yes, you suspected some kind of kidney problem?'

'Our John Doe was suffering from a kidney disease called IgA nephropathy. One of its symptoms is blood in the urine, something very few people would choose to ignore.'

Monty felt his spirits lift. It was breaks like this that kept him on the job. 'Which means a sweep of doctors' surgeries and clinics might well lead us to the identification of our mystery man — you beauty!' Monty clapped her on the shoulder, forcing her to step back to keep her balance.

'Steady on there, King Kong.'

He walked her back to her car and then joined Barry who

was standing with Wayne Pickering at the edge of the underground car park of the half finished shopping centre.

DS Wayne Pickering introduced him to Geoffrey Browne, a stick-thin old man wearing a security officer's uniform.

'You found the body, yeah?' Monty asked him.

'Not only found it, he saw it dumped,' Wayne said.

'Really?' Monty raised his eyebrows. 'Tell me what you saw …'

'I've already gone through it all with these fellas,' the security man said with a nasal whine.

'And you're more than likely going to have to go over it again another dozen times I'm afraid, sir,' Monty said.

The old man sighed deeply. Monty met Wayne's look of concern with one of his own, wondering just how much they could rely on him.

'I was boilin' up some tea over there, see?' Browne pointed a crooked finger to a card table and folding chair set up alongside one of the car park's concrete pillars. A kettle sat on the table with an industrial length extension cord trailing into the shadows.

Monty scuffed his way over the concrete slab to the makeshift tearoom and gazed between the pillars to the clear view of the floodlit skip. It was hard to ascertain quite what the old man might have seen earlier in the grainy darkness and the dazzle of car headlights.

'Go on then, what did you see?' he asked when he returned.

'I heard it first, the squeal of brakes, then I saw a four-wheel drive crash through the fence and fishtail across the building site.'

He peered in the direction the man was pointing. One section of the cyclone fence had been knocked down and the supporting poles bent out of shape. A police officer was taping up the gap. Traffic on the highway beyond the fence-line had slowed to a crawl as motorists sought to take in the drama. Bloody ghouls, he thought.

'Then a bloke come out, opened up the back door and grabbed hold of this heavy thing,' the old man said. 'At first I thought he was just some mug dumping rubbish illegally. He threw the thing onto the skip and climbed onto it, scrabbling around for a bit like he was trying to bury something. I radioed it in from here while I watched him.'

'He drove through the mesh fence, and you just stood and watched?' Monty said.

'What the hell else was I supposed to do at my age and with my back? Besides there was another fella sitting in the front seat, I wouldn't have stood a chance if they got aggro. The fella on the skip must have seen me, I reckon, cos he jumped down real quick and scarpered back to his truck and took off.'

Wayne frowned and said to the man, 'You didn't mention this second person before, Mr Browne, did you get a look at him?'

'Yeah, well, I only just remembered him didn't I? Nah, I didn't hardly see him.'

Monty wondered how he could have forgotten this, wondered just how drunk the old man really was.

'And this second man didn't get out and help the first man at all, he just sat there, watching?' Wayne said, meeting Monty's eyes.

Browne must have sensed their doubt. 'I'm telling you what I saw, mate, no more, no less.'

'But surely you weren't alone here?' Monty spun on his heels and waved his arms around. 'This place is huge.'

'George was over the other side with the dog. Every half an hour or so we take it in turns to do a circuit.'

'And where's George now?'

'I sent him home, boss,' Wayne said. 'He saw nothing. But Mr Browne here got a good look at the bloke who took the body from the car and he's given us a detailed description and the rego.'

Fair enough, Monty thought, calming himself; old Mr Browne had probably done them the greater service. If he had tried to apprehend the men they might very well have had two victims on their hands.

Wayne read from his notebook, 'Khaki coloured Toyota Troop Mover licence number MDG 76X. Scene of crime officers also found skid marks and tyre prints matching that kind of vehicle. The guy is described as short and stocky with darkish curly hair, late forties to early fifties.'

'Anything else you can add, sir?' Monty asked the old man.

'Nah, can I go home now, mate?'

Monty said he could. The detectives stood in a group and watched him hobble off until he was out of earshot.

'Jesus,' Barry smoothed his bald head. 'Iron Bar Security must've scratched the bottom of the barrel for that one.'

'He had a half bottle of bourbon sticking up from his holdall,' Wayne added. 'Not exactly a reliable witness, he never even mentioned a second man the first time around.'

'He's all we've got at the moment,' Monty said.

'I hope to God he's wrong. One child killer is bad enough, a team of them's a bloody nightmare.'

'At least we've got the rego — have you run it?' Monty asked Wayne.

'Waiting on it now. Meanwhile the developer of the site and the builder are on their way. They're not going to be too happy when they hear that work will have to be halted for a few days.'

'A darn sight happier than the kid's mother, I'm sure,' Monty muttered.

There was an uncomfortable silence, some shuffling of feet. Barry cleared his throat. 'So who gets the short straw?'

Monty had no idea how Mrs Webster would react to the news that they had found her daughter's body. All he knew was that he couldn't face her alone. Angus Wong, his first choice, was briefing the local police and unavailable. That left bald Barry with the grin of Alfred from *Mad* magazine, or Wayne Pickering who looked like something freshly exhumed from a graveyard — on a good day.

'Don't worry, it won't be either of you.' He turned to Wayne. 'As soon as we get a name for that car, haul the owner in.' Then to Barry he said. 'You stay here. No comment to the press yet. I'll give a statement when I've informed the next of kin. Help with the search, tell SOCO everything in that skip needs to be sifted, the whole building site thoroughly scoured and secured. You'll need to get more uniforms in and get some door knocking underway.'

Monty reached for his phone and called Stevie.

6

Excerpt from chat room transcript 071106
BETTYBO has entered the chat room
HARUM SCARUM: were u been?
BETTYBO: Sry. Things bad hear. He cam round agin.
HARUM SCARUM: wats rong? He hrt u?
BETTYBO: pir
BETTYBO has left chat room

There wasn't much traffic at ten o'clock at night and it didn't take Stevie long to drive from Cottesloe to Shenton Park where the heady scent of frangipani replaced the briny tang of the sea. She parked her unmarked car between the other police Commodore and a white Ford Escort, outside a block of state housing flats. A beige rectangle with clunky concrete balconies, Shenton Rise wasn't much to look at, but it did offer a pleasant view of the floodlit park on the other side of the road.

Monty joined her on the footpath and briefly took her hand. 'Was there any problem getting Mrs Nash to mind Izzy?'

'She was watching the late movie, didn't seem to mind switching venues to watch it at your place. I said I wouldn't be long.'

He filled her in on the details as they scuffed up the stairs. They climbed slowly, the caged lights on every level casting a crisscross of shadows across the graffiti-streaked walls. Had this been a prison or a place of refuge for little Bianca Webster? Stevie wondered.

They heard a door slam from the floor above, then the sound of heavy footsteps echoing around the stairwell. Seconds later a man pushed passed them on the stairs, shoving Stevie against the handrail.

'Hey, watch where you're going, mate!' Monty called out.

Stevie glimpsed a stocky, denim-clad figure. 'Go fuck yourself,' the man said, leaving a trail of beer fumes behind him.

Monty mumbled under his breath and moved quickly down a couple of steps as if to follow him. The feint worked, the footsteps sped up and the man made a hasty escape, slamming the door of the stairwell behind him.

Stevie and Monty made their way along the verandah until they came to number 34.

Monty took a breath and knocked. 'Here goes nothing.'

Stevie would never forget the first time she'd been the bearer of tragic news; a twenty-two year old PC telling a forty-five year old woman that her son had died in a car crash had seemed unnatural. She knew it was only the authority of her uniform that had let her get away with it. No uniform necessary these days, she mused, with age and parenthood the universal leveller.

The thin woman who opened the door had one arm in a greying sling. The sudden movement of her free hand to her mouth sent a draught of cigarette smoke wafting at them through the flyscreen. Despite their civvies they radiated the unmistakable aura of cop to Stella Webster.

They'd decided earlier that Stevie would do the talking. 'Mrs Webster? I'm DS Stephanie Hooper and this is Inspector Monty McGuire. May we come in?'

Stella Webster barely glanced at the ID Monty pressed

against the screen door. Her nose was red and inflamed and her watery eyes fixed on Stevie, searching her face for assurances she could not give.

They were led into a small, airless lounge room. The furniture was dated and minimal, the place clean except for an overflowing ashtray on the coffee table, an empty beer can on its side next to it. A few knick-knacks on the shelf above the gas fireplace saved the place from total sterility and dreariness.

The woman wrapped her free arm around her injured one. She turned her back to them and spoke to a movie poster of *The Titanic* tacked to the wall. Stevie stared at it too, thinking how appropriate it was.

'I hope you weren't trying to reach me earlier. I had to get out for a bit. I shouldn't have gone, the cops said I had to wait near the phone, but I had my mobile with me, so I thought what difference does it make? I went into Subiaco, couldn't bear waiting around at home for news on my own. If she'd been kidnapped and they'd wanted a ransom, they'd have rung me on that wouldn't they, I mean —'

The woman dropped her head and her thin shoulders began to shake. Stevie noticed a red area on her neck where the knot of the sling had rubbed. She crooked her head at Monty, indicating the kitchen, which was separated from the lounge by a breakfast bar. He nodded, a look of relief on his face. Taking off his suit jacket he began to bustle about.

Stevie guided Stella Webster to a cracked vinyl couch and sank down beside her. She could tell by the woman's stiff posture she knew the news was not good, but she still had to spell it out. 'Stella, I'm afraid a dead body matching Bianca's description has been found.'

Stevie tensed and waited for the barrage of anguished questions: where, when, how, by whom? And, most critical, did she suffer?

Monty was filling the kettle at the kitchen sink. He turned the tap off and stood as if holding his breath. Like her he was thinking of Izzy, thinking how it would be for them if the tables had been turned.

'I shouldn't have gone out,' Stella managed before the tears began to fall.

Stevie resisted the temptation to put her arm around the woman. In her experience, overt gestures of sympathy often did more harm than good. 'It doesn't matter, Stella, it wouldn't have made any difference,' she said, gently.

'Not today maybe, but all the other times, the double shifts, the overtime, I left her alone too much.' The woman patted the pocket of her shapeless pinafore dress and frantically looked around the room. Stevie offered her a cigarette and lit it for her, her own hands shaking so much it was hard to catch the tip with the flame. She could imagine herself reacting in the same way if something happened to Izzy — the guilt first, always the guilt.

She said, 'We're going to need to ask you some questions, Stella. We can come back in the morning if you like …'

'But now would be better,' Stella finished for her. 'I know all about this, seen it on TV often enough. You have to act fast; every hour that passes lessens the chances.' She choked on a sob. 'But time has run out for Bianca, hasn't it?'

'Time is still imperative. We need to catch this man before he does it again.' And when we do catch him, I might consider leaving him alone with Tash, Stevie thought. Or I might even give Tash a hand.

The phone in Stella's kitchen rang. Monty pointed to it and Stella indicated for him to answer it.

'Stella's phone,' he said and listened. 'Just a minute.' He covered up the mouthpiece and called out to Stella, 'A bloke here wants to speak to you. Won't give his name.'

Stella shrank towards the back of the couch as if she'd just glimpsed a poisonous snake and shook her head.

'It's all right, Stella, you don't have to speak to anyone. A lot of people take their phones off the hook at a time like this.' Stevie put her hand over Stella's, which trembled like a wild mouse under her touch. 'Who do you think it was?' she gently enquired.

Stella took a breath and gave a dismissive wave of her hand. 'Probably Bob, some guy who's been asking me out, that's all. He often rings at this time.'

It wasn't what she said so much as how she said it. Stevie paused as she puzzled over the reason for Bob's brush off. 'You don't seem to like him much.'

'Hey, got that right in one.'

Monty unplugged the phone from the wall, then he put a tray on the coffee table before them. 'Did you have a visitor before we came around? We passed a man on the stairs, he seemed angry,' he said.

'No, I've been here on my own. He was probably from upstairs.' She pointed to the floor above with her good hand. 'The woman up there has a different fella every night.'

'How did you break your arm, Stella?' Stevie asked, still thinking about Bob.

'I was carrying a basket of laundry downstairs and missed my footing. It's getting better, plaster's coming off soon.' She flexed the fingers of her left hand, moving the arm in the sling to show how much it had improved.

'Is there anyone we can call to sit with you?' Monty asked.

Stella shook her head.

'Are you sure? It's not good for you to be on your own at a time like this.' He handed them each a chipped blue mug, ladling a generous amount of sugar into Stella's without asking if she wanted it. As gently as he could he told her that someone would pick her up in the morning to formally identify the body.

'Where was she found?' Stella turned red-rimmed eyes to Stevie.

'In a half-built shopping centre in Midland.'

'She's never been to Midland. I don't even like the place, never took her there. How was she, was she …?'

'She died quickly, but I'm afraid there is evidence of sexual assault,' Stevie said.

Stella covered her ears with her hands. 'That's enough, please, I don't want to hear any more.'

Discarding her earlier caution, Stevie put an arm around the woman. 'And we won't tell you any more, not if you don't want to hear it.'

Stella ignored the gesture of comfort, reached for her tea and took a shaky sip. 'I'll tell you anything you want, just as long as you don't tell me anything more about how she died.' She put her mug down and buried her face in Stevie's shoulder.

Stevie remained with Stella long after Monty left to relieve his neighbour of babysitting duties, promising to stay until the distraught woman was asleep. She contacted the medical officer who dropped by with some sedatives, then called Stella's sister in Esperance who said she'd arrive in Perth about lunchtime the next day. In between talking to Stella and making phone calls, Stevie briefed the team of uniformed officers assigned to question the neighbours.

Stella had taken the sleeping tablets and was now having a shower before going to bed.

Clothes scattered the floor of Bianca's bedroom and the residual tang of salt and vinegar chips salted the air. The top of the Formica desk was scarred with slash marks and pitted with tiny holes as if from multiple compass stabbings. 'I ♥ Daniel'

— a boyfriend, a rock or movie star? — had been scratched into the surface.

Stevie cleared the desk chair of shoes and sat down to make notes of the key points of her conversation with Stella.

Bianca was the product of a one night stand with a New Zealand backpacker on a Darwin beach. Stella remembered the man's Christian name, Nicholas, but that was it. After their brief encounter he'd returned to New Zealand none the wiser of Stella's pregnancy.

It had been a struggle to bring up Bianca alone. Stella worked a regular shift at Lotus Lodge as well as moonlighting at several nursing homes in the metro area. She averaged a sixty-hour working week and was saving up to take her daughter to Queensland for a holiday.

Bianca grew up well able to amuse and take care of herself. Last year she'd chucked a tanty (Stella's words), insisting she was too old for after-school care. Stella had conceded and bought her daughter the laptop which had provided hours of amusement — much more educational for her than the TV, Stella had said.

Stevie had been unable to reply.

No, Bianca didn't seem to enjoy school much, was often teased. She was a bit of a loner — her teacher had reported often seeing her alone at lunchtime, playing with her iPod. She didn't have many friends, despite the effort she took to fit in: the belly button ring, the dyed hair, even the rock stars on the wall. Stevie tried not to react when Stella had mentioned the belly button ring — the early sexualisation of girls Bianca's age seemed almost the norm these days.

Stevie gazed at the posters, recognising the Veronicas, Pink and a boy band whose name she couldn't remember. Her talk with Stella had given her enough insight into the child's personality to make her wonder whether the posters were only there on the off chance that one day a school friend might come over to play.

Bianca had wagged school several times last term, promising her mother after their last blow up that she wouldn't do it again. Her mother thought it was because a kid called Zoë Carmichael was bullying her. When she'd approached the school about it they'd done nothing.

Despite her absenteeism Bianca's school grades had been improving, especially in reading and story writing, and she even had a story published in the school newsletter. Untidy piles of type-written paper formed a nest where the laptop should have rested on the desk. Stevie shuffled through the scattered sheaves, hoping she might find some printed emails, but she only found doodles of brick walls, more Daniel hearts, and piles of half finished stories. 'Once upon a time in a place far, far away.' Or 'It was a dark and stormy night …' Nothing particularly original; atrocious spelling, but not bad for a child of this technological age where DVDs and computer games were the entertainment of choice.

Stevie searched through the wastepaper basket next to the desk and found a few more screwed up stories, some used tissues, chocolate wrappings and several empty potato chip packets.

A row of sagging shelves above the desk was weighed down with paperbacks — the Harry Potter series, Alex Ryder boy detective, C. S. Lewis's Narnia books, Paul Jennings and several others. Despite the strained finances of her mother, it didn't seem as if Bianca had gone without. Next to the books were jumbled piles of CDs, an iPod and a small-screen combo TV and DVD player.

'Did you ever see what Bianca was doing on the computer?' Stevie had asked Stella earlier.

'Don't know anything about computers, all I know is I get a

whacking great bill for the Internet every month.'

'Did she use email?'

'Yes, with her Internet friends. I encouraged it. I couldn't write a proper letter when I was her age. I was proud of her.'

If the woman had known anything at all about kids' activities on the Internet, Stevie thought, she would have realised the letters were probably far from proper.

'Why's everyone so caught up over the computer, anyway?' Stella had queried.

'We think it might have been taken by her abductor to cover his tracks.'

'You mean he took it when he grabbed her? But why would he do that?'

'This man is probably a cyber predator, a paedophile who picks up children through the Internet and tricks them into meeting him. I doubt he came here to take the computer. A common ploy is to get the child to bring their laptop, if they have one, to the meetings. In that way they can destroy the computer and any evidence of their activities.'

At that point Stella had buried her face in her hands. 'I never knew any of this. She was always so good. So quiet.'

Stevie heard her own mother's voice across the chasm of the years: 'You're too quiet, you're up to something.' And usually they were, either putting laxatives in the shearers' tea or hiding the hand-reared calf from their father at market time. There were no computers then, no Internet chat rooms and no mobile phones.

Stevie was thirty-five years old, but her childhood could have been a century ago.

Thursday

7

Her parents were at it again; Emma Breightling heard them yelling at each other in the kitchen. She padded through her bedroom door, still in her nightie, and peered down into the kitchen from behind the wrought iron banister, wondering what it was about this time. Three guesses: money, money or maybe even money; Emma wasn't usually wrong. She looked down at her mother's head and saw the gleam of scalp shining through the dark sculptured hair. Miranda would be mortified if she knew how exposed and vulnerable — how *old* — she seemed from this height.

Emma took hold of the decorative balustrade on the mezzanine with both hands and wiggled at it. The ornamental railings were loosening nicely in their concrete beds and would soon be more of a danger than a safety feature. God help the stumbling drunk who might one day lean upon it for support. Emma smiled to herself and continued to watch Miranda.

Her mother hit the side of the table with the rolled up morning paper, making the Spode cups rattle in their saucers, the milk shiver in the matching jug. Emma's father flinched but said nothing. Emma could imagine the little muscle in his jaw twitching, one beat short of a facial tic. It was as if there was something lurking there just under his skin, bursting to get out. He reached for a paper napkin and placed it under his cup to absorb the slops.

'You've got to do something, Christopher! I can't take much more of this — this not knowing. Have you any idea what it's doing to me?'

'Miranda, I told you, everything's fine. It was just a temporary cash flow problem; we're back on track now.'

Compared to his wife's hysterical shriek, her father's voice sounded calm and slow, though Emma could tell by the twitch and by the clenching and unclenching of his fist on the table, how close he was to snapping.

'Aidan said —'

'You shouldn't be listening to Aidan,' Christopher interrupted.

'He said we might have to sell the house.'

'That stupid nouveau prick doesn't know what he's talking about. Just leave everything to me, it's going to be fine.'

'That's no way to speak of your oldest friend,' Miranda pouted. '*And* our accountant — if anyone should know, he should.'

'*Your* oldest friend, Miranda; not mine.'

Christopher said no more, refusing to be drawn into a conversation about Aidan Stoppard. Funny, he never listened to Emma either, when she tried to tell him what her godfather was really like; it seemed he never listened to either of them any more.

Miranda bided her time, drumming her long fingernails on the breakfast table, clicking them like metal balls on strings. Emma knew the signs; her mother was dredging for something else to hurl at her husband.

At last she seemed to find it. 'That man was hanging around outside the agency again the other night,' Miranda said. 'I told you to do something about him. I've not been sleeping; my nerves are shot to pieces. You'll have to give me another prescription. Imagine if he tried to do something to one of the girls?'

Emma had to stop herself from laughing out loud; Miranda was even dumber than she thought. You'd think that after fifteen years of marriage, she would have realised the only thing that got Christopher Breightling flustered was money; money and Aidan Stoppard, which were one and the same thing really.

'When was it you saw this man?' Christopher asked calmly.

Miranda lifted her chin. 'Monday.'

He took several measured sips of coffee before answering her. 'I spoke to him weeks ago, I told you that.'

'Well it can't have done much good, whatever you said. He was hanging around outside the agency again, ogling the girls, just like before. And you're off to your stupid conference in Queensland this afternoon. What do I do if he comes back?'

'I'll only be away a couple of days. Get Julian to talk to him if you're worried.'

'Huh, some help he is.'

'Are you sure it was the same man? What did he look like?'

'It was dark, so I couldn't see his face but he was smallish, and thin, and he was wearing a hooded windcheater.'

Christopher paused with the coffee cup halfway to his lips. For a moment he appeared to stare right through Miranda. Then he gave a slight shrug. 'There are always men hanging around waiting to get a glimpse of the girls, and he sounds like a different man to me. I'm sure the one I spoke to won't be coming back.' After some deliberation he said, 'Maybe you should just go to the police.'

Emma was sure she saw the hint of a smile on his face — yay, one for the old man at last. After Miranda's last disastrous contact with the police, he'd have to know she wouldn't dream of involving them in this.

Emma turned back into her room, stopping when she reached her desk to gaze at the photo on the pin up board. The picture showed a small dark-skinned boy standing in front of a mud shack, grinning. His name was Josef, he lived in Morocco and he was her World Vision sponsorship child. She rummaged in her school bag and plopped yesterday's lunch money in the tin under the photo. Then she kissed her finger and tapped the small boy's face with it. Every morning Christopher gave her money to buy lunch and every morning she put it in her tin and made her own lunch after he'd left for work.

She selected her wardrobe for the day, an old pair of school track pants with torn knees and saggy waistband. The other girls would doubtless be wearing their sexy pleated sports skirts. This was the thing she liked the most about her state school, the compulsory school uniforms — not.

In her pink en-suite bathroom, designed by her mother to keep her out of hers, she brushed her long dark hair one hundred times. Then she bent over and mussed it all up again. Satisfied with the unkempt look, she went downstairs to make some toast for breakfast, planning on taking it back up to her room to eat as she scanned her morning's email.

The tension between her parents had eased by the time she joined them in the large open plan kitchen which merged into the family area. Her father was crunching cereal, her mother reading the newspaper horoscope.

'Huh,' Miranda scoffed as she read her stars aloud. '*A work colleague might surprise you.*' Maybe it means Julian will at last come up with the photos for the catalogue. God know, he's had the proofs for weeks. I can't stall Hartley Macs for much longer. Before we know it, they'll be hassling me for the autumn shots.'

'Sack him,' Christopher said dispassionately. 'He's already got you into enough trouble as it is.'

'That's easier said than done. Good photographers are almost impossible to find these days.'

'Do you need a lift to work?'

'No, I'm fine; Julian's picking me up. Or so he said.' She glanced at the watch on her wrist. 'He's late of course. I can't believe how long the panel beaters are taking with my car. It was only the smallest of dents.'

Miranda rattled the newspaper and Emma caught a glimpse of the headlines, something about a missing girl. The few words she read made her breath jam in her chest. She cocked her head and tried unsuccessfully to peer at the front of the paper as it quivered in her mother's hands above her breakfast grapefruit.

Then the phone rang.

'Always at meal times, guaranteed,' Christopher grumbled as he picked up the phone, quickly switching to the unctuous cheer of his bedside manner. Emma had once overheard one of his professional colleagues saying that despite what he might once have been, these days Christopher Breightling had the bedside manner of a vet. Emma didn't understand the comment; vets were usually nice.

He listened for a moment, then said, 'Yes, certainly, here she is.' He held the phone out to Emma without looking at her, his attention already back on his breakfast.

'Hello Emma, my name's Stephanie Hooper,' the voice on the end of the phone said. 'I live quite close to you in Hill View Terrace. I've been speaking to Mrs Carlyle — apparently you babysit her twins when she goes shopping.'

'Uh, yes, that's right,' Emma said.

'Mrs Carlyle is very impressed with you and thought you might be looking for more babysitting work. I was wondering if you might be interested in doing some after-school care for me? I have a six year old daughter who goes to your school. It would be a case of walking her home from school and staying with her until her father or I get home. It'll be regular for a week or so until my mother comes back from holiday, then just occasionally after that. I'm a police officer, so my work hours are a bit erratic.'

'I remember you, you're the lady who talked to us at school the other day.'

'That's right.'

Emma could hear the smile in the woman's voice. 'Cool.'

'You'd better check with your parents then, make sure it's okay.'

'Sure.' Emma put her hand over the receiver and left it there for a moment. Her mother got up from the table to make herself another cup of tea. Taking advantage of her turned back, Christopher took the paper and spread it open at the finance pages, now obscuring the headlines completely.

'Yes, they said it would be fine,' Emma said into the phone after a suitable lull. 'When shall I start?'

'Come over to my place after school today to meet Izzy, number 25 Hill View terrace. We can take it from there.'

Forgetting the disturbing newspaper headline for a moment, Emma gave an excited little jump, which neither of her parents noticed. Every job meant more money for Josef and the Cause, more freedom and another step towards getting away from this place. Her toast popped and she smothered it in butter and lashings of honey. She was ready to make her escape when her mother said, 'You're not going to school dressed like that are you?'

Emma shrugged, causing her toast to fall from the plate and land honey side down on the faux marble floor.

'Please, let's not start again, Miranda,' Christopher said with a long sigh. 'Just let her wear what she likes.'

'But she dresses like that just to spite me, she knows it upsets me. She knows it, but still she goes to school dressed like a tramp.'

'The way kids dress these days is no reflection on their upbringing. Everyone knows Emma comes from a good home, that I have money.'

Miranda's sigh was worthy of Greek tragedy. 'Well I certainly haven't seen much of your money recently. Besides, this isn't *only* about you, or *only* about money, Christopher.'

'Don't worry, Miranda,' Emma said as she mopped up the honey from the faux marble tiles. 'Not too many people know I'm your daughter — it's not something I care to advertise.'

'For heaven's sake, stop calling me by my first name!'

Emma glanced at her father. He looked up from his paper, met her eye and gave her a wink.

The doorbell rang but no one moved to answer it. Julian Holdsworth, Miranda's photographer, let himself in and wandered through the house to the family room just as Emma was making her way back upstairs. One glance at his beaming face and droopy blond noodle of a moustache made her quicken her steps. 'How's my gorgeous girl then?' he called up to her. The look he gave her as she beat her retreat made her relieved she wasn't wearing a skirt. She pretended she hadn't heard him and closed her bedroom door.

The voices had long since gone from downstairs, her parents and Julian having left for work. Emma looked at her watch; she still had half an hour before she was due at school.

The breakfast table had been left in disarray for the housekeeper. The paper lay where her father had left it, the finance pages spread across the dirty plates. She stopped for a moment, not daring to touch it. As she downed the half finished glass of orange juice her mother had left she thought how unusual it was for Miranda to leave any. The pervert at the modelling agency and mention of the police must really have left her rattled. The slippery smart of the vodka gave her the courage she needed to turn to the front page of the paper: 'Missing girl's body found at Midland building site.'

Another victim, another miserable story and this one with an ending of the worst kind. She read on until her glasses misted, and she was forced to remove and clean them on her T-shirt. Her hands shook. Breathing deeply, she tried to pull herself together — this was not the time for tears.

Back in her room, her fingers flew across the keyboard with little conscious thought from her. Emma hated to be late for school, but today she would have to make an exception. She would tell the teacher there'd been a trauma at home. Her father had run over their dog in the driveway and they'd had to make an emergency dash to the vet. In the car she'd held poor Snuffy in her arms, one side of his dear little head caved in and covered in gore. The vet was going to wire the dog's jaw and set his broken leg, but he didn't think he'd survive the operation. The tears Emma had held back while she read the newspaper would be allowed to gush freely. Everyone would believe her and everyone would feel sorry for her. Emma Breightling was a good actor; Emma Breightling was good at everything she chose to do.

And she was also an exceedingly good liar.

8

CHAT ROOM TRANSCRIPT 100207
TIMTAM: did u get the pix of the mullets I sent?
ANGEL12: yeah thnx
TIMTAM: what do u think?
ANGEL12: squeeeeeee!!!!
TIMTAM: did they make u feel horny?
ANGEL12: ur baaaad lol!

Robert Mason had been denied bail. He would be held on remand at Hakea prison, pending trial.

'The bus from Hakea will be here soon, but there's a few more things we need to ask,' Stevie said as a uniformed officer escorted Robert Mason into one of Central's interview rooms.

She glanced at Tash and gave her a discreet nod. It would be interesting to see how she handled their pre-planned tactics, if she could strike the right balance in her 'bad cop' role. It would also be a good indication of how seriously Tash had taken her earlier warning. This was a fact-finding mission only and hard as it might be, it was paramount that they leave their personal prejudices outside the interview room door.

The uniformed officer pushed Mason into a chair and closed the door behind him. Mason leaned on the table and pushed his fingers through his spiky hair, looking first at Tash then at Stevie.

'You two again?' he whined. 'I've admitted it, I'm gonna

plead guilty, what more do you want?' Swamped in regulation overalls, he looked ridiculously young, almost young enough to be a victim himself.

Stevie couldn't have cared less.

'Just a few more questions, that's all,' she said.

'But shouldn't my lawyer be here?' Mason looked around the barren interview room as if his lawyer might appear out of one of the sludge green walls.

'It's okay, we've discussed this with him, it doesn't involve your actual case.'

'Then w-what ...'

'Cooperate with us now and I guarantee it will be taken into consideration during the trial,' Stevie said.

He was interested; Stevie could tell by the way his deep brown eyes stopped flitting around the room to focus on hers. Tash had called them 'gravy eyes', but bottomless cesspools might be a more appropriate term, Stevie reflected, keeping her face blank.

He touched his brow. 'I have a headache.'

'I'll get you something for it in a minute,' she said. When she was ready to get him something, she would, and not before. To get the optimum amount of information from him he had to be shown that his every physical need was under their control.

'How can I make this easier?' he asked.

'A young girl's body was found in a builder's skip yesterday. She was the victim of a paedophile,' Stevie said.

His eyes widened with panic. 'You had me locked up yesterday, I couldn't have done it!'

'No one's saying you did, but this murderer and you seem to share a similar approach ...'

'So?'

'Listen to Sergeant Hooper!'

Stevie tensed, expecting a barrage of Tash's dirtiest insults: *rock spider, hanging Johnny, shit head, scum of the earth*. She let out a silent sigh of relief when none seemed forthcoming. Well done, Tash.

'We think you're involved with some kind of Internet club where people like you can swap information and methods of picking up kids,' Stevie said.

Mason wriggled in his seat, adjusting his overalls in the crotch area. 'There are groups like that all over the net.'

'But this one is locally based and contains a list of chat rooms and websites frequented by Perth kids. In fact, I think you got the address of the *Stoned Mullets* chat room visited by Angel12 from this site, yeah?'

He looked away.

Tash circled the table like a shark. During an interrogation, detectives can move around as much as they like but they can insist the suspect remain seated. It was all a part of the tactics of maintaining control.

'You can probably also obtain photographs from this site,' Tash said, keeping her voice level. 'You had two hundred and fifty photos of children on your computer ranging from soft to hardcore abuse and everything in between.'

'They're just pictures,' Mason mumbled.

Tash placed her palms on the table and leaned in towards him. 'Oh yeah, so they have no grounding in reality; that's what you're trying to say?'

'Yeah, well kinda …'

Tash slammed her hands upon the table, making Mason start. Good one, Tash, Stevie thought, that's just the right amount of fright we want from him. Too much and he'll clam up all together. She caught Tash's eye and mouthed, 'My turn.'

Tash stepped back and leaned against the wall, rubbing her stinging palms.

'Strangely enough it's the soft stuff we're interested in at the moment,' Stevie said. 'Our experts tell us that these photos bear a strong resemblance to each other, were taken in the same location and probably by the same photographer.'

'Soft, what do you mean soft?' He looked at the detectives blankly until realisation finally dawned. 'Oh, you mean the *art shots*?'

Tash pushed herself from the wall. 'That's what you call them, *art shots*? Now it's high culture is it? Give me a break!'

'You can't say there's anything wrong with them — Jesus, what's wrong with you people? The kids are dressed ...'

'Yes, Robert, most are dressed, but often in revealing, sexualised clothes and provocatively posed,' Stevie said.

She saw the 'art' pictures lined up in her head, in particular a snap of a little girl sitting up proud and straight in her school uniform, like the one she had of Izzy on her mantelpiece. It was innocent, it was unsuspecting and it made her stomach lurch. 'If we can find the source of these art shots we might also be able to nail the origin of the hardcore photos and videos,' she said.

'I don't know where any of the photos come from, the webmaster ups them.' Mason's voice rose. 'But jeez, what's the big deal about all this? I've never even touched a kid, all I do is look at pictures.'

'But you were planning on doing more than look at Angel12, weren't you?' Tash asked.

'Look, it was just an experiment, right? If anything had happened with her, it would have been what she wanted too.'

'What, with the help of money, drugs, CDs?' Tash said.

They were getting off the point; if the interrogation were to turn to Mason's court case, they'd be obliged to turn the tape on. Stevie guided Mason back to where she wanted him.

'We think the man who murdered Bianca Webster might belong to this Internet group of yours. Your computer log shows us you visit a site called the Dream Team — you may've run your files through a shredding program, making the information hard to access, but it's not impossible.'

'Next time buy a better shredding program, Mason — though I suppose there's not much left in the coffers once you're done spending up on kiddie porn,' Tash said.

'It's not porn, why do you have to make it sound so degrading? It's all just natural, kids are still sexual beings, they enjoy it, just like the rest of us,' Mason said.

Tash clenched her fists at her sides. 'Oh yeah, the girl being raped in the video looked like she was having the time of her life.'

'I don't know how that clip got there, someone must have planted it. I don't do violence.'

Tash consciously unclenched her fists. 'I was called to the hospital not long ago, to a toddler who'd been so brutally sodomised he'll be wearing a colostomy bag for the rest of his life.'

'And I'm not into boys either.'

Tash slammed her fist onto the table again, ramming her face up close to his. The pulse throbbing through the flush at her neck looked fit to burst; she wasn't playacting. 'You just don't get it do you? People like you should be burned alive!'

Stevie pulled her away from the table. Tash rubbed both hands over her face and took a breath. 'I'm okay,' she murmured, shaking her head when Stevie offered to continue.

To Stevie's relief, Tash changed tack, dropping the subject of the rape video; they'd been through it with him before and maybe it was a one off. 'Our experts will be able to piece together the data from your computer, but it would save time if you just gave us the information,' Tash said, in control again.

'I can give you the password, but I don't think you'll get much further than the home page. There's all sorts of security there — even I couldn't get through it.'

'But we need to know where the soft photos have come from. Some shots are of a candid nature, of girls getting dressed in what looks like a change room,' Tash said calmly.

'There's a hotmail address of a photographer,' Mason said, shoulders slumped, mouth turned down in defeat. 'We can buy the photos from him and download them from a file sharing site.'

'How much?'

'Twenty bucks a hit.'

'Your habit doesn't come cheap,' Tash said.

Mason rested his chin on his hand and thought long and hard. 'You said if I cooperated, the judge might be more lenient.'

'We're going to take you up to our ops room in a minute and you can show our experts as much about this site of yours as you can.' Stevie flicked him a tight smile. 'Is there anything else you'd like to add while we're still down here?'

Mason pressed his fists into his eye sockets and sniffed. 'Well, these photos I told you about that cost twenty bucks? For forty you can get the personal details of the kids in the art shots. Names, addresses, ages, email, the lot.'

Stevie and Tash exchanged glances. *Shit.*

Mason narrowed his eyes and glared at Stevie, 'But I wish I'd seen a genuine photo of Angel12 and not that fake one you sent me.' He curled his lip. 'Jesus, that was wishful thinking, eh? You'd never have looked like that in your dreams, baby!'

'How's it going?' Stevie addressed the plump middle-aged constable hunched over her keyboard in the ops room. Clarissa D'Silva, computer nerd extraordinaire, was one of a bunch more than happy to sit behind a screen for eight hours a day, leaving active duty to the likes of the more physically inclined like Tash and herself.

'It's like Mason said, this website has a minefield of security measures. I've found the hotmail address of the photographer, but its ISP is listed as coming from Turkmenistan, so matters are somewhat complicated.'

'Terrific,' Tash sighed.

'I said it complicates matters, I didn't say it puts an end to them. I'm going to have to sign up if I want to get further in. What shall I call myself?'

'How about Peter File?' Tash suggested.

Clarissa laughed. 'They're not paedophiles remember, they merely love children.' She put on an arch vaudeville accent, in imitation of an elderly rock spider they'd apprehended a few weeks ago. 'There's nothing unnatural about what we do. In ancient times it was common practice for older men to go with young girls — and boys. It's no different to how it was when people got shocked if a woman showed her ankle. Who knows, in one hundred years, it might be considered normal again ...'

Tash laughed, 'Yeah, right, and I'm running off to join a nunnery.' Stevie laughed too, glad to see that Tash had recovered her humour.

'What's the latest on the dead girl from last night?' Clarissa asked Stevie, back to her normal voice.

'They traced the rego to a Miro Kusak from Mundaring,' Stevie told her. 'When our guys turned up with a warrant for him, all they found was the ex-wife. Separated nearly a year, pending divorce, so she said; claimed she didn't know where he was living. They pulled the house apart, found enough high tech stuff in his den to launch a space shuttle, but nothing incriminating. His wife said he took his main computer and flash drives with him.'

'You want me to go and have a talk with her, Stevie?' Tash asked, jumping down from the desk. Her face clouded when she read the look on Stevie's face and she pulled her away from Clarissa's earshot.

'What's the matter, don't you trust me? You think I'm going to take it out on his missus?'

Stevie hesitated. 'No, of course not. Go on,' she indicated the door with a tilt of her head. 'Find out everything you possibly can about Mrs Kusak's estranged husband.'

9

People in various stages of physical or emotional distress lined the corridors of Royal Perth Hospital. In fact the casualty department wasn't much different to Central Police Station on a Saturday night, Monty decided. He sat on a bench next to an old man whose chest rattled and wheezed like the water pipes in Stevie's kitchen, and watched the parade of walking wounded. A bikie in leathers staggered by with blood streaming from his head, another followed with a bunch of reddened tissues to his nose. A couple were screaming abuse at each other near the automatic doors until a security guard came to escort them from the hospital. A listless child was wheeled past on a trolley, his mother crying and wringing her hands by his side.

God, there was no getting away from it.

For the third time in half an hour he checked his mobile phone for messages. He doubted he'd be hearing back yet from the team he'd dispatched to China Town, but his restless hands needed something to do, some kind of distraction from the misery surrounding him. He yawned, wiped tears of exhaustion from his cheeks and massaged his jaw. An intermittent toothache seemed to be flaring up again.

Izzy had shown him how to work one of the games on his phone and he wondered if he could remember her instructions. Even with his glasses on, he had trouble finding the right keys and hit several in error before he was in. Ah yes. He had to get one of the heads with the gaping mouths to devour …

'Inspector McGuire?'

He gave a start and quickly turned the phone off. A young nurse stood above him with a look of amusement on her face.

'Doctor Sutcliffe will see you now. Please come with me,' she said.

He followed her past several cubicles of quivering curtains to the last one. A middle-aged doctor stooped over a trolley, finishing his notes.

'Good of you to see me, Doc, I appreciate how busy you are,' Monty said.

The doctor looked over the rims of his glasses. 'Sorry to keep you waiting, Inspector, a hectic day.' He pointed to the empty trolley. 'An infarct right here, a man only about your age, your build, stressful job — chronic smoker of course.'

Monty felt himself being examined. He shifted his feet and cleared his throat. 'You said you had some luck with my query about an Asian man with kidney necro …' he struggled to remember the rest of it.

The doctor smiled, 'Nephropathy.'

'That's the one.'

'You suggested the patient might have been an illegal migrant. Well, you were right in assuming he might have presented here for treatment. We get quite a few at Royal Perth — no Medicare cards, just a wad of sweaty cash, and of course we treat them with no questions asked. I spoke to one of my registrars and she remembers seeing just such a man. She'd talk to you herself only she's just come off a week of nights. I told her I'd handle it.'

'Okay, you might start with telling me about this disease, keeping it simple, please,' Monty said with a smile.

'The common name for IgA nephropathy is Berger's disease. It affects three times more men than women, with Asian men at the top of the list. It's a kidney disease characterised by abnormal deposits of the protein IgA in the kidney's filtering system and one of the symptoms is blood in the urine — that's what the man presented with when he checked himself in.'

'Did he speak English?'

'A bit.'

'Name?'

The doctor smiled. 'Bruce Lee.'

Monty smiled wryly. 'Of course.'

'As well as the blood in his urine, he had a history of upper respiratory infection and high blood pressure. My registrar made the preliminary diagnosis and arranged tests to confirm. But when she mentioned the possibility of a kidney biopsy, he jumped off the trolley and became quite aggressive, forcing her to press the emergency button for security assistance. He was eventually escorted from the hospital, having refused treatment altogether.'

'How sick was he exactly?'

'Still in the early stages of the disease so he would've been able to function relatively normally for a while. Left untreated however, the disease would most likely have slowly progressed to acute renal failure and possibly death.'

'Did he know the dangers do you think?'

'My registrar explained them. She said he seemed to take them on board because he got more and more agitated with everything she said.'

Monty rubbed his chin thoughtfully. 'When you tell something to patients that they don't want to hear, what do they tend to do?' he asked.

'I see your point,' the doctor nodded. 'They usually get a second opinion.'

Monty thanked the doctor, stepped into the corridor and phoned Wayne Pickering, asking him to make some enquiries at Northbridge Chinese herbalists and medicine centres. If the guy thought he'd been let down by the western medical system, he might very well have gone down the street to one of these for a second opinion.

He pocketed his phone, about to turn on his heel and leave the hospital when an unsettling thought stopped him in his tracks. He looked back into the examination cubicle where Doctor Sutcliffe was still finishing his notes.

'Just one more thing, Doc,' Monty said through the parted curtains.

'Yes Inspector?'

'The bloke you had in here before, the one who had the heart attack. What happened to him, where did he go?'

'He didn't go anywhere. I'm afraid he died.'

Monty felt the blood drain from his face.

The doctor looked concerned. 'I'm sorry, did you know him?'

Monty shook his head vigorously. 'No, I didn't. No.'

He tried to call Stevie as he was leaving the hospital, but all he got was a message from her answering machine. He told her to ring him.

Later that afternoon Monty caught up with Wayne, Barry and Angus Wong in his office. It seemed his hunch about their mystery victim seeking a second opinion about his diagnosis had proved correct.

'It was about the third herbalist shop we visited, wasn't it fellas?' Barry checked with his colleagues.

Angus nodded, said to Monty, 'Mr Cheng's shop — he speaks practically no English.'

'But he had a pretty dolly of a Chinese interpreter with him,' Barry added.

'Angela Nguyen is multilingual Vietnamese,' Angus answered with a long-suffering sigh.

Barry shrugged, 'Same diff.'

'I went into the back room to talk to Cheng,' Angus told Monty, 'while Barry and Wayne spoke to Angela in the front, in between serving customers.'

'It was interesting, Mont,' Wayne added. 'When we got together to swap notes, we discovered a discrepancy in their stories.'

'Yeah, Mr Cheng told me the man's name was Zhang Li.' Angus spelled the name for Monty. 'Cheng had never met him before but had heard on the grapevine that he was a money lender, an illegal who'd only been in the country for a couple of months. He wanted something for the blood in his urine and Mr Cheng mixed him up a herbal concoction …'

'And Cheng said Zhang Li had a kid with him.'

Angus scowled, 'Yes, Barry I was getting to that. He had an Asian kid with him of about fourteen or fifteen, a scruffy little bugger who wasn't introduced to Cheng.'

'But Angela Nguyen's version wasn't nearly as helpful,' Wayne said. 'She said she remembered the man with the blood in his urine, but not his name. She also denied seeing a boy.'

'It's because you got her all in a fluster,' said Barry, straightening the collar of his Boss polo shirt. 'You should have let me do the talking. You just have no idea about handling women, you have no couth.'

'And I suppose you would have done better?' Wayne said.

Angus muttered under his breath in Chinese, having little patience with the love-hate relationship between these two. Barry and Wayne went back years and had worked with each other long enough to know exactly which buttons they could press to good effect. Despite their constant bickering, they were a good team though, complementing each other in their differences.

Angus brought a different set of skills to the job: a cool professionalism and an almost obsessive eye for detail. Monty could see Angus being selected to take the reins should he decide to toss the job in. Tossing it in — he had no idea where that thought came from, what else he wanted to do or even what he was capable of doing.

His attention kicked back in when he heard Wayne say, 'I'm going back to see Angela Nguyen later. Alone. She's hiding something, I'm sure of it.'

10

Excerpt from chat room transcript 121206
  BETTYBO: wanna meet F2F?
  HARUM SCARUM: Y?
  BETTYBO: I wan 2 rt Katy Enigma stories wit u
  HARUM SCARUM: Me 2 but not yet. we cn rite on line 4now

It was Stevie's turn to cook. She ran through her mental shopping list as she hurried from the lifts in Central. For seafood chowder she'd need prawns, a few snapper pieces, mussels maybe, coconut milk, coriander and crusty bread. With any luck Izzy would be out of school on time and they could pick the ingredients up before Emma came around.

She spotted Monty in the front foyer, standing half a head taller than most of the bustling figures. He held up his hand to stop her, hurrying over before she could pass through the revolving door.

'Mont, I've got to go,' she said before he could speak. She jumped into the revolving compartment and Monty joined her. 'I have to collect Izzy then meet the new babysitter.'

They stepped outside into a wall of heat.

'Just hang on a minute will you?' Monty took hold of her arm to keep her in the shade.

With so much on her mind, Stevie didn't have time for his

quick words that always became long, but she listened patiently to what he had to say about Wayne's investigations at the Chinese herbalist. As she listened, part of her brain pondered the suitability of a thirteen year old for a babysitter. She also managed to slide in a thought or two about Tash, wondering what she'd learned from Mrs. Kusak.

Talk about multi-tasking.

It seemed as if Monty just wanted an excuse to linger for a moment, but it was a luxury she didn't have time for right now. As Monty talked on, she bounced from one bubble soled trainer to the other, scanning the car park. It was chock-a-block with overflow from the the cricket ground and she couldn't see the car she'd borrowed from her mother anywhere.

The crack of leather on willow and the crowd roared. 'The cheek of it,' she muttered when she finally got a word in, 'illegally parking at a police station.'

A youth barged past them carrying a long parcel wrapped in brown paper and tied with string. It didn't take a genius to work out what was inside it. Monty had just introduced an amnesty on illegal weapons — they could be handed in to the police station without prosecution in exchange for tickets to the test. The scheme had been going well for everyone except the officers in charge of the armoury, who'd been so inundated they'd run out of storage space.

'Are you listening to me at all?' Monty asked, slapping his thigh with exasperation.

'You said you were about to phone me but then you saw me in the lobby and decided to speak to me now. You filled me in on the latest on the floater case, then you said you wanted to arrange a team meeting for the Bianca Webster case.' She spotted the bonnet of her mother's white Citroen sticking out from behind a four-wheel drive. 'Beauty, there it is.'

'Shit, this is ridiculous,' Monty grumbled, increasing his pace to keep up with her. 'We never seem to get any time to talk.'

'Come with me to collect Izzy and we can talk in the car,' she said, and as an afterthought added, 'She's your daughter too.'

He reddened. 'Yes, I am aware of that. If I organise a meeting for five this afternoon can you leave Izzy with the girl while you attend?'

'If I think she's suitable, yes.'

'You should look into that after-school centre.'

'I have. They've too many kids and not enough staff.'

'And call Natasha Hayward, I want her in on the meeting too.'

Stevie looked at her watch. 'Will do. She's visiting Mrs Kusak now, but she should be back on time. Okay, I've really got to go. See you.'

Monty stood in the shade of the entrance for a moment and watched Stevie run through the glare of parked cars. Tyres squealed as she left the car park and darted into the traffic.

Tash didn't turn up for the team meeting, nor did she answer her phone. Stevie dropped by her place on her way home, but only Terry was home, and he hadn't seen Tash all evening. Stevie then had to spend precious moments assuring Terry that if his sister had been involved in a car accident they would have heard by now. She asked him to get Tash to give her a call as soon as she got home.

The meeting at Central had gone longer than expected and the deviation to Tash's place meant Stevie was later home than she'd planned. She was hoping this hadn't caused Emma any problems — Izzy tended to play up when she was late to bed. Stevie let herself quietly into the house, interested to see how the babysitting session was going.

Emma sat on the couch with Izzy on her knee, slurping on an icy pole, rapt in a blanket of attention. Stevie tiptoed closer, wanting to hear but not wanting to break the spell.

Izzy interrupted the girl's narration by thrusting the icy pole under her nose and offering her a lick.

'No thanks, I have germ issues,' Emma smiled. 'Do you want me to go on?'

Izzy nodded and snuggled closer.

'It was a magic, fairy-tale kind of a place,' Emma continued, 'part castle and part luxury villa, and it was built over a lake where a billion water lilies grew. It had towers and battlements and an inner courtyard with a pond and a statue of Peter Pan for a fountain. A high wall surrounded the courtyard, and the only way you could get into it was through one of those little doors like they have in the walls of prisons …'

'Daddy says they're for little prisoners,' Izzy interrupted, her whisper whistling through her missing front teeth.

'Then he must be right, Izzy. And because of all these barriers and the very small door with the very big lock, Katy Enigma knew that in this place she would always be safe from her enemies. If by some bad luck one of them was to get into the castle, she could escape by the secret passageway hidden behind the bookcase in her bedroom, or the other one that led from one of the kitchen cabinets and ran under the lake. If they came upon her outside in the courtyard, she could climb the one thousand steps to the highest tower, the one with the dome on top of it, and throw herself off to make her escape by running across the water lilies …'

'And the baddies would try to follow and then be drownded,' Izzy interrupted.

'Drowned,' Emma corrected. 'That's right, because they don't have magic powers like Katy Enigma.'

'Or her jet-propelled backpack,' Izzy said.

Much as she was enjoying the story, Stevie could play the voyeur no longer. She cleared her throat.

Emma looked up and smiled, flashing Stevie a mouthful of coloured braces. 'Oh, hello Mrs Hooper.'

Izzy jumped from her babysitter's knee. 'Mummy's not Mrs Hooper! She's not Mrs anything — silly!'

Emma reddened. 'Oh, I'm sorry,' but made a quick recovery. 'We laid the table and made a salad. Izzy said she doesn't like fish, so I gave her baked beans on toast, I hope that's okay. I wasn't sure how you wanted the soup cooked, so I've left that for you to do. Izzy's had her bath and done her reading.'

Stevie was almost speechless. Mrs Carlyle hadn't been wrong when she'd said this girl was a model of efficiency.

'Thank you, Emma, you've done a terrific job.' She smiled as she looked around the lounge room, at the cushions set straight upon the sofa, the hearth rug smoothed and the toys in the toy box — the place seemed to be tidier now than when she'd left it. She rummaged in her bag and handed Emma a twenty-dollar note. 'I'll give you a lift home.'

'Thanks, but I'm okay. It's only a short walk.'

'I don't think your parents would want you walking home so late — it's nearly dark.'

'They don't care,' the girl shrugged. 'But do whatever you want, it's cool.'

Stevie would have liked the opportunity to talk some more with Emma, but the short drive was monopolised by Izzy eager to hear the rest of the story. Apparently the waterlily lake was the home of a friendly dragon with eyes like ginormous stuffed olives and a tongue which, when unfurled, could stretch the length of their school oval.

Number 64 Riviera Place dwarfed its neighbours, taking up almost every available metre of the sloping riverside block. Stevie's headlights lit up a white, double storied, flat roofed building, easily visible through an inadequate row of pencil pines. Look at me, look at me, the house seemed to cry, but upon closer inspection, there was little to see other than the even stripes of the front lawn and the dead eyes of huge reflective glass windows. Like looking at black ice, Stevie thought.

'What do you think of it?' Emma asked her.

'Your house? It looks great.'

'Liar,' Emma said with a grin. 'But it looks better than it did before. When it was grey it looked like Hitler's bunker. I got them to paint it.'

Stevie smiled, but said nothing. Talking to someone about their house was like talking to someone about their children. They were allowed to be critical, but more fool you if you agreed.

Emma jumped from the car and ruffled Izzy's head through the open back window. 'I'll tell you some more of the story when I come over next, but first we have to finish reading your schoolbook.' She turned to Stevie. 'You wouldn't want her watching too much TV would you?'

Stevie shook her head vigorously, the model parent to a stern schoolteacher. *Shit* — how old was this girl again?

'Same time tomorrow, Emma?' she queried.

'Sweet.'

The return to teenage vernacular was reassuring. The front porch light came on and Stevie saw a plump figure bathed in light. She unclipped her seat belt and made to leave the car. 'If that's your mother, I'd better come and introduce myself.'

Emma gave a slight start. 'Um, no, that's not Mum, that's our housekeeper. Mum won't be home yet.'

Stevie relaxed back into the car seat. 'I'd like to meet her sometime.'

'Sure, I'll arrange it.' Emma turned on her heel and ran towards the house, disappearing into the light before Stevie could get a firmer commitment.

Izzy was asleep in her car seat by the time they got home.

'Emma, where have you been and whose car was that?'

'Oh, hi, Mrs Bamford, great to see you too.'

The housekeeper shook her head and clucked her tongue. 'Your mother never said anything about you going out after school. I've been worried.'

Emma kissed Mrs Bamford on her cheek and squeezed her floppy arm. 'Mrs Carlyle wanted me to do some extra babysitting this week. I did tell Miranda, but you know what she's like, she must have forgotten to pass on the message. The lady who dropped me off was one of Mrs Carlyle's friends who called in for a visit when I was there. She lives nearby and offered to drive me home.'

'I'll go and heat up your tea in the microwave.' Mrs Bamford headed toward the kitchen, her slippered feet yawing inwards as she negotiated the shiny sea of marble.

Emma stopped at the stairs, gripped the wrought iron balustrade with one hand and swung outwards, making her body star shaped. 'I ate at Mrs Carlyle's,' she called out. 'When are my parents getting back?' The balustrade groaned.

'Stop doing that dear, it's becoming quite loose,' the housekeeper chastised.

Emma continued to swing; Mrs Bamford would expect nothing less.

Mrs Bamford said, 'Your mother's at one of her cocktail parties and your Dad's gone to his conference in Queensland.'

You mean, Emma thought, Miranda's off with her boyfriend and Christopher's looking for a big chunk of Queensland sand to bury his head in.

Her father used to play with her sometimes: she had vague memories of soccer on the oval when she could barely walk, let alone kick a ball. And there were the stories too, always the stories before bed. She tried to remember when they stopped and couldn't; it must have been a long time ago.

'You staying over?' Emma asked.

'Yes. Now you be a lovey and get on with your homework. There's a new series of "Grey's Anatomy", I mustn't miss the start.' She rolled down to the TV room on thick stockinged legs which always made Emma think of the maid in Tom and Jerry.

The babysitter being baby sat, how stupid was that. Then again, not much made sense in this strange, dysfunctional family. Emma waited until she heard the music blast from the TV. Poor, dear, lovey Mrs Bamford, just as well you're so deaf, so trustful.

Emma strode past the TV room where the shadows flickered beneath the closed door. In the kitchen she double clicked the deadbolt and stepped into the paved back courtyard. The garden pond shone like black ink, reflecting the splayed trumpets of day lilies, golliwog heads of agapanthus and spear-shaped irises. She'd chosen and planted the flowers around the pond herself after extensive research on the Internet for the most colourful and longest blossoming. The citrus hues of the day lilies crowded with the yellow daisies and pale native orchids, gradually merging with the blues and purples of iris and agapanthus. The gaps between the stone steps leading to the pond were carpeted with tiny blue-flowered bindweed and English violets.

A jet of water from Peter Pan's pipe carved an arc of silver through his silhouette. Miranda didn't know who the statue was supposed to be. She'd had some men dig the pond and put up the fountain chosen at random from the garden shop. 'What a charming little boy,' she'd said.

Peter Pan had been Emma's best friend. When she felt sad or lonely she would come out here and talk to him. She imagined him teaching her how to fly and taking her off to Neverland where she'd help him fight the pirates and help Wendy to look after the lost boys.

The dream had faded as she'd grown up, but the pond was still one of her favourite places, rarely visited by anyone in the household except her and the gardener. She turned on the garden light, then the green pond light, and sat on the stone bench for a moment to watch the goldfish glide, tails swirling through the water like chiffon in a breeze.

A scuffing sound from the other side of the garden wall broke into her thoughts. She looked up from the pond to see two hands clasping the top of the wall as if someone was trying to heave himself up on it. Or herself, Emma automatically corrected. You should never assume anything. She stopped breathing, her eyes strained as she peered through the shadows. The top of a dark head appeared above the wall, then a young face. It was a boy, his face pale as the moon. One of 'her' kids, she wondered? *Squeaky*? If so, how had he managed to find her here?

Emma stood up. 'Hi,' she called.

The head disappeared. There was a thump and then the sound of running feet on the other side of the wall.

Emma ran to the wall and stood on the pot of a cumquat tree to see over. 'Hey stop! It's okay! *Squeaky, Howzat, Cheeky Charlie* — is that you?' The figure didn't turn back, continued running along the river's edge until he rounded the bend.

Emma jumped down from the plant pot feeling vaguely disappointed. It was a silly idea; the boy couldn't have been one of 'hers'. Sometimes she wondered if it was a mistake, remaining so anonymous, maybe if she had been more open ...

She shook her head to rid it of the crazy thought. He was probably nothing to do with her, just someone casing the joint, checking to see if there was anything in the garden worth pinching.

She returned to the pond. The palm tree groaned, an owl hooted. The reticulation from the front garden announced itself with a soft fizz. She had about twenty minutes to go before the sprinklers here would be activated. Kicking off her trainers, she removed her tracky pants and reached for Peter's hand. He helped her into the pond and warm yoghurty sludge slid between her toes.

Careful not to slip, she felt her way down the statue's body, holding onto his leg with one hand and lowering the other hand into the water. She groped around feeling for the jut of the underwater plinth and slid the metal box from its hiding spot. The slimy bodies of fish slithered against the bare skin of her legs and the blood-warm water tickled at the sleeve of her T-shirt. She glanced around, shivered. No face at the wall this time but there were still plenty of gaps in the wall for prying eyes.

She couldn't shake the feeling that she was still being watched.

11

It was the same kind of cloud, Stevie mused, that floated in the sky when they'd been doing controlled scrub burns on the station. Nothing dramatic and billowing, just low slung and greasy, indicative of a gentle simmering heat from the ground below.

The cloud had started gathering at the team meeting. By the time Monty came home with it hanging above his head, Stevie could smell it, could almost see it. She soon realised this was not the time to tell him about the phone call she'd just received from a hysterical Mrs Kusak. He was angry enough with Tash as it was.

'It's totally unprofessional, that's what it is,' he grouched as he plonked his keys near the phone. 'We needed her at that meeting. I make sure my team members keep their phones switched on day and night. You should too if you ever want to get beyond acting officer in charge. You have to set some kind of boundaries, discipline your people.'

Stevie sighed and returned to the pot bubbling on the stove. He'd bust a valve if she told him the rest of it now.

'I called round at her place on my way home, but she wasn't there. Her brother said she hadn't called and he didn't know when she was coming home. Her phone probably had a flat battery,' she told him.

'But you left a message?'

'Yes Monty, I've told you that. Twice. And I told Terry to get her to ring me when she got home.'

Monty tore at his tie and flung it across a kitchen chair and stormed out of the room, his heavy tread making the jarrah floorboards lurch under her feet like the deck of a ship. She heard the banging of drawers, the slamming of the wardrobe door. Within seconds he was back.

'Where are my clothes?' he demanded.

'Where you left them.'

'In your wardrobe, but they're not there now. I've never seen such a mess, I'm surprised you can ever find anything in it — talk about the bloody black hole of Calcutta.'

Stevie tasted some soup from the wooden spoon. 'Then they must be at your place. Or in your car.'

'This is crazy, this whole situation is fucked.'

She slid the saucepan off the hotplate and turned to face him. 'Then maybe you should go home. We can try for a rerun tomorrow night.'

Monty stared at her for a moment, then his shoulders suddenly dropped. 'I'm hungry. And that smells good.'

She gave him a nonchalant shrug, kept her smile to herself.

He moved over to the soup pot and took a sample from the spoon. Then another. 'It is good,' he said, 'but it needs more salt.'

'Then hand me the salt and grab us both a beer while you're at it.'

Monty's mood improved as they ate. She told him about the new babysitter, Emma Breightling, and what a hit she'd been with Izzy. He even laughed when she described how the girl looked. 'Sounds like a female version of Harry Potter,' he said.

'Harriet Potter aged thirteen, going on fifty.'

He was as good as he was likely to get, she decided; it was time to broach the topic. 'Mrs Kusak rang me a couple of hours ago. She wants to make an official complaint about Tash.' She lowered her voice half hoping he wouldn't hear her. 'She was in quite a state, almost hysterical.'

Monty clattered his spoon into his empty bowl and jumped to his feet. It didn't take much of a change in the wind to turn a controlled burn into a raging inferno. 'So now Natasha's gone AWOL. That's just bloody marvellous!'

May as well cut to the chase now, Stevie thought, things couldn't get any worse. She took a breath. 'Mrs Kusak said Tash was intimidating, that she threatened her with violence if she found she was holding things back about her husband. Apparently she even showed her Bianca's autopsy pictures, made her physically sick.'

'Christ — would she really have done that?' Monty pressed the heel of his palm into his eye.

'I don't know. She was a bit heavy handed with the guy we caught in the park the other day, I had to warn her off him.' She gave him an airbrushed summary of the incident at the DNA tower.

'You'll have to have a talk with Mrs K,' Monty muttered, already calming down. 'See if you can persuade her to drop the complaint, or at least find out exactly what happened. And find Natasha and talk to her first. They'll be two sides to this, there always are,' he said.

'I will. I'll call on her at home again if I have to. And I've arranged to see Mrs Kusak in Mundaring tomorrow afternoon; I'm bound to have caught up with Tash by then.'

They cleared the table and did the washing up and made the fifty-year old kitchen as clean as it ever would be, though Stevie could still smell mouse in the cupboard under the sink.

She'd been planning on doing the house up ever since she'd bought the 'renovator's dream,' but had become so used to the place now, the torn lino, the sagging floor and the rattling water pipes, she wasn't even sure if she wanted a new house any more.

Monty picked up his keys from where he'd left them near the phone.

'I'd better go,' he said as he kissed her.

'Really?' She put her hand up the inside of his shirt.

'I have no clean clothes for tomorrow and I have a meeting with the commissioner first thing.'

She felt goose bumps on his skin. 'But you don't need clothes now.' The only thing she enjoyed about their rows was the make up afterwards.

Friday

12

Terry answered the door of the Inglewood townhouse.

'Stevie!' he said, grabbing her and pulling her into a bear hug that almost squeezed the breath out of her body. He had no idea of his strength.

'Oh, I'm sorry, so sorry,' he said as she attempted to push him off. He let her go, blushed and stared at his feet. 'I'm just happy to see you, that's all.'

Stevie laughed, she'd only seen him the night before, but you'd think it had been years ago. He was looking 1950s smart in a nylon shirt tucked into high waisted trousers, his vinyl trainers with the Velcro tabs perfectly matched. He clung to the doorframe for balance and hefted up a foot. 'New shoes,' he said as the hot easterly wind lifted his thinning hair. He was five years older than his sister. 'Tash bought me them.'

Stevie stooped to inspect. When she'd finished admiring them she said, 'Off to work, Terry?' She knew he loved the sheltered workshop he attended and never missed a day if he could help it.

He looked sad and shook his head. 'Tash is sick. I have to stay home.'

'That's too bad. What's the matter with her?' Stevie asked.

Terry slapped himself on the head with a blow that could have knocked a lesser man down. 'Mee-grain.'

'Migraine?' Stevie queried. 'She hasn't had one of those in

ages.' She gently pushed past his bulk. 'Is she in bed?' Without waiting for an answer she made her way down the short passageway and knocked on Tash's bedroom door.

'No visitors, no noise, no light,' Terry said as he lumbered after her, his enormous hands twisting with anxiety.

Stevie turned and placed a hand on his arm. 'It's all right; I know what she's like when she has a migraine. I won't stay long. I just need a quick word. Has she got plenty of water?'

Terry scratched his head.

'Well, you go and get her a jug of water — from the tap, no ice, and a glass. And better grab a warm flannel for her head.'

It took a while for her instructions to sink in. Terry was a sensitive soul, easily upset and she knew they couldn't talk shop in front of him. She hoped the task would keep him occupied long enough for her to have a private word with his sister.

The curtains in the room were closed, but enough light leaked through the cracks to produce a dim visibility. The small mound on the bed stirred as she approached.

'I'm sorry Stevie, I should have rung, but this is a bad one,' Tash gingerly rolled over, in obvious pain.

Stevie could barely hear her, and sat close on the edge of the bed.

'I was sick as a dog last night. Vision like an out of tune TV — the works,' Tash continued. 'I tried to get Terry to call you, but you know what he's like with phones.'

'Have you had your pills?'

'I have now.' Tash indicated to the prescription medication on her bedside table with a limp hand. 'But I didn't have my pills when it started yesterday. If I'd taken them when it began on my way to see Mrs Kusak, I could've nipped this thing in the bud.'

Stevie thought for a moment. Should the shit hit the fan, the migraine might work in Tash's defence. She would attempt to discover the facts from Mrs K then hopefully smooth over the offence caused. It made sense that the migraine attack would account for irritability and, with any luck, memory loss too.

The room was hot and airless. 'Do you want me to put the air conditioner on? It's going to be a stinker of a day.'

Tash shook her head as if it was only held onto her neck by a thread. 'Too noisy.'

It was pointless trying to question her now. The stress of Mrs Kusak's accusation would only increase her headache. 'Just take whatever time you need. Ring me when you're ready to come back,' Stevie said.

A smile flickered at Tash's mouth. 'Don't worry, Terry will look after me.' She managed to raise the volume of her voice. 'Just make sure you get that prick of a child killer, okay?'

The sound of shattering glass at the doorway made them both jump. Tash groaned and put her hand to her head. 'Shit.'

'Don't worry,' Stevie said, 'I'll deal with it, but I'll have to put the light on so cover your eyes.'

Stevie flicked the switch and Tash groaned again. Terry had already dropped to his knees and was scrabbling through the broken glass and water in a futile attempt to clean up. He cried out to Stevie and held up a finger dripping with blood.

'It's okay, it's okay, I'll clean it up,' Stevie said, trying to pull him to his feet, away from the mess.

'My shoes,' he moaned. She looked at his feet. One of the trainers was splashed with scarlet, as if it had been dipped in a can of red paint.

With her softly-softly approach to Mrs Kusak clearly thought out, and a plausible explanation for Tash's behaviour, Stevie's hands relaxed on the steering wheel and she began to enjoy the drive to the hills. She turned the volume of the police radio down and the golden oldies station up. Leaving the last of the traffic lights behind in Midland, the road took on a more countrified appearance. She passed a bloated kangaroo lying on the gravel shoulder, shredded truck tyres next to it, curling in the sun. The external temperature recorded on the dash was 41 degrees. She turned up the air conditioning.

Properties became larger, gardens browner except in those where windmills marked the locations of dams or bores and where the owners allowed themselves the luxury of a small patch of green. At Mundaring townsite she turned off the highway; Mrs Kusak lived somewhere along Weir Road.

A throaty Eartha Kitt song came on the radio and she increased the volume.

Most of the houses Stevie passed were small but the blocks large, many with cottage gardens and even the occasional white picket fence. She could picture herself living up here. It wasn't the kind of country she grew up in, but she wasn't ready to give up proximity to the city yet. They'd have chooks, a vegie patch; Izzy could have a pony and a dog.

Stevie began to warble along with the song — an old fashioned house and an old fashioned fence didn't sound too bad at all.

But it was a bit far from the beach.

The crackle of static from the police radio intruded into her fantasy. She turned off Eartha and strained to hear. The male voice sounded young, inexperienced and panicky as he struggled to report the discovery at Mundaring Weir of a dumped four-wheel drive matching the description of Kusak's. Through the gabble she caught the code three-thirty-eight — sudden death, repeated several times. She was less than five minutes from the location, so she radioed in to tell the patrolman to stay where he was and wait for her arrival.

The blue and white police car was parked at the lookout next to an overflowing rubbish bin with a halo of flies. The heat wriggled up from the bitumen car park; it was the hottest time of day. She twisted behind to the back seat and reached for her peaked cap and heavy police vest and reluctantly put them on, then started to make her way down.

The track beyond the busted 'No Vehicular Access' sign was rough, but wide enough to take a vehicle — indeed, fresh tyre tracks made it clear she was at the right spot. Loose gravel and gumnuts rolled under her feet like ball bearings as she made her way down. The dirt between the bare-knuckle rocks was red from iron oxide, as if the earth had bled into it, the air still and weighted with the scent of eucalypt. It didn't take long for the sweat to gather into cooling circles under her armpits. The heat sucked at her breath and soon all she could hear was her own laboured breathing.

A rustle from somewhere to her right.

She skidded to a stop.

Pebbles rolled and the humidity pressed.

A twig snapped.

She peered into the surrounding bush, saw nothing, not even the tremble of leaves. Whatever had made the snap was too big for a snake or a goanna. A country girl, Stevie knew the variety of noises the bush could make.

She took another step, slid a foot or two on the loose gravel and was forced to cling to a sapling for support else risk slithering the rest of the way down on her backside.

A scrap of blue and red fabric hanging from a prickle bush at the side of the track caught her attention. It could only have come from a checked shirt, and the bright colour told her it hadn't been there long. A lucky find? Maybe it was. She teased it into a paper evidence bag and tucked it into one of her vest pockets.

Another sound, this time from the opposite side of the track. She whirled in time to catch the dying shiver of a nearby bush. Just a roo, she told herself as she rubbed the back of her neck, sticky with sweat and dust. Uneasy now, she continued down the track, spinning into sharp turns every now and then to surprise her phantom stalker.

With a sense of relief she rounded the curve at the bottom of the hill and found herself within a few metres of the four-wheel drive. The front end of the vehicle was concertinaed into a tree near the shoreline. The peaceful waters of the weir lapped at the fringe of rocks and sand. To her right she saw the old pumping station standing above the water on concrete pylons. Long abandoned, its small windows were boarded up with planks, though a new padlock glinted on its heavy wooden door.

There was no preamble from the tall, beet-faced constable who rushed over to her. 'Oh Christ, Jesus,' he spluttered. 'Thank God you're here, ma'am, the last ten minutes seemed like ten hours. Assistance is on its way, but I'm just glad you were so close.'

'You shouldn't have radioed in the three-thirty-eight, you use your phone for sudden death, remember?'

'Shit, I'm sorry, wasn't thinking.'

The fact that the probationer was alone in the patrol car in the first place was something else his superiors would no doubt be taking up with him. But Stevie had more than police procedure on her mind.

She gave him the barest nod and hurried over to the vehicle. It was an older model Toyota four-wheel drive, a 'troop carrier' with bench seats in the back to seat up to ten people. MDG 76X — this was it. Even from where she stood it was obvious to Stevie that the man in the driver's seat was very dead.

'You didn't touch anything?' she asked the constable.

'You said to wait. I could see he was dead, nothing I could do. I only quickly checked the back to make sure there was no one else in it.' The officer ran his palms down his pants and stuttered. 'Look, you're going to think I'm crazy, but …'

'But what?' she squinted at his nametag, 'Constable Nagel.' He looked hardly more than twenty.

'Well, while I was waiting down here, I got the strangest feeling I was being watched, y'know?' He gestured to the surrounding bush. 'And I was wondering,' he lowered his voice, 'if this is the guy who dumped the kid's body, then maybe the other guy is hanging around.'

'The other guy, meaning the second guy the security guard saw in the vehicle?'

The young man nodded. His shiver spread to her like a yawn and she felt the hairs prickle on the back of her neck. She decided not to tell him about the strange noises she'd heard on her way down. There was no need to get him even more anxious than he was now.

He pointed to the star-shaped hole in the driver's side window, the brown misting on the glass and what appeared to be flakes of dry tissue clinging to the jagged edges. Keeping his voice low as if someone might be trying to listen, he said, 'Looks like a bullet hole. I reckon they had a fight in the Toyota, the other guy shot Kusak — if it is Kusak that is …' He trailed off and looked nervously around with one hand resting on his Glock, the safety clip of his holster already unfastened. 'And he's still hanging around.'

Controlling her voice to hide her own concern, Stevie said, 'I suppose it's a possibility, Constable, but a long shot all the same. This might even be a simple suicide, he just couldn't live with what he'd done — hardly surprising, really.' She nodded to the body in the Toyota and pulled a face. 'By the looks of him he's been in there all day at least.'

Nagel cleared his throat as if to rid it of bile, and affected a smile. 'Yeah, err, slowly cooking.'

In a few years he'd be a master of the black joke, Stevie

thought, but he needed more practice on the delivery if he ever aspired to being the stereotypical, fat-bellied, the-job's-fucked kind of sergeant.

'Anyway, why would his murderer hang around that long unless he was hurt?' she said. 'And if he *was* badly hurt, he won't be much of a threat to us, would he?'

Stevie scanned the ground as if they might be lucky enough to spot the bullet or shell casing twinkling in the sun. She saw no sign of it of course; this wasn't a TV cop show. In her head she worked out the perimeter they would need to tape and search.

She circled the Toyota, taking in the damage. The impact from the tree didn't seem as bad as it had first looked; and was probably not violent enough to have caused the death of the seat-belted man in the driver's seat — if he hadn't been shot dead already. She tried to look through the back windows, but could see little through the grime. Upon opening the back door, she noticed that the rear bench seats had been removed to make room for a mattress and boxes of supplies. She saw no sign of another occupant. A thorough search would be undertaken when the scene of crime officers arrived.

'How did you find him all the way down here?' Stevie asked.

'I stopped at the lookout to take a leak, noticed the smashed barrier and fresh tyre tracks and thought I'd check it out.'

'When was that?'

The constable looked at his watch, 'No more than twenty minutes ago. You reckon this really is that Miro Kusak guy?'

'Who knows, but it's his vehicle all right. And there's only one way to find out if it's him for sure, isn't there, Nagel?'

Beet red turned turnip white. 'I was worried you were gonna say that.'

'Have you got gloves?'

'In the car.' He looked helplessly back up the rocky track.

She rolled her eyes and reached into her jeans pocket for a

pair of latex gloves. 'These are too small for you, must be your lucky day,' she said, snapping them on.

She wiped her brow with the back of her arm and moved over to the passenger side of the Toyota. 'Stand back.' She took a breath, knowing what to expect but still not prepared for the initial shock, the feeling of pebbles in the face as the blowies vacated the car in an angry cloud.

And the smell.

Holding her breath for as long as she could, she leaned across the empty passenger seat and patted the pockets of the dead man. She extracted his wallet and swiftly drew back to fill her lungs. The driver's licence was visible through a plastic window inside the wallet and she steeled herself for a look at his face, comparing it with the picture. As bloated as the roo she'd passed on the road, he looked barely human, though the greying curly hair did resemble the man's in the photo, as did the bulbous nose and broad forehead. 'Miro Kusak, 41 Weir Road Mundaring, DOB 23/10/54,' she read aloud for the constable's benefit.

The left side of Kusak's head was plastered with congealed blood, originating from a two-centimetre entrance hole above his ear. His left hand was empty and there was no sign of a gun on the floor or among the folds of the dirty blanket bunched upon the passenger seat — this was no simple suicide, this was murder.

Her mouth dried as she recalled the fear she'd felt when scrambling down the slope. She turned and peered into the back of the truck to have a closer look at the supplies she'd glimpsed before: a rolled up swag, camping equipment, boxes of food and bottled water. Miro Kusak had presumably been planning on lying low until the search for him had scaled down. The countryside around the weir was dense with forest, one park leading into another. With local knowledge and adequate resources a man could lose himself for months in a place like this.

She took a few short breaths. Even with the door open, the smell in the Toyota was overpowering and she was forced to vacate and gulp long drafts of fresh air. The search would have to be continued by police with breathing masks.

The constable handed her a fistful of tissues and she used them to wipe the body fluids from the outside of the wallet before riffling more thoroughly through the contents. As she searched she told the constable about the camping equipment she'd seen in the back of the van, shaking her head as she talked to clear the air of the hovering flies. Her fingers felt the outline of something solid in one of the wallet's compartments and she found a newish key. 'To the pump station you think?' she said.

When the constable didn't answer she looked up to find him nowhere in sight, she'd been talking to herself. Frowning, she turned slowly, shaded her eyes from the glare and scanned the surrounding bush.

'Constable Nagel?' Only the gentle waters of the weir lapping against the shore answered her call. Flies buzzed, a parrot squawked, but other than that, silence.

Then from the nearby scrub, the painful sound of retching.

Seconds later, the retching morphed into a scream of terror.

Stevie slapped her hip. No gun, *shit*. A stout stick lay across the track. She picked it up and charged through the bush to a burnt clearing where rubbish had been dumped. She found the constable on the ground beside a pile of empty bottles, one arm thrown protectively over his face and the paws of a giant dog resting on his chest.

'Oh God, oh God, get it off me,' he moaned.

Stevie approached cautiously. The dog turned from his busy licking of the constable's arm, fixed her with spooky yellow eyes and wagged its tail.

Stevie swore, partly from relief and partly from amusement. She grabbed the dog by its collar and hefted it off the stricken man.

'Are you okay?' she asked him.

'Oh, yeah, jeez ma'am, I'm sorry,' Nagel gasped, 'the dog came from nowhere, gave me one helluva a shock.' He struggled to his feet and began to dust himself down.

She took off her belt and threaded it through the dog's collar, holding him back a lot more successfully than she could her smile. Nagel smiled back sheepishly. 'He seems quite friendly, but,' he said.

Stevie ran her hand down the pinky-brown fur, feeling the prickling highway of hair scratching at her palm. 'Looks like a Rhodesian Ridgeback,' she said.

'Must be a stray, lucky he's not vicious. Wonder where he comes from?'

Stevie thought for a moment. 'Try the front seat of the car. There was a dirty old blanket on it, covered with dog hair.' She paused to pat the dog. 'Constable Nagel, this just might be Miro Kusak's mysterious passenger.' She bent to examine the disc on the dog's collar. 'Meet Bonza. 41 Weir Rd Mundaring.'

13

The late afternoon sun weighed on the heads of the investigating officers, yet the mood remained buoyant as they combed the area around the crashed Toyota. This prick was no loss, Monty heard one of the SOCO officers say, the killer had saved them all a pile of bother. Another answered that he'd shake the killer's hand, buy him a beer if he ever ran into him. Fine, he thought, but at this stage, despite the discovery of the dog, he wasn't discounting the possibility that two men were involved, and who could say which was the nastier piece of work.

Monty was sitting under a tree, filling out an evidence label, when he heard the crunch of approaching footsteps.

'"Thwackum was for doing justice, and leaving mercy to Heaven."'

He looked up. 'What?' he asked Angus Wong.

'Henry Fielding, *Tom Jones*.' With his Asian looks, his ocker accent and his propensity for producing a literary quote for most occasions, Angus was a maze of incongruities. Monty stared at him for a moment and wondered if he was also a mind reader.

Angus flopped onto the ground next to Monty, reached into one of the folds of his overalls and handed him a bottle of water. A television news chopper slashed through the air above their heads. Monty thanked him, took a long draught and returned to the task of labelling two small paper evidence bags.

'What've you got there?' Angus asked.

'A bullet and a shell case; the slug was embedded in a tree at the lookout, the shell case near the rubbish bin.'

'Beauty, can you tell what they're from?'

'Looks like a point 40 S&W cartridge.'

Angus met Monty's eyes. 'Semi-automatic pistol? Interesting.'

'Could be.'

'Anything else?'

'They found several of what appear to be Bianca's short bleached blonde hairs in the Toyota, subject to confirmation of course. Plus a long dark brown hair on the dashboard.'

'Another victim?'

'Who knows? The results will be sent to missing persons, there's always a chance it might match someone in their database.'

They fell silent. Monty put the bags into the top pocket of his overalls.

He spotted the mortuary van bumping along a rough weirside track. They'd sensibly decided not to come down the steep path. Upon vacating their van, the assistants grappled with the Stokes stretcher while Henry Grebe buzzed around them like a blowfly. At the Toyota, Grebe raised a hand to signify a halt and beckoned his team around him for a briefing.

'Found anything else of interest?' Angus asked Monty.

Monty switched his gaze from Grebe and pointed to the red-brick structure at the water's edge. 'That's the old pump station, long since abandoned but with a new padlock. Stevie found the key in Kusak's wallet.'

'You think that's where he kept the girl?'

'More than likely. Forensics have swept it clean — already sent their samples back to Perth for analysis. There was bedding in there.'

'His own private hideaway,' Angus looked sickened. 'Anything else I should know about?'

'No sign of Bianca's laptop, but we found a PC in the back of the van. It's had the sun glaring down on it like a laser beam for most of the day so I'm not sure what kind of nick it'll be in. It's on its way to Central. Also found camping stuff and enough food supplies for about a month in the wilderness.'

Angus gazed at the enormousness of the vista. 'Looking at this place, I'd say he might have got away with it too. How are the others going?'

'Stevie's visiting Mrs Kusak, breaking the news about Miro's death and returning the dog, and Barry's conferring with the Mundaring police. Wayne wasn't doing much except whinging about jock itch, so I sent him with some uniforms to start questioning Kusak's neighbours.' He paused, gave Angus a faint smile. 'And I'm supervising the crime scene.'

'The press are gathering at the lookout. Want me to give them a statement?'

Monty nodded gratefully, took another pull on his water bottle and watched as Angus made his way back up the track. He felt like shit, his toothache had become a headache and his stomach churned. The last time he'd felt this lousy was when he was a kid when he'd been out all day on the mustering at Stevie's family station and got heat stroke. He poured some water from the bottle over his head, rubbed it into his scalp and attempted to lose himself in the activities of the crime scene investigation.

The photos had been taken, the pathologist long gone.

But the body snatchers seemed to be taking their time. It should have been a routine job, but for some reason they seemed to be discussing the body's removal at length.

From where he still sat under the tree, Monty saw Henry Grebe beckon to the probationer, Constable Nagel. After a few moments, Nagel nodded and walked with hesitant steps to the Toyota. Monty hauled himself to his knees and squinted through his aviation sunglasses. As far as he knew SOCO guys wearing breathing apparatus had thoroughly searched the back of the van, photographed and removed the camping gear. It was hard to believe the body snatchers had noticed something in the Toyota the experienced searchers had missed.

The SOCO team had worked their way in a radius away from the Toyota and were now out of sight in the bush. The police divers had not yet arrived to search the surrounding waters. A group of local police were positioned at the lookout, holding the media and the curious at bay. As far as Grebe and his assistants were concerned, there was no one in their immediate vicinity. *They don't know I'm sitting here under the tree*, Monty thought.

Nagel opened up the back door and stepped inside. Right behind him, Grebe closed and latched the back door, then skipped over to rejoin his men who were laughing themselves stupid a few metres away.

Monty had seen enough. Heat exhaustion forgotten he leapt to his feet and strode towards the Toyota. He could hear the blows hammering upon the doors from within, and the anguished cries from the constable trapped inside. He turned the handle and wrenched the door open. Through the sickening miasma of methane gas the hapless constable all but fell into his arms.

'It's okay, son, it's okay,' Monty said, guiding him away from the vehicle and into the shade. Tears ran down the young man's face as he gasped and choked down his anger, humiliation and fear. Monty handed him some water, which he promptly threw up.

'You're fresh meat, that's your problem,' Monty said, turning his back on the kneeling, puking kid. If he wasn't careful, he'd soon be joining him. 'But this is above and beyond.'

When the constable had recovered, Monty handed him the evidence bags containing the bullet and case. 'Take this up to the lookout and get the exhibit officer to make a record of it, then I want you to take it personally to the ballistic lab in the city, lights and siren, top priority. I'll ring and tell them to expect you.'

Nagel wiped his mouth, flicked Monty a grateful smile and headed up the track.

The body snatchers were scowling around the Toyota when Monty returned, at last getting on with the job in hand. They'd laid the body bag open on the Stokes stretcher and two of them were struggling to remove Miro Kusak from the car seat. Henry Grebe watched the proceedings from the shade of a nearby tree, still smiling, hands on hips.

Monty walked over to him and met his arrogant glare head on.

And then he punched Henry Grebe, smack on the end of his long beaky nose.

14

Mrs Kusak nodded and dabbed at her eyes with a lace hanky. This was the second round of bad news Stevie had had to break in forty-eight hours, but this time, her sympathies could not have been less stirred. Mrs Kusak's eyes streamed, and her plump fingers traced the cross at her neck, but her beady black eyes conveyed no sense of grief.

The knock at the front door came as a welcome reprieve. There was an unpleasant odour about the place of rancid oil and stale cheese and she was glad of an excuse to escape. She found Wayne on the front step, patting the head of a white concrete swan.

The day was cooling, but Wayne's thin hair stuck to his head like a helmet, feathery sideburns plastering his cheeks like beached seaweed. He wore herringbone flares and a floral nylon shirt bright enough to give you a headache. When he lifted his arm to give his head a scratch, Stevie caught an unpleasant whiff and stepped back, making an obvious point of fanning herself. Wayne couldn't have cared less; Stevie even detected a slight smile on his craggy features. She suspected he enjoyed the distaste he stirred in others. Here was another one who followed a carefully rehearsed act. But given the choice, she'd take Wayne's BO over the cloying cheesiness of the Kusak house any day.

He pointed to the Christmas lights threaded through the

porch eaves and the melting 'Merry Christmas' written in fake snow on the window.

'It's weeks past Twelfth Night,' he said. 'Miro's certainly had his dose of bad luck. What about her?'

'I'm not sure if she regards this news as bad luck or heaven sent,' Stevie said.

Wayne had gleaned some interesting information from the neighbours. As he made his report Stevie wondered if Tash had discovered the same when she'd visited yesterday.

She returned to the small, black-frocked woman in the cluttered lounge room, and couldn't help but think of Rosemary West, Catherine Birnie, Myra Hindley. Was it the dog, or could Mrs Kusak have been the figure in the passenger seat when Bianca Webster's body had been dumped? And if she wasn't an accomplice, how the hell could she have been so oblivious to her husband's activities?

She offered to make Mrs Kusak the traditional cup of tea, keeping her voice as gentle as possible, struggling to resist falling into any kind of judgemental trap.

Mrs Kusak shook her head and reached down to pat the dog at her feet. Bonza seemed exhausted from his harrowing experience at the weir; he twitched as he dreamed. Stevie wondered what he had seen, wondered if dogs suffered from nightmares too.

'When the police first told you that your husband was a suspect in the murder and abduction of a child,' Stevie said, trying to keep the accusation from her voice, 'why did you tell them that you had been separated for over a year?'

The woman spread a puffy hand over her mouth and said nothing.

'You see, we've been given reason to doubt that,' Stevie continued. 'Apparently on the day after the child's abduction, your neighbours spotted you with a trailer load of things, believed to be your husband's possessions, and then another neighbour saw you at the dump with them. These same neighbours said they'd seen your husband's four-wheel drive parked outside the front of your house many times over the past few weeks.' Stevie let the silence linger. 'Can you see what I'm getting at Mrs Kusak?'

The woman sniffed but said nothing.

'It makes us think that maybe you knew what your husband had been up to and were trying to get rid of evidence — had he told you to get rid of evidence, Mrs Kusak?'

The woman twisted her hands on her lap and spoke in heavily accented English. 'We were separating. Miro was a worthless piece of shit. He's a Slav, I'm Italian, I should have listened to my mamma, but I didn't. I should have thrown him out years ago, but I didn't. When I went to the dump I didn't know what Miro had done, all I knew was that I wanted to be rid of the worthless shit Slav and all his worthless shit things.'

'Our crime scene officers will be able to recover his things. If anything incriminatory is found you might find yourself charged as an accessary to murder.'

'No no, only clothes, books and shit.'

'What about a computer?' She knew that a hard drive and a flash drive had been found in the Toyota, but she wondered how much the woman knew.

'He took the computer with him when he left.'

'Which was when? Not a year ago? When was he last here?'

'Three days ago was the last time I saw him.'

After Bianca's abduction but before her death, Stevie calculated, when she was most likely being held prisoner in the pump house.

'Did he spend a lot of time on the computer?'

Mrs Kusak nodded. 'Always, he spent all his time and money on computers. Always the latest and the best.'

'Doing what?'

'Looking at filth. He made me sick.'

'Did you know that he had an unhealthy interest in young girls?'

The woman inspected her rings. They were hardly visible between the folds of fat on her fingers. 'Maybe. It was filth.'

'Your neighbours said he used to stare at their children. They never let their kids near him. Or you.'

'He only looked. That's all. I told him it was wrong but he never listened to me.' She sniffed. 'My neighbours are nosy bitches, I'm gonna move.'

'Do you admit to lying to the police then, about the separation?'

'I no speak good English, they heard wrong. I told them we was separating, that's all. He was looking for somewhere to rent. This week I told him to take his computer and leave.'

'Where did he work?'

'Samson's factory in Welshpool, he worked shifts. I never know if he was coming or going.'

Stevie's gaze slid across the mantelpiece, taking in the colourful religious cards, noticing the absence of family photos. 'Do you have children?'

'No. He was married before. There was,' she hesitated, 'problems with the kids of his first marriage. We think better not to have them.'

Stevie could guess what the problems were. Jesus Christ, lady, you'll think twice about marrying a Slav but not a paedophile? This exercise in patience was getting harder by the minute.

'Was he capable of killing a child, Mrs Kusak?' she asked, suppressing a shudder. Talking to this woman was testing enough for her — she flinched at the thought of the effect she would have had on Tash. She wished she'd listened to her instincts and seen the woman herself yesterday.

The woman shook her head vehemently. 'He never would, no, never. He couldn't kill nothing. He hated blood, he even hated fishing. If she died, it was accident. He didn't kill her.'

For all that the woman filled her with revulsion, Stevie believed her. It helped too that the pathologist had determined the murder to be a sexual assault gone wrong.

'The child had been missing for nearly two days when her body was found. Have you any idea where he might have taken her after he abducted her?'

Mrs Kusak seemed to ponder the question, but who knows where her mind was.

'Mrs Kusak?'

The woman let out a sigh and rolled the hem of her black dress between her fingers. 'Yes, I think I know,' she said. 'Mundaring Weir. He always takes the dog to a special place there where no one else goes — it's a good dog, but it always fight other dogs.' She nodded to herself, 'Yes, he would have taken her there.'

'Where is this special place?'

Mrs Kusak stopped her fidgeting but still couldn't look Stevie in the eye. 'Near the old pump station, by the water. People aren't supposed to go there. They've closed off the track but Miro parks at the lookout and walks down with the dog. He always hangs about down there. He even takes me sometimes. It's what I told that bitch woman cop yesterday.'

Stevie kept her face impassive while she thought hard. Tash had known this yesterday and not told her. Damn her for not saying anything, damn her bloody migraines. How could she have said nothing? What the fuck was she playing at?

'Does anyone else know about this place where he takes the dog?' Stevie asked, her eyes fixed on the cross hanging on the wall above Mrs Kusak's head.

'Why you need to know that?' Mrs Kusak asked.

Why do you think, you stupid bitch? 'Because we need to find out who killed him, Mrs Kusak,' Stevie said with brittle patience.

Mrs Kusak narrowed her eyes. 'Then why don't you ask that woman cop from yesterday?'

Stevie stood up. 'Are you accusing Constable Hayward of your husband's murder?' she asked.

The woman's eyes dropped. 'Yes — no — I dunno.'

'You have to be very certain Mrs Kusak, before you start making accusations. What time yesterday did Constable Hayward come to see you?'

Mrs Kusak shrugged and touched her hair, making the pendulous folds at the top of her arms swing. She looked through the window at the pink-flossed sky. 'Before now, four o'clock maybe. My neighbour's kids was having a party, they start at lunch and go all night. I asked her to go and see them, warn them to shut up. She said no, tell me I no deserve to ever sleep good again.'

Now that did sound like something Tash might've said. Stevie cleared her throat. 'What time did she leave?'

Mrs Kusak shrugged. 'I dunno, about five maybe.'

Stevie had called at Trish's at about six thirty and she was still not home. 'Do you wish to proceed with the harassment charges against Constable Hayward? If you do, you'll need to put your complaint and any other suspicions you might have about the constable in writing.'

There was a momentary pause before Mrs Kusak answered, 'No.' She dropped her head into her hands and began to sob, her plump body wracked with self-pity.

'You told me on the phone that Constable Hayward showed you pictures from the child's autopsy. Is that true?' Stevie asked, unmoved.

Mrs Kusak didn't look up. She spoke through her hands. 'No, I said that to make you listen. But she was still a bitch. She told me all about how she died, that little girl …'

'You lied about the separation, you lied about the autopsy photos. What else have you lied about, Mrs Kusak?'

When the woman looked up, Stevie saw for the first time genuine tears of grief carving their way down the powdered cheeks.

'My Miro, what am I gonna do without him, the dirty no good Slav …'

She loved him, Stevie realised. Despite it all, she still loved him.

15

Monty drove while Stevie sat in the passenger seat of the unmarked police car, pondering the various forms of love. Mrs Kusak had told the officers making the initial enquiries that she and Miro were separated, then she'd told Stevie they were in the process of separating. It was obvious upon the search of the house that despite her trip to the dump, he was still very much in residence. They'd found his shaving equipment in the bathroom, his underwear in the bedroom drawers, even his pyjamas folded under the pillow. If she had really planned on chucking him out, they would never know. What made a woman stay with a man like that, she wondered, when she was so aware of his foul proclivities?

And what about you, her inner voice nagged. *You lived with a man who raped you and caused misery to countless others. You're a cop, you of all people should have seen through him — you are in no position to judge.*

I threw Tye out as soon as I knew he was up to no good, Stevie answered in her defence, reaching for the water bottle at her feet. She took a swig and tried to wash down the lump that rose like bile in her throat. She looked over at Monty as he drove and wondered how she could ever have thought that she loved anyone else. The problems she faced now with Monty were a walk in the park compared to what she'd endured with Tye. The demands of the job affected plenty of other police couples too.

Or so she tried to tell herself.

But tonight there was such a crackling tension in the car between them. Monty was answering her questions in grunted monosyllables, turning what could have been a comfortable silence into a bed of nails.

His flat delivery suited the subject matter when at last he began to speak at length. 'You remember that case of the abducted girl in Mundaring a couple of years ago?' He kept his eyes on the road, his face glowing in the dashboard light. 'She was found tied to a tree in the state forest after an anonymous tip off.'

Stevie hadn't worked the Mundaring case, but she remembered the frustration of all concerned. 'Yes, the victim had traumatic amnesia, couldn't remember much about her ordeal. She was sexually interfered with, but otherwise physically unharmed.'

'The state forest where she was found borders the east side of Mundaring Weir,' Monty said. 'The anonymous caller who raised the alarm was male and had a slightly foreign accent. We always presumed he was the perpetrator, though the only leads we had at the time were some dog hairs found on the girl.'

Stevie smacked her palms upon her knees. 'It's Kusak, it has to be,' she said. 'He didn't mean to kill her; he was planning on leaving her tied up like he did the first girl. He must've panicked when he realised she was dead, had no kind of plan for the body disposal and did the first thing that came to his mind — dump her at the building site.'

'SOCO found a rape kit in the back of the Toyota: duct tape, mask, more or less what he used on the first girl. Kusak's undoubtedly our guy and, yes, Bianca's death was probably an accident.'

'Any signs of a double act?'

Monty shook his head. 'Evidence suggests that Kusak

abused her alone, although that doesn't rule out Mrs K as an accessory of some kind. The pathologist said Bianca had a bad head cold; she wouldn't have been able to breathe through her nose and probably suffocated when she was gagged. They also found dog hairs on her body.'

Monty's despondency spread to Stevie like a virus. *At least he'd acted alone. I should be elated*, she thought, *but I'm not. We should be going out for a celebratory drink, but the thought sickens me. We've solved the crime; this man will harm no more children, and there will be no protracted court case. Someone has done us all a huge favour by knocking the creep off, yet I feel cheated, unsatisfied.* She wondered if this was Monty's problem too.

He started to speak, hesitated, moistened his lips and glanced at her. 'Is Mrs K going to pursue her complaint about Natasha?'

No, she realised, his problem ran a bit deeper than one murdered paedophile. His tone of voice, the way his eyes left the road to glance at her face, made her wonder if he was already aware of her doubts about Tash. She felt a sudden rush of anxiety. *Shit, am I that transparent? What has he found out?*

She shifted in her seat; the air conditioner didn't seem to be working properly, it felt like a hair drier aimed at her face. She fiddled with the angle of the vent and turned down the fan. 'No, she's dropped the complaint.'

No more questions about Tash please, Monty, she silently begged. *I have to get a few things straight in my own mind first.*

'Emma's minding Izzy,' she said. 'Her mother said it was okay for her to sleep over when I said I might be back late. I think Emma will be disappointed when Dot comes back,' Stevie rattled on, hoping to draw Monty into conversation.

No such luck.

'The bullet that killed Miro was fired at the lookout from an automatic pistol,' Monty said. 'I found it embedded in a tree with the casing on the ground near the bin. There was also broken glass and a small amount of what looks to be blood splatter. I think someone either sat in the passenger seat or leaned through the open passenger window and shot him while he was sitting in his car. '

'When I arrived, the passenger window was closed.'

Monty shrugged. 'It could've been wound up again. SOCO have found fingerprints, but none yet that are identifiable with anyone other than Kusak.'

She took a breath, wondering where he was going with this. 'Go on.' *Let's get this over with.*

'The dog was probably out of the car when the shot was fired,' Monty went on. 'We found its tracks at the lookout and also plenty of tyre tracks. After Kusak was shot, the gear stick was placed in neutral and the Toyota pushed down the hill. There are some fresh dents in the side where it clipped vegetation on the way down.'

Stevie thought for a moment. 'Maybe someone went down the track on foot after to check all was as it should be. That could explain the piece of torn shirt I found on the bush.'

'Possibly. The Toyota's been towed away for forensic examination. One of the first things we need to do is eliminate Mrs K as a suspect in her husband's murder or as an accomplice in Bianca's murder and abduction.'

'She's never had a driver's licence,' Stevie said. 'I can't see her getting herself the ten kilometres home from the lookout without a car.'

'Unless she had some help. She might have paid someone else to knock him off. I'm going to get people onto her bank accounts. I've also asked the media to put out a plea for public assistance, see if anyone saw anything from the road that night.'

Close family members of a victim were always the first suspects, but Stevie couldn't discount the feeling, despite the unpalatable taste it gave her, that Mrs K had actually loved her husband.

'I was looking through Wayne's witness statements while I was waiting for you to pick me up,' Monty went on. 'Some local kids were having a gathering that started at lunchtime and went on into the night. Mrs K rang them several times to complain, first in the afternoon about a car parked across her driveway, then about beer cans tossed over her fence. By the time it was dark and the party really cranked up, she was threatening them with he police. They finally conceded to her wishes at about midnight and turned the music down. Wayne's got records of the times.'

'Still a bit dodgy. Kusak was apparently killed sometime between early evening and midnight.'

'The time of death is just a preliminary estimate. We won't know until the autopsy. Whatever the TOD, she's still not clear, she could have paid someone else. Then again ...' Monty tapped his fingers on the steering wheel for a moment and frowned. The dense bush on either side of them was dark as they headed down the hill to the city. Stevie felt disorientated, had no idea how far they were from the well-lit highway below.

'Early evening.' She cleared her throat, reluctant to tell him what she knew, but his silence compelled her to speak. 'That was about when Tash visited her,' she said, deliberately vague about the time.

Monty took his eyes off the road for a moment and searched her face. 'Find out the exact time,' he snapped. 'And find out where she was when she was supposed to be at the team meeting in Central.'

Jeez, can a couple know each other *too* well? 'She was home with a migraine,' Stevie said.

'But she wasn't there when you called around. Do you know exactly when she did get home?'

'For God's sake, you're acting like you think Tash had something to do with ...' A bounding shape leapt out into the road from the bush. He braked hard, only just missing the roo.

'Watch out, there'll be another,' Stevie warned.

Sure enough, a joey darted out, bouncing after its mother.

Monty expelled a pent up breath. 'I'm pulling over,' he said as he glided the car to a stop on the shoulder of the road. He left the lights on but turned off the ignition, swiping his forehead with the back of his hand.

There wasn't another car on the road. A recent bushfire had burned the surrounding vegetation into a moonscape and she could smell the acrid dead smoke through the air conditioning vent. Darkness and silence closed in upon them.

Monty's face appeared green and distorted in the dashboard light, his forehead glistening with sweat. People in relationships reflected each other like mirrors, Stevie decided. Right now Monty's was a magnifying mirror, sending all her flaws and faults right back to her.

But she was not going to make this about her. She touched his arm. 'Are you all right?'

'No, I've had a splitting headache all day. It started in my tooth. Is there any Panadol in the glove box?'

'You need to take some time off and go to the dentist. That tooth's been bothering you for a while.' She found a packet jammed between the maps. After popping the pills out of their foil she handed them to him with the water bottle that had been rolling around at her feet.

'These migraines must be contagious,' he said, giving her a pointed look before swallowing the pills. When she didn't reply, he slapped the steering wheel in frustration, the sudden sound making her flinch.

'I don't understand you,' he bellowed, at last losing any semblance of self-control. 'I saw Mrs Kusak not long after you saw her and she mentioned then that she told Natasha Hayward where her husband was most likely to be hanging out. She told you too, yet you've said nothing to me about it. Why are you protecting her? Is it because her parents died tragically and she's nobly dedicated herself to looking after her retarded brother? Or is it because she's gay and you figure she needs all the help she can get in a job that's dominated by a mob of overbearing straight males?'

Stevie struggled to maintain her composure; one of them had to. 'Forget the stereotypes, okay? Try loyalty, trust and friendship instead. But protecting her? I don't know what you're talking about.'

'Oh come on, Stevie,' he slapped his thigh in frustration. 'Miro Kusak was killed by an automatic pistol that uses point 40 S&W ammunition. I got the bullet and cartridge dispatched to ballistics as soon as I found them. I heard back from them about half an hour ago while I was waiting for you to pick me up.'

Stevie swallowed. 'So?'

'So, we happen to have a couple of Glock 22s in the armoury, which could easily match the murder weapon. They were handed in for the weapons amnesty.' He lapsed into the interrogator's most effective weapon, silence. It gave the suspect the chance to incriminate herself.

Stevie wouldn't fall for it. After a lengthy pause she said, 'I can't see what you're getting at.'

'How about the gun used to kill Miro Kusak was *borrowed* from the armoury at Central? I called the property sergeant and he had something interesting to tell me. It seems ...' Monty hesitated.

Stevie became aware of an ache in her jaw and forced herself to unclench her teeth. 'What?'

'It seems Natasha was hanging around the armoury the other day, chatting to the property sergeant and looking at the confiscated weapons. We have so many in there at the moment, there's not room enough in the gun cabinets for all of them. When the week's up, they're going to be moved to the firearms repository and destroyed.'

'Get to the point Monty.'

'The point is, the property sergeant didn't worry too much about a missing imitation Glock, which was actually a very well crafted water pistol. It was handed in with a bunch of genuine weapons and he didn't get the chance to check it properly before the guy bolted. He was quite pissed off that someone received tickets for the test with a bloody toy, and he didn't report it missing because a) he knew he'd be in the shit for it and b) he knew it was harmless.' Monty paused. 'But at least he was being straight about it with me.'

Not like me you mean, Stevie thought. *Shit, I've been sprung. Shit shit shit.*

'So ... have you seen Hayward brandishing a water pistol around the place?' Monty demanded.

She knew what he was intimating. If Tash had been able to spirit out a water pistol, she could just as well have been able to spirit out the real thing, use it to kill Kusak and then return it to the armoury with no one the wiser.

Stevie avoided a direct answer. 'I'd have put her on report if she'd been out of order.'

Monty's face lit up with the headlamps of a passing car. He rubbed his face with his hands and placed them back upon the steering wheel. Under the glow from the dash she noticed the knuckles of his right hand glistening like split cherries.

Monty spoke softly, with no hint of anger. In Monty McGuire this was not a good sign. 'Robert Mason has filed a complaint at the remand centre, alleging he was intimidated by

Tash with a water pistol at the time of his arrest.' Monty moistened his lips. 'An incident which you seem to have conveniently brushed under the carpet. I imagine Dolly will want a little chat about it with you. The complaint form was put on my desk by mistake, I'm going to have to hand it over to her.'

Fuck, oh fuck, oh fuck! Inspector Dorothy 'Dolly' Veitch was head of the Sex Crimes Division and Stevie's immediate superior. Stevie opened her mouth to speak but it took a few moments before she could form the words. 'I have had a word with her about it, everything's fine now, it was just a momentary lapse on her part.'

'I've ordered tests to be carried out on the confiscated Glocks in the armoury. They should be able to tell us if the guns have been fired recently. I know Natasha has had it rough, she's been in Sex Crimes for a long time …'

'I said I've spoken to her, fuck it! She assured me it won't happen again.'

Stevie dug her fingers into each side of the car seat and twisted her head to look at him. 'How did you hurt your hand — hit someone?'

'I felt frustrated. I thumped a tree at the scene.'

She clamped her jaw. 'You're lying to me, Monty.' How cool she managed to make her words sound.

He shot her a glare. 'Yeah, I've had a good teacher.'

He said nothing more, turned the key and glided from the shoulder back onto the road. Soon they were close enough to the city to have the benefit of streetlights. She gazed at the ring on her finger where it sparkled under the passing lights like a small crystal of ice.

Saturday

16

Excerpt from chat room transcript 150107
BETTYBO: I metta nic boi in book chat called danil
He red KE & likd her storeys
HARUM SCARUM: gr8, he has good taste
BETTYBO: hes smart lik u
HARUM SCARUM: no 1s as smart as me roflmao

Stevie dreamed she was in the car with Monty, hurtling down a dark hill, the car brakes had failed. It was a white-knuckle ride; they were gaining speed, struggling to keep the car from careering out of control …

It wasn't her own scream that jolted her out of the nightmare and it wasn't Izzy's either. Stevie struggled with her fuddled mind to put it in context. The scream was high pitched and keening, like an animal in distress. And it was coming from the spare bedroom.

Emma.

She turned the spare room light on to find the girl sitting bolt upright in bed, hair over her face like a yeti, arms crossed at her chest like a corpse.

The light woke her. She shook her head as if to shake off nightmarish images and pushed a damp clump of hair from her face.

'I'm sorry, I'm sorry,' she repeated as she dragged herself

back to reality. 'Oh God, this is so embarrassing.' She turned her face to the wall as Stevie came over to the bed.

'Don't worry, most people have nightmares Emma.' Stevie sank onto the edge of the mattress and touched the girl's arm. 'Do you want to tell me what yours was about?'

Emma wiped her bare arm across her face and glanced at her watch on the bedside table. 'I'm sorry I woke you, it's Saturday, you should be having a lie-in.'

'Usually, yes, but things are very busy so we're working today. Luckily Izzy has a play date with a school friend.' She took in the tear-smudged face. 'How about I make us a hot chocolate?' she said.

'I'd rather a cold Milo if that's okay.' No hesitation. Despite the state she had woken in, she remained polite but forthright. Here was a girl who knew her own mind.

Emma followed Stevie into the kitchen, sat at the table and watched her make their drinks. It was too warm for dressing gown and slippers, too warm even for hot chocolate. Stevie slapped across the lino in her bare feet and oversized T-shirt and made two cold Milos. Just after seven in the morning and the light shining through the kitchen blinds was already the colour of warm honey.

'I go through phases where I get the same nightmare over and over again — is that what happens to you?' Stevie fished.

'I usually control my nightmares or I use my wings and fly away from them. But I couldn't control this one. Something horrible was happening to someone else and all I could do was watch, helpless.'

Stevie saw Emma's eyes stray to the newspaper on the kitchen table. Bianca's murder was still on the front page. The girl visibly paled and her eyes began to well again.

'Emma, are you okay?' Stevie folded the paper in half and pushed it away. She hadn't taken the child to be quite this emotionally delicate. 'You didn't know her did you?'

Emma placed one hand over her mouth and gestured to the paper with the other. 'No, but I hate all that. I don't know how you do your job.'

'I sometimes wonder too.' Stevie took a sip of Milo and decided a rapid change of subject was necessary. 'What do you want to be when you leave school?'

'A teacher,' Emma replied without hesitation, brightening up immediately. 'I want to teach underprivileged children, you know, kids from homes where education is not considered important, especially if the child is a girl, like in third world countries. I believe lack of education is the root of all the world's troubles. I want to encourage literacy, I've already got my own …' Emma broke off mid sentence, as if she thought Stevie might be bored or might reproach her for her enthusiasm.

Stevie didn't want her to stop, she was fascinated by the animation in the small intense face. The girl was way older than her years. Emma Breightling didn't fit at all with the image of what a girl her age was supposed to be.

'Go on,' Stevie encouraged.

'You might think this sounds dumb, but I want to have my own website for kids, to encourage reading, have story writing competitions, prizes and stuff. One of the teachers at school has one, but I want mine to be totally kid friendly, do you know what I mean? Not preachy and teachy. It's a good idea, don't you think?'

'I think your ambitions sound fantastic. I'll bet your parents are very proud.'

Emma fell silent, as she always did when her parents were mentioned. She took a sip of her cold drink.

'You've given yourself a Milo moustache,' Stevie said.

The girl wiped her mouth on the back of her hand and

laughed; she had a wide mouth, designed for laughter.

'Izzy always does that,' Stevie said.

Emma had become serious again. 'Apparently,' she said, in a voice dripping with sarcasm, 'I cause my Dad nothing but anxiety. I was kept down a year at school you see. I should have started high school this year. I'm glad I didn't because they want to send me over east to boarding school and I don't want to go. I had bad hearing when I was little — glue ear — and they seemed to think it set me back.'

'And did it?'

'No way, if anything it's helped me more. I don't care about being kept down at school; I like it there. I learn what I want to learn, no one bothers me and I know where I'm going — that's the main thing, isn't it?'

To know where you're going? Lucky you. Stevie's gaze fell to her left hand. She usually kept the ring on while she slept, but last night she'd taken it off and put it on her chest of drawers.

'You're not wearing your engagement ring,' Emma said with a frown, 'did you lose it?'

Stevie waved away the child's look of concern. 'No, it was … it was getting in the way.'

'If you don't mind me saying, the set up you have here is kind of funny,' Emma said, licking the crust of Milo from the edge of her glass.

'Funny?' Stevie queried, 'In what way?'

'The way you and Mr McGuire don't live together and you never even have. It's like Izzy comes from a broken home, only the home was never fixed in the first place, was it?'

Was the girl lumping Izzy among her clutch, settling her within her nest of disadvantaged children? If Stevie hadn't had such a bad evening with Monty she might not have taken the statement so much to heart. She found herself curling her toes into the lino under her feet. 'Maybe you should think about going back to bed,' she said. 'You might be able to snatch a second sleep; they're always the best.'

Emma put her hand over her mouth, eyes widening behind the magnifying lenses. 'I'm sorry, I've offended you.'

'Not at all,' Stevie lied. Jeez, the girl didn't miss much. She was better than most adults at seeing through the crap and getting to the very heart of things. And not big on self censorship.

'I can go home now if you like. I've got a school assignment to work on and lots of other stuff to do. I was planning on going early anyway.'

There was something about the hurried way Emma spoke, the way she eagerly jumped to her feet that made Stevie ask, 'Emma, you really did get permission from your parents to stay over, didn't you?'

'I left a note.'

'Yes, but what did your note say?'

'Look, they don't care where I am. Dad's at a conference in Queensland and Mum's always so busy worrying about something or other she doesn't even know if I'm at home or not.'

Stevie searched the little face intently for a moment. 'Busy with work you mean?'

The girl's face lit with a cheeky smile. 'Yeah, that too, but mostly what to wear out to lunch, laser or electrolysis for hair removal, worrying if collagen gives you Mad Cow — if it does she's living proof.'

Resisting the urge to return the smile, Stevie repeated her question with more firmness. 'What did you say in your note, Emma?' She climbed to her feet and stood over the seated girl, suddenly feeling as if she was interviewing a suspect.

Emma gazed into to her Milo and said softly, 'I left a note saying I'd gone to bed early. She never checks up on me once I've gone to bed.'

Stevie folded her arms. 'Emma, does she even *know* you've started working for me?'

Emma nibbled at her bottom lip and shook her head.

'But she knows you work for Mrs Carlyle, right?'

'Yes, she doesn't mind that,' Emma said quickly.

'Then why didn't you tell her you were working for me?'

Emma's eyes had not strayed from her glass. 'Because you're a cop. My mother doesn't like cops.'

Stevie sat down again. 'Look hon, this isn't acceptable, whatever your reasons I can't be party to this deceit. We're going to have to get dressed, go and see your mother and explain the situation.'

'But then you'll be stuck without a babysitter!'

'My mother will be back soon. This arrangement was only temporary, I explained that.'

'But I love it here, I love Izzy …'

'We might still be able to persuade your mum to let you come over now and then to play with Izzy.'

The girl's face crumpled and the huge brown eyes filled. Stevie reached for her hand and gave it a squeeze. 'It'll be all right,' she said, 'we'll sort something out.'

Emma shook her head, letting fall a single tear. 'You don't know my mother.'

17

Stevie struggled to make conversation as she drove Emma home. 'Is your father some kind of specialist?' She shot a look at the girl sitting rigidly beside her. He had to be more than a GP to afford the Hitler's-bunker by the river's edge, she thought.

'He's supposed to be a plastic surgeon, specialising in the treatment of burns. He used to be famous for the work he did in war torn countries. Maybe you've heard of Christopher Breightling.'

Stevie mused over the name. Yes, it did have a familiar ring.

Emma's top lip curled as she continued. 'Now he's into cosmetic surgery — there's more money in it you see, and my mother has expensive tastes.'

Stevie smiled to herself. At the traffic lights she stopped and angled the rear vision mirror to inspect herself. She made a play of pushing up the skin of her forehead and stretching it away from her cheeks. 'A handy man to know, maybe I'll give him a call someday,' she said, attempting to lighten the mood.

'Don't,' Emma said with surprising vehemence.

Stevie glanced over at her as she took off from the lights.

'Plastic surgery sucks. One more nip, one more tuck, then I'll be perfect. People are never satisfied with what they've got. And only vain rich people can afford to have it done while the people who really need it, the people my father used to treat, don't have a chance.'

'I was joking.'

'It's not funny,' Emma said. 'People in the west spend too much time and money worrying about what they look like and then in the end you can't tell what's real and what's fake.'

Christ, the kid will be preaching hell and damnation soon. *Never satisfied with what they've got.* Stevie untwisted her seatbelt and attempted to make herself more comfortable.

In the back seat Izzy played with a computer game. A series of beeps came as a welcome distraction.

'How're you going back there, Izzy?' Stevie asked, for once wanting a conversation interrupted by her daughter

'Good,' Izzy answered. End of topic. Great.

'And what does your mum do, apart from go out to lunch?' Stevie glanced at her passenger.

Emma's face screwed up with distaste. 'She runs a modelling agency. And a school of etiquette.'

Stevie paused to digest this. 'And I gather you don't approve of either?'

'You wouldn't if you saw what went on there. Girls younger than Izzy turned into baby beauty queens by stupid mothers who wish they could change places' — Emma broke off, giggled and pointed to an old woman trundling down the footpath with a shopping trolley. 'Hey, look Izzy, there goes old Mrs Do-as-you-would-be-done-by, the lady I told you about, the one with all the cats.'

Izzy wriggled in her harness with excitement. 'The witch, the witch!'

'She's a good witch, remember, that's why she takes in all those strays.' Turning back to Stevie she rolled her eyes. 'Sorry about that, my going on about cosmetic surgery and modelling schools I mean.' She smiled. 'Oh and that's not really the old lady's name, it's the name of a character from the *Water Babies* — just part of an imagination game I play with Izzy.'

Stevie smiled back, but said nothing. What a strange kid you are, she thought. You know you're strange and you play on people's reactions to it too. Somehow she found herself liking the girl all the more for it.

Emma straightened as they came to her house. 'Oh-oh, here goes nothing,' she said, a thirteen-year-old again.

The black lacquered doors of the mansion opened as they pulled alongside the curb and a man stepped onto the porch. He seemed to be saying goodbye to someone inside. His head and shoulders disappeared from sight, the hidden movement suggestive of a kiss.

Emma shivered and slipped further down the car seat. 'Oh shit,' she breathed.

Stevie threw her a startled glance. 'Who's that?'

The girl twiddled quote marks in the air. 'The family friend — my godfather. Please, let's just stay here a moment, wait for him to leave.'

Stevie studied the man as he strode towards a black Porsche parked a little further down the road. Here was a man who knew he cut a dashing figure. His jaw jutted forward in a manner very like that of a male salmon, his longish brown hair was wet and curled carefully behind his ear. In his pink polo shirt, white pants and boaters without socks, he could have been sauntering down the road to the yacht club.

'Actually,' Emma said in a matter of fact tone, 'he's Aidan Stoppard and as well as my godfather he's my parents' accountant.' Then she said casually, as if it were an afterthought, 'He's also my mother's lover. He always visits when my father's away.'

Emma shrugged her shoulders in response to Stevie's gob-smacked look. Stevie wondered if she was being manipulated. Was the child making up stories, trying to provoke sympathy in order to avoid being dobbed in for her deceit? That must be it, she decided as she regarded the small, deadpan face. Mature beyond her years, Emma had already proved herself quite capable of manipulation and deception. Perhaps it was just as well the babysitting was coming to an end.

The Porsche took off with a throaty rumble at about twenty over the speed limit. Had she been in uniform, Stevie would have relished the job of booking that one.

'C'mon Emma,' she said, twisting around to the back seat and unclipping Izzy's belt. 'Time to face the music.' Izzy held Stevie's hand and skipped up the path towards the house with Emma dragging her heels behind them.

Miranda appeared a model of cool poise when she opened her door to find her daughter on the front step with a stranger and a small child. The only sign of surprise on the beautifully made up face was a deepening of the almost imperceptible lines between the startling violet eyes. 'Emma, what an earth are you doing out here? I thought you were in bed.'

'I need to get some homework done.' Emma brushed past her mother, dragging her bag across the marble floor, leaving skid marks of dirt behind her.

The mother rolled her eyes. 'Teenagers,' she sighed.

Stevie said, 'There seems to have been a bit of a misunderstanding, Mrs Breightling. I believe you've been under the impression that Emma has been doing some extra babysitting for Mrs Carlyle, when in fact she's been working for me. She slept at my house last night and I thought you knew about it, but you obviously didn't. I've come to apologise; it seems we've had our wires crossed.'

From somewhere within the house, Stevie heard the sound of footsteps scraping up a stone staircase.

Miranda Breightling pursed plump lips and touched her short, immaculately styled hair. 'I'm afraid I lost control of

Emma a long time ago. This is very embarrassing, you'd better come in, Mrs …'

Stevie put out her hand. 'Just call me Stevie,' she said. 'Stevie Hooper.'

The woman flinched under Stevie's firm grip. 'I'm Miranda Breightling. Come in.'

Miranda glided ahead, a small woman, walking as straight as if she had a book balanced on her head. Stevie followed, trainers squeaking on the white marble tiles. A ditty of her father's popped into her mind and the memory made her smile. *When you use this marble hall, use the paper not the wall.*

The house was more interesting on the inside than it was on the outside, although the ultra modern décor was not to Stevie's taste. She preferred old things, things with warmth and character. More black lacquer doors to the right of the front entrance opened into a formal lounge dominated by an oversized cream modular couch. As she progressed through the house she discovered the soft furnishings to be the exception, not the rule; the place consisting mostly of wrought iron, stone and sharp angles. The kitchen contained more stainless steel than a hospital morgue. Light streamed in from a stained glass skylight in the adjoining family area. There was no evidence of a TV. A shiny black couch stood next to a blocked up fireplace.

At the granite breakfast bar, Miranda pulled up a wrought iron barstool for Stevie to perch on. She turned to a coffee machine, whose milk frother sounded like an old-fashioned steam train. Stevie wondered if the sound effects were a ploy on Miranda's part to delay what was sure to be an uncomfortable conversation for both of them.

In her white linen skirt suit, Miranda looked as cool as ice cream, although Stevie did detect a slight tremor in her hand and an almost imperceptible quivering of froth on the cappuccino placed before her.

They made small talk. Stevie could tell that the woman couldn't wait to get rid of her, but courtesy demanded a show of gratitude to the scruffily dressed woman who'd brought her daughter safely home.

It was patently obvious that Miranda wasn't interested in Stevie's polite answers to her polite questions, and was even less interested when Stevie tried to reintroduce the topic of Emma's deceit. The restless eyes indicated a mind far away on more important things — lunch? Hair removal? Surely the woman couldn't be as shallow as her daughter had made out.

Stevie knew she'd failed the etiquette test the moment she'd gripped Miranda's hand too tightly. She shook hands the way her father had taught her. She tried to make up for it now by mimicking her perch upon the barstool, but failed in this too. The stool wasn't built for comfort, and in jeans the natural tendency was to flop the legs, not keep them taut and together like Miranda's, constricted as they were in the tight skirt.

Coffee from the overfilled cup slopped onto Stevie's jeans at her first sip. Damn, another fail, but it could have been worse. Once when she'd been out at a restaurant with Monty, a gulp of coffee had gone down the wrong way and she sputtered it all over the white tablecloth. They'd laughed so much they'd had to leave. Under different circumstances it would have been quite fun to take the piss out of this woman, give her a bit of a shock. No wonder Emma was such a reactionary.

She wondered what Monty would have thought of Miranda. She was very beautiful, no doubt about it, but that wouldn't have fazed him. He wouldn't have felt as uncomfortable here as Stevie did, he was at home anywhere, in an outback pub or a reception at Government House. With a good education behind him and well travelled, he could be smooth as molasses when he wanted to be and probably would have charmed the be-Jesus out of her. She shook her head to stop her mind from wandering any further.

Miranda's fingers were long and graceful and adorned with a tasteful array of rings; nothing too big or garish. Her large eyes followed Izzy as she explored, worried perhaps about sticky fingermarks on the pristine surfaces.

Izzy stopped when she came to an abstract arrangement of steel and glass rising out of the floor, gazing up at it, no doubt trying to figure out what it was. She reached to touch one of the sharp edges and Stevie called out to her to stop, worried she would damage herself on one of the steel points which rose to the vaulted ceiling like spears.

Izzy dropped her hand and turned, bestowing an angelic smile upon the two women seated at the breakfast bar.

Miranda's smile in response was probably as genuine as she was capable of through the eggshell smooth skin. 'What a beautiful child,' she murmured to Stevie, 'those Shirley Temple curls —'

'Can I go upstairs and see Emma?' Izzy asked her.

'Of course you can, darl,' Miranda said.

'Just for a minute, it's nearly time to leave for Georgia's house,' Stevie said as her daughter scuffed up the stairs to the mezzanine landing, calling for Emma.

Stevie's coffee tasted like mud. She forced down a final swallow, resisting the urge to pull a face. Give her instant coffee any day. A breeze cooled her cheek and she became aware of the musical sound of trickling water, tracing its source to an open window at the back of the family room. Next to it French doors opened into a high walled courtyard blocking the view of the river beyond. The paving and wall were made of recycled bricks, rustic and charming and quite incongruous with the style of the rest of the house.

'Have you ever thought of signing Izzy up with a modelling agency?' Miranda's violet eyes were now focused intently on

Stevie's for the first time since they'd met.

Stevie dragged her gaze from the inviting view outside. 'Nah, not really, not my scene,' she said, roughening up her voice just for the hell of it. 'I suppose I might let her if she was keen when she was older, but frankly I haven't got the time as things are.' Now might be a good time to test out one of Emma's possible lies. 'I'm a police detective you see, which means a lot of after hours work. I don't think I'd ever find the time to get her to the shoots, the make-up courses and what-nots.'

Miranda visibly paled under the layer of foundation. Her eyes widened and her hand crept to her throat. *Sheesh*, Stevie thought, Emma wasn't lying, not even bending the truth on this one. The mention of police had left the woman looking like a roo in headlights.

Miranda composed herself, slid from the barstool and looked at her wristwatch. 'My goodness, is that the time?'

Stevie followed suit. 'I suppose we should get those girls moving,' she said, heading towards the stone stairway. She called out for Izzy, heard footsteps thumping on the mezzanine and saw her daughter peering down at them through the decorative balustrade.

'Thank you for telling me what Emma's been up to. I think it's best that Emma stops working for you. It's the only way for her to learn.' Miranda looked pointedly at her daughter who was coming down the staircase. Stevie agreed, adding that Emma was more than welcome to call by any time for a visit.

'But I want Emma's stories!' Izzy cried.

Stevie stopped on her way to the stairs, feeling something cling to the wisp of a thought in her mind, something connected to the Bianca Webster case. But like a feather in the wind, it blew away before she could grasp it.

18

Monty stared down from his office window, watching the white figures spill onto the oval while the seagulls circled in a cloud above. He was a rugby man; cricket had never held much interest for him although the view from the window provided a handy focus for his restless gaze. He couldn't count the times he'd had to put up with the grumbles of colleagues that his fifth floor corner office was wasted on the likes of him.

He sat at his desk looking at Stevie's photo, gazing into her clear blue eyes. He traced the high ponytail that accentuated the curve of her neck, at the little gold kinks still visible even when her hair was pulled taut against her head. She hated the kinks, but wouldn't be bothered doing anything about them — not a straightening-iron kind of girl, she'd say, occupied with more important things — Izzy, the job, even him he liked to think. He knew the grunge fashion and offhanded manner belied a girl with old-fashioned tastes and a passion for real family values. Her reluctance to move in with him was a mystery, even more to her than to him he suspected.

The funny thing was that once he'd felt pretty much as she did now. For years he'd punished himself for a mistake he'd made one night when he was drunk, a mistake that in the long run turned out to be no mistake at all. But he'd put himself on the wagon, desperate to take control of his life. Now he could take or leave a drink, the same as the next man.

Couldn't she see that she was doing the same thing now, punishing herself for something that wasn't her fault? *If only I could explain it to you in a way that wouldn't make you turn your back on me*, he muttered to the photo as he put it back in his drawer. Whatever was going on with Natasha Hayward seemed to be stretching her loyalties like a spinnaker in a storm and he worried she would snap.

He had been relieved and genuinely pleased to find the fax waiting for him on his desk from ballistics, stating the bullet that killed Kusak could not be traced to any of the confiscated guns in the armoury. Nevertheless, his suspicions of Hayward niggled no less than his aching tooth; at the very least he thought, she was a major incident waiting to happen.

Monty stretched, unable to get comfortable; his toothache seemed to have travelled down his neck and into his arm. It dawned on him then that his anger stemmed largely from the fact that Stevie had failed to tell him, failed to trust him. If it turned out Hayward was involved in Kusak's death in any way, Stevie would go down for it too. She'd be accused of ignoring the possible breakdown of a team member, which subsequently led to that team member committing murder; her career would be in ruins. Why the hell hadn't she told him at the start, got his advice when she first had trouble with Hayward in the park? Why hadn't she let him help her with this? Why sacrifice her career for a loose cannon like Natasha when she must know he'd do anything for her?

He looked up at the phone, willing it to ring. Stevie would doubtless be talking to Tash today, but he had no idea when. The pain in his arm worsened. It seemed to be spreading to his chest. He took some deep breaths and, deciding it was better to err on the side of caution, phoned his doctor. The receptionist said there was a space in two hours time, sooner if it was urgent. Monty said it wasn't.

He put the phone down, his gaze dropping to some unconscious doodling on his notebook — Natasha's name woven into a maze of Celtic knots. To his dismay he discovered that her name had pressed its way through all the pages that lay beneath.

That afternoon, after a piece of news that had initially dumbfounded him, Monty called an impromptu progress meeting with the senior detectives involved in the Zhang Li case. The three men grabbed swivel chairs and clustered around Monty's desk, sipping coffee from foam cups and balancing notebooks on knees.

'Firstly,' Monty said to his gathered team, 'the report from ballistics on the bullet that killed Miro Kusak was waiting on my desk when I got in. Apparently it's an exact match for the bullet that killed our Asian loan shark, Zhang Li.'

Wayne put his cup on Monty's desk and leaned back in his chair. 'Well, well, that is interesting.'

Angus beamed. 'I thought two murders by an automatic pistol within weeks of each other was a bit of stretch for Perth — I mean this is hardly downtown LA. Looks like there is a God.'

'And it seems he wants to help us out for a change,' Barry said. 'Though he could have waited till after the weekend.'

'Don't get too excited, fellas,' Wayne cautioned. 'The bullets might have been fired by the same gun, but we don't have the gun. What about the impounded guns, Mont? With the state of the armoury since the amnesty, anyone could have lifted one and then put it back.'

So Wayne had been thinking along these lines too. The thought left Monty feeling slightly vindicated.

'One of us you mean?' Barry sounded incredulous.

Monty nodded. 'Yes, we couldn't rule out the possibility

that we might have a cop playing vigilante — but rest easy, there's no match.'

Wayne shrugged. 'Without the gun then, we're not really any the wiser.'

'Only now, Wayne, we have a link, bizarre as it might seem, between the death of a loan shark and the death of a paedophile,' Monty said.

And I have no reason to be suspicious of Hayward, he thought. *So why then am I still plagued by these doubts, this deep sense of foreboding, as if she is still some kind of a threat?* He thought back to what the doctor had told him that morning; that he must attempt to cut down on his workload and reduce the stress in his life. He had to drop the subject. He slashed a pen through his doodles and tore the page from the book.

He attempted to pull himself together and pointed at Wayne. 'You and Angus said you thought the Vietnamese girl at the herbalist's was hiding something. Have you followed that up yet?' Monty asked Wayne.

Wayne shook his head. 'The dead rock spider put paid to that yesterday, boss. I'll pay her another visit this afternoon.'

Barry smirked at Wayne from where he sat spinning in his chair. 'He's sweet on her,' he said with one of his infuriating Alfred-E-Newman grins, 'that's why he hasn't done it yet.'

Monty listened to the exchange with the distance of a weary headmaster.

'Don't be ridiculous, I've been flat out,' Wayne said, a faint blush circling his collar line.

'Turned into quite a softy in your old age … You should have seen him, Mont, carrying on and laughing with this babe, making bad jokes about herbal aphrodisiacs …'

Monty had had enough. He slammed his hand down on his desk, forgetting it was the one he's damaged on Henry Grebe, and let out a blue streak of obscenities. When he'd recovered he pointed to the door and snapped, 'Shut it or just swivel out of here, Barry.'

Barry touched his chest, 'Who, me?' but he still didn't make a move.

Angus climbed to his feet. 'I need to go, I have some leads to follow on the kid running around with Zhang Li.' He flicked his hand at Wayne. 'Keep your phone on, I think I might have you a name soon.'

When Angus had gone, Monty said to Barry, 'I'm sure you can find something to do. Go over the statements from the Kusak neighbours and chase SOCO up over the evidence reports we're still waiting on. Oh yeah, and check Mrs K's bank statements too.'

Barry nodded complacently, but the only move he made was to take another bite of his doughnut. Monty gave him a heated look, and even that didn't penetrate the kid's thick skin until he registered the flexing of the fingers on Monty's left hand.

Barry wiped sugary fingers down the legs of his pants. 'Okay, keep your hair on, I'm going.'

When he'd gone, Monty leaned back in his chair and closed his eyes for a few seconds.

'He can't bear to miss out on anything, the nosy little prick.' Wayne looked with concern at Monty. 'You okay?'

'No.' Monty wondered if Wayne had heard about his altercation with Henry Grebe. It was unlikely that Grebe would have reported it, given that he had behaved so atrociously. The fear that had been gripping Monty didn't have anything to do with the possible fall-out, it was more about his own lack of control, a control that seemed at the moment to be increasingly shaky.

Monty opened his eyes at the sound of the loosening of a screw cap, cocked an eyebrow at Wayne's hip flask, but said nothing. Wayne took two glasses from the tray, poured a generous measure of scotch into each, and added water from the jug on Monty's desk.

They clinked. Wayne took a sip and said, 'You going to tell me about this morning's appointment?' Wayne was the only person Monty had told about his chest pain and subsequent visit to the doctor.

Monty leaned back in his chair and scowled, keeping his eyes focused on something invisible above the office door. 'Bloody scare-mongering doctors.'

'I take it it didn't go so well?'

Monty swirled the whisky in his glass and put it down without a taste. 'Did a few simple tests in the surgery, doesn't think it's too critical, but wants to book me in for an angiogram ASAP. I said I couldn't possibly take time out at the moment, not with my current caseload, at which he got rather shitty with me. My caseload, huh!' he threw his hands into the air. 'The murder of two low lifes who, truth be known, I really couldn't give a flying fuck about.' He patted his chest. 'High blood pressure and some problems with the old heart too, thinks it's stress related. He's given me some pills and a spray pump thing to tide me over.'

'Does Stevie know?'

The crowd roared from the WACA and a flock of parrots jetted passed the office window as if fired from a cannon. 'Bloody cricket,' Monty grumbled.

'I'll take that as a no.'

'I haven't had the chance to tell her yet.' Monty felt a sudden need to change the subject. 'Okay, so the paedophile and the loan shark were killed by the same gun, and I want you to find the connection.'

Wayne's jaw dropped. 'Me? how …'

'The Vietnamese girl in the herbalist shop?'

'It was just a gut feeling of mine, don't set your hopes on it.

Angus still has some more digging to do.'

Monty steepled his fingers and tapped at his teeth. Those who didn't know Wayne well would be excused for seeing in his face nothing but a wall of rock split by a million year old frost. Monty knew better.

'Wayne,' he said. 'Far be it to teach my grandfather how to suck eggs, but I hope Barry's wrong about all this …' He waved his hand trying to find the right words. 'I mean, you're not getting too involved here, are you? Not letting your personal feelings get in the way of the case?'

Monty grunted to himself — he could talk. Again he thought he detected a faint blush in the face of older man. 'Shit, Wayne, an old codger like you should have more sense.'

Wayne pushed himself up from the desk and attempted to pull the frayed cuffs of his mustard coloured shirt further down his hairy wrists. Rumour had it that Wayne had not bought new clothes since the death of his wife twenty years ago.

'Nah Monty, it's nothing like that, I just feel like looking out for the girl, that's all. Now is there anything else?' Wayne said, his face back to its usual wall of granite.

19

Excerpt from chat room transcript 260107
HARUM SCARUM: u shld nvr meet up wit some1 u don't no
BETTYBO: bt hes soooooo nice!
HARUM SCARUM: u need anotha KE story. U need her powa. U don't need a boy 2 giv u that
BETTYBO: I want KE to kill some1 this time
HARUM SCARUM: okaaaaaaaay ... lets see what she's got

The high temperature in the van hadn't hurt Miro Kusak's hard drive as much as they'd feared. In Central's operations room Clarissa explained in a steady stream of techno-babble how she'd managed to extract the valuable information. Unfortunately none of Kusak's correspondence with Bianca had shown up yet. Stevie loved her new job, but found the technical side of it a bit of a stretch. She rubbed her gritty eyes and did her best to focus on the screen, but without much success.

This was like no incident room she'd ever worked from before. No cigarette smoke in here, no fusty odours of unwashed clothes and sweaty sandshoes, cheap bourbon and cheaper aftershave. Someone had received a bunch of roses for her birthday and put them on the windowsill, and the scent mingled with the different perfumes of the room's occupants. A collection of cuddly toys stood sentry in the workstation next to Clarissa's, while the partitioning of its neighbour was papered with children's colourful artwork.

'Okay, I can see by your blank expressions that the details of my cyber investigations are less to you plebs than pearls before swine. In a nutshell …' Clarissa stopped for a moment to see if anyone was listening and let out a martyr's sigh when she realised they were all looking vacant.

Stevie dragged herself back from her mental wandering. Tash, who'd been hovering over an open box of chocolates on Clarissa's desk, looked up and pointed to herself. 'You talking to me?'

Clarissa turned her eyes to the ceiling.

Stevie put the lid on the chocolates, pushing them out of Tash's reach. 'Bad for your migraine. You were saying?' she reminded Clarissa.

'Yes, sorry, I'll translate. Miro Kusak and Robert Mason were both members of the Dream Team paedophile ring. Kusak's hard drive and flash disk contained similar photos to Mason's, which they'd both purchased from the webmaster who may also be the photographer — I've found email correspondence that suggests this. The webmaster calls himself Lolita and sends his picture files from an Internet cafe in Mt Lawley.'

'That wouldn't be very private would it?' Stevie queried.

'No one would be able to see the files if they weren't open on the screen. He probably wouldn't use the cafe for everything, maybe just the most sensitive stuff, like the jpegs,' Tash said.

'There's something else,' Clarissa said. 'It's not as obvious as it was in the so-called *art* shots, but I think several of the hard core pics were taken in a common location.'

'What, in the same place as the art shots?'

'No. Have a look at these.' Clarissa tapped some keys and the screen filled with a photograph of a young girl lying naked and in a degrading position on a bed. Stevie swallowed, and was glad to let her gaze follow the cursor to the rough plaster wall behind the bed. There was something hanging on the wall.

Stevie squinted at the screen. 'A crucifix? Can you make it any clearer?' She tried to remember the last time she'd noticed a crucifix on a wall. It was in Mrs Kusak's house, but this one was more ornate, and did not bear the figure of Christ. There seemed to be some kind of filament hanging from it.

'What is that, a crack in the wall, a piece of string?' Stevie tapped the screen.

'Sorry, that's as good as it gets.' Clarissa tapped the keys again, bringing up other images taken in the same room. Some of the shots were taken at different angles and showed several unidentifiable objects on the walls, just visible within the frames.

'So, where do you go with these?' Tash asked Clarissa.

'I should be able to get the dates of the transactions from Miro's computer, so that'll help you narrow your search down. You'll need to look at the cafe's records, see who was on line when the pictures were sent and start grinding through the names. After that, it'll be a question of how easily we can subpoena the bank accounts of those we think might be involved. It's a bummer Bianca's laptop never turned up.'

'Oh but it has,' Tash said with a triumphant grin.

'Where?'

'At the bottom of Mundaring reservoir.'

Clarissa scowled at Tash. 'You love building people up just to cut them down, don't you?'

'Okay, that's enough,' Stevie said. 'Clarissa, get us a report typed up in plain English, summarising everything we need to ask and be looking out for at the cafe.'

'Give me an hour or so to get it organised,' Clarissa said.

'Time for us to grab a bite of lunch,' Stevie said to Tash. If she was ever to get a decent night's sleep again, she and Tash needed to talk. 'Also,' she added to Clarissa, 'print out all the photos of the *art* girls on Mason's and Kusak's computers and start trying to ID them.'

'Was Bianca Webster's picture among them?' Tash asked.

A phone rang from a few workstations down and was answered.

'Not so far, but I'm not through all of them yet,' Clarissa said.

Stevie jumped down from the desk. 'Then finish that first, even before you get those reports typed.' She thumped Tash on the shoulder. 'Ready for lunch?'

'All right for some,' Clarissa grumbled.

From further down the line, a young man's voice called, 'Hey, Stevie! Dolly wants a word in her office. Now.'

Stevie's stomach back-flipped. 'Shit.'

'Guilty conscience?' Tash teased.

'Don't ask, you really don't want to know. We'll have to skip lunch.'

Tash shrugged, 'I've got plenty to do. I'll gather the troops and start on the Internet cafe.'

Stevie reached for Tash's elbow before she could leave the room. 'We really do need to talk, Tash.'

'Come over this evening if you can bear to drag yourself away from your fella.'

Stevie was used to Tash's jibes, they usually didn't worry her, but now she prickled. 'It's not that, it's a question of whether Mont can be there with Izzy or not.'

'Of course it is, Sweets. Bring over a bottle of red.' And she was gone.

Inspector Dolly Veitch smiled and indicated the spare office chair to Stevie. 'Take a seat, I'll be with you in a moment,' she said as she finished filing some documents.

Stevie liked her inspector. Fair and popular with the officers under her, Dolly was the prime reason Sex Crimes was considered such a plum appointment. The ghastly reality of the job was more bearable with a respected boss behind you and the moral support of contented colleagues.

Dolly lowered herself into her desk chair as if she had a sore back, which she didn't as far as Stevie knew. It was just that everything she did she performed with slow and deliberate care; the fine linen pantsuit she took off at the end of the day was doubtless as clean and crease-free as it was when put on that morning. If she hadn't been a police officer, Stevie could have imagined Dolly as the editor of a stylish woman's magazine. Tash often joked that 'when she grew up' she wanted to be just like Dolly Veitch.

Putting on a pair of metallic-framed designer specs, Dolly picked up the complaint form in front of her. Stevie's stomach fluttered as she tried to interpret what was going on behind the unflappable visage.

Dolly finished reading and handed the report to Stevie. 'Read what Mason said and tell me if this is a fair account of what happened.'

Stevie's mouth dried when she first started to read, but by the time she'd finished, she was smiling. 'This is ridiculous, she did not kick him when he was on the ground,' she said. She might have placed her heel upon his head but she didn't kick him. 'And the water pistol was so obviously a fake, he would have known that.'

'But she was out of order with it.'

'Yes she was ma'am and I've had a firm word with her.'

'It was a stupid thing to do.'

'She won't be doing it again. I don't think she realised quite how stupid it was; to her it was just a joke.'

Dolly leaned back in her chair and took her glasses off. 'I can't really see that there's anything to worry about, Stevie, or any need to mount an internal investigation. I spoke to the boss of the remand centre earlier this morning and was told that Mason has also lodged complaints against the staff there, ridiculous accusations. They're all getting a proper going over of course, but lucky for us he's lost any credibility he might have started out with.'

Stevie sank back in the chair; she could hardly believe they were getting off so lightly

'It looks like Natasha is off the hook for the time being, but I'm concerned about her attitude …'

Stevie held her breath.

'She needs to be watched, there are times when that girl plays too close to the edge. It's hard dealing with friends, I understand that, especially when everything is new and you're still finding your way. If anything like this happens again, you're to file a report and send it straight through to me, is that understood? What happened to the water pistol after she threatened Mason with it?'

'I destroyed it, ma'am.'

'Good, rest easy then.' Dolly gave her a reassuring smile.

Monty, you lying bastard, you got me all worked up over nothing. But at least he hadn't told Dolly that Tash had stolen the water pistol from the armoury. Yet.

'Is that all ma'am?' Stevie asked as she rose to her feet.

Dolly motioned her to sit back down. 'No, I haven't finished.'

Stevie dropped back into her chair.

'I had a call from Kate the other day, she's having a hard time coping with the new baby. I tried to warn her what it would be like, but you know as well as I do that all the advice in the world can't prepare you for what you're up for when you first come home from hospital.'

Stevie agreed. When she'd had Izzy, she naively expected life to go on as before, the baby fitting into her world and not the other way around. She hadn't expected two years of broken nights and exhaustion which, combined with the nightmare of dealing with her ex, sent her only a whisper away from full blown depression. If it hadn't been for Tash's support back then she probably would've cracked up.

'So is she extending her maternity leave?' Stevie asked.

'She's resigned.' Dolly fanned the air with a letter plucked from a pile on her desk. 'She's not coming back.'

Stevie paused as the news sank in.

Dolly opened her mouth to speak, but Stevie's mobile rang, cutting her off. She indicated for Stevie to take the call.

It was Clarissa. 'Sorry to interrupt, but this is important. I've found a photo of Bianca Webster on Kusak's computer, along with some of her personal details. He bought the photo from the webmaster, Lolita. The photo's maybe a year or so old, but it's similar in format to others we found on Mason's hard drive.'

Stevie thought for a moment. They were dealing with two problems now, both offshoots of the Bianca Webster case: the death of the paedophile and the cracking of the paedophile ring run by Lolita. She mentally reorganised her day, hoping she could slot in another visit to Stella Webster.

'Have you spoken to Tash?' Stevie asked.

'Yes, she was talking to the staff in the Internet cafe when I rang, going through the logs of users at the time the photos were sent. There are a few names that keep popping up. The guy we want is probably using an alias, or more than one, but it's a start.'

Stevie glanced across the inspector's organised desk, caught her eye and put up her thumb. After she thanked Clarissa and hung up she said, 'Looks like we're getting closer to this Lolita character, ma'am.'

'Good, keep me informed.' Dolly clasped her hands and leaned forward, indicating a change of subject. 'The job vacancy, sergeant in charge of the Cyber Predator Team, was part of the agenda at the senior staff meeting yesterday.'

Stevie wondered if this was the meeting Monty had had with the commissioner, the one he needed clean clothes for.

'Your name was put forward as Kate's replacement. It would mean promotion to senior sergeant, of course.' Dolly smiled and raised elegantly arched eyebrows as she waited for Stevie's reaction.

Stevie found her words disappearing before she could get them out, she didn't know what to say. This was totally unexpected — why the hell hadn't Monty said anything?

God, she must look like a complete moron. She was pleased to be considered up for the job, yet her mind flooded with reasons to turn it down. 'Thank you ma'am, but there are things I need to think about. Childcare is my first priority; the new job will mean longer hours …'

Her words dried before they could leave her mouth. Dolly didn't attempt to break the silence, giving Stevie time to organise her staccato thoughts. *I've not been in the Cyber Predator Team long enough — I don't understand the complexities of computers — am I up to it? — do I deserve it? What effect will it have on Izzy?*

Dolly broke the silence. 'I know; childcare; same old, same old. But you have a good support group I believe.'

Stevie nodded. Yes, but for how long?

'How long have I got to think about this, ma'am?' she asked, finally able to get some sensible words out.

'They'd like an answer by next week — think you can manage that?'

Stevie attempted to smile but her face felt stretched and tight, as if coated with cosmetic peel. 'Sure.'

Dolly must have read the doubt in her expression. 'You know Stevie, you're a bloody good officer, one of the best I've had. Your capture of Robert Mason was masterful. For all of our sakes, I hope you give the job serious consideration.'

Stevie rose to her feet. 'Thank you, ma'am, I will.'

Dolly regarded her for a moment then smiled. 'You'd damn well better, girl.'

20

Wayne drove most of the way to the herbalist with his jaw clamped, Barry's words 'he's sweet on her' playing over in his mind like an unwelcome tune. Damn Barry for choosing just the wrong moment to enter the herbalist's, just as he'd been having a harmless flirt with Angela Nguyen.

He sighed as he pulled into a parking space outside the shop, hoping things would go better this time. He had to put his discomfort aside and concentrate on the case. It didn't help that he was brooding on the information Angus had just given him about the boy who'd been associated with Zhang Li.

The signs outside the herbalist shop had already been brought in, even though it was still an hour before closing time — they can't have been expecting much more business. He gave his paisley tie one last reassuring tug before stepping across the threshold.

There was no one at the counter, no one else in the shop. He could hear Angela Nguyen speaking on the phone in the back room and decided to let her finish her conversation.

A row of colourful boxes caught his eye from one of the aisles and he wandered over to inspect. The aisles were so narrow he couldn't stand far enough away to read the names of the products and was forced to put on his reading glasses. The flimsy metal shelving shuddered as he reached for a box. Some kind of hair-restorer, he surmised, if the picture on the front was any guide. He looked around. The counter was still empty, the only noise came from a humming fridge and the voice of the girl on the phone. He saw no evidence of security cameras in the ceiling corners — it wouldn't do to let the beautiful interpreter catch him in the act of inspecting boxes of hair-restoring lotion.

Prising open the cardboard box he plucked out the enclosed leaflet, looking for some English instructions. The Chinese seemed to have a way with herbs; they, if anyone, should have found a cure for baldness. Not that he was thinning too badly, he reassured himself as he smoothed down his feathery hair, and certainly not enough to do a Barry and shave it all off.

He examined the leaflet, finding nothing but Chinese writing. *Shit*. And now he must attempt to straighten up the box and squeeze it back into its original condition.

Busy as he was behind the shelving, Wayne only noticed the boy when he was already at the counter, leaning against it, cocking his head as if trying to hear the phone conversation in the next room. He looked to be about fourteen. A small fourteen. Swamped in camouflage army pants and a jungle green military jacket, his clothes were totally unsuitable for the current heat wave. As he pulled away from the counter, the boy scratched his head, his neck, then his arm, gazing around the shop in much the way Wayne had when he'd been looking for security cameras.

Wayne froze behind the shelving; he didn't want to give his position away before he knew exactly what the boy was up to. The boy straightened his shoulders as if taking a breath of courage and then slipped behind the counter and pinged the till.

Wayne now had a clear view of him. This was the same boy in the photo Angus had shown him earlier. But the face was skeletal, the eyes wide and wired, skittering around the room like black beetles. The boy hesitated at the open till, picking at a sore on the side of his mouth. Wayne cursed his bad luck. Give him a grown man any day over a teenage boy with something to prove and a habit that left him with no boundaries.

Like a starving man snatching food, the boy began to stuff his jacket pockets with cash from the till.

Wayne had seen all he needed. He stepped out from behind the shelving. 'Hold it right there, son. Police.'

At that moment, Angela emerged from the back room. Her timing couldn't have been worse. He couldn't have reached her even if his mind had registered the split second whirl of movement. The boy lunged towards Angela, clasping her in front of him like a shield. With one hand clamped around her neck, the other reached into the folds of his jacket and pulled a machete from its hidden scabbard.

Wayne's gut twisted with a painful lurch. He'd be paying for this later if he survived, damn his weak belly. Holding his hands up in supplication he said, 'It's okay, son, it's okay. Put the knife down. You don't have to do this. Let her go and we'll have a talk.'

'Stay there, stay there, I'll kill her!' the boy screeched through a spray of spittle.

The girl looked to be on the verge of fainting. Her eyes rolled and her knees sagged. In this state, without her mask of self-confidence, he realised how much younger she was than he'd first thought. Christ, he'd been bantering about aphrodisiacs with a girl who was only sixteen if she were a day. Now he understood Barry's tasteless jibes.

The boy staggered back as he tried to support her, barked something in Vietnamese and placed the gleaming blade to her throat. She swallowed her scream and straightened, making herself several centimetres taller than her captor.

He's a wild animal, Wayne thought. Any sudden move from me, and the girl's throat will be slit from ear to ear.

'Can I close the shop, mate?' he said. 'We don't want anyone crashing our friendly little party, do we?' He fought to keep his tone steady; he'd seen first hand the damage a machete could do to the human body when he was in Nam. Without waiting for an answer and keeping his movements slow, he moved to the front door and flicked the 'open' sign to 'closed'. Over his shoulder he said, 'I'll close it too,' and slipped the bolts.

He took several steps towards the counter. The boy yelled at him to stay back, his eyes darting about the room.

Wayne stood and waited for the silence to do his work for him. He stared hard at the boy, saw him lick his dry lips, jacket moving in and out with rapid, shallow breaths. The fridge by the counter hummed, the sound of a leaking tap dripped from the back room. Eventually the machete began to tremble in the small white-knuckled hand. As the blade began to waver, Wayne could see the kid's grip upon the girl weakening.

'So, what'll it be, boss?' Wayne kept his voice soft and low to force the boy to listen closely. 'The way I see it, you either let her go, take the money and run, or you let her go and have a nice friendly chat with me.'

There were other options too of course; one involved slicing and dicing them into stir-fry. 'C'mon Sammy, I know you speak good English, I know all about you. Put the knife down so we can have a talk. You don't really want to hurt your sister, do you? She's the only family you've got.'

21

Excerpt from chat room transcript 081206
  BETTYBO: I wagged scool agin 2day
  HARUM SCARUM: Bad grl!
  BETTYBO: I hate zoe carmkel
  HARUM SCARUM: hate cn b good. Use it. I do
  BETTYBO: I hate that pig he maks mum cry. I wish I was KE
  HARUM SCARUM: let KE empowa u
  BETTYBO: I wanna c u f2f
  HARUM SCARUM: No sme

Stevie finally answered one of Monty's missed calls while she was driving to Stella Webster's house.

'I've been trying to call you all day,' he said.

'And I called you back mid-morning and your phone was off — where were you?'

'I had an appointment.'

She waited for him to offer something else. He didn't. 'Right then,' she said. 'What's new? Other than you dobbing Tash and me in to Dolly, that is.'

'Stevie, I had no choice. The complaint form was handed to me by mistake. I warned you about it, it should have gone straight to her anyway.'

'She offered me a promotion.'

She thought she detected a sigh of relief from his end of the phone. 'There you go then. No harm done.'

'What were you ringing me for?'

'There's so much going on I don't know where to start. Firstly, you'll be pleased to know that none of the impounded Glocks matches the one that killed Kusak. Look, about Natasha...' He hesitated. 'About last night, I'm sorry; I got a bit carried away. I've not been feeling ...'

'Okay, apology accepted, what else?' She was being overly curt, she knew, but didn't seem able to help herself. What they both needed to do now was detach from their personal relationship and behave like professionals.

There was a long pause from Monty's end of the phone; she heard the flick of a cigarette lighter, could imagine him taking a long drag. 'The bullet was matched to the gun that killed our loan shark, Zhang Li,' he said, his voice stronger again.

So much for her resolution. How the hell could they possibly work this? Two linked cases meant they'd be thrown even closer together. And what on earth could the cases have in common?

'Any leads?' she asked.

'First we have to ask ourselves who'd want the two dead — a contract killer, some kind of vigilante? Someone they've both had business dealings with? Wayne and Angus seem to think they have a witness to Zhang Li's murder. He's a street kid and Wayne's following a lead on him now. Seems pretty hopeful.'

Stevie thought for a moment, cautiously passing a school bus spilling out a group of jostling children. 'Could Zhang Li and Kusak have been hit by the same contract killer hired by two different people for two different reasons?' she asked.

'Could be, they were both killed execution style with a single bullet to the head. Apparently Mrs Kusak withdrew six thousand dollars from her account a couple of weeks ago, Barry's going to have a word with her about it. But everything's just speculation until we can talk to that street kid and find out what he saw. What are you up to now?'

'I'm visiting Stella Webster; want to show her the picture of Bianca we found on Kusak's computer. I also want to have another look in Bianca's room, see if there's anything I missed the first time around.'

'Good idea.'

Stevie's voice softened. 'Are you feeling better today?'

'Great.' He didn't sound it. 'Do you want to meet for fish and chips on the beach tonight?' he asked with forced jocularity.

'I have to go over some stuff with Tash after I've seen Stella.'

'Natasha.' He paused. 'Ah.'

She counted to ten in her head. 'But I should be able to meet you after that. I'll bring food.'

From the balcony outside number 33, Stella's sister pointed to the park and the lone figure sitting on the bench near the lake.

'How's she doing?' Stevie asked. She could see the family resemblance despite Gail's extra fifteen kilos and apple cheeked, outdoorsy complexion. Had she reached adulthood, Bianca might've looked like this.

'Oh, up and down, you know. I'm hoping she'll feel a bit better after the funeral.' She gave Stevie a weak smile, not reflected in eyes that were deeply shadowed with sleeplessness.

Stevie glanced toward the lake and hesitated, not sure if she should intrude upon Stella's solitude. No, she'd leave her alone for a bit longer, she decided. The picture of Bianca from Kusak's computer could wait. She cocked her head to the door of the flat. 'I need to have another look in Bianca's room, do you mind …' Her words trailed. Out of the corner of her eye she saw the vaguely familiar shape of a stocky man wearing a checked shirt and jeans, swaggering towards Stella on the bench. Even from this distance, she could see the woman stiffen as he drew near.

'Any idea who that is? I'm sure I've seen him before …' Stevie spoke her thoughts aloud, making a hesitant move toward the stairwell. 'I might just …'

'I dunno,' Gail shrugged, then did a double take and Stevie saw why. The man was leaning towards Stella now, one hand on the back of the bench. Stella cringed and shook her head, her panic obvious even from where they stood on the balcony.

Gail pushed past Stevie and stormed towards the steps. 'The bloody creep, as if she hasn't been through enough …'

'Leave this to me,' Stevie put a hand on her arm to hold her back.

Gail flicked the hand off, voice rising as she looked helplessly toward the park. 'Look, he's grabbing her!'

'Stay there!'

Stevie hurtled down the concrete steps two at a time, four when she jumped the landings. She swung out from the stairwell at ground level, sprinting across the weedy verge, across the road and into the park.

The man saw her coming. He dropped Stella's arm and took off at a run towards a car parked on the perimeter road. Stevie gave chase, but he had reached the car and was pulling out when she was still metres away. Hands on hips and panting, she watched him move into the traffic and splutter away. She was too far away to catch the number plate, but she caught the make. And she'd seen the white Ford Escort before, on the night she and Monty had brought Stella the bad news. It had been parked in the street outside Stella's flat.

When she reached the bench, Stella was leaning forward, elbows on knees, as if fighting back nausea. Stevie sank down next to her, still puffing, and patted Stella on the back. 'Are you okay?'

Stella straightened, wiped her eyes. 'I think so. Thanks for that.'

'That wasn't Bob, was it, Bob of the pestering phone call from the other night?' And the man who almost pushed me down the stairs, she added to herself.

Stella shook her head and spoke quickly, 'No, I've never seen him before.'

Stevie scrutinised her for a moment in silence. When Stella continued to avoid eye contact she said, 'Stella, are you sure …'

'Of course I'm sure, he was just some creep, that's all.'

'What did he want?'

Stella hesitated. 'Money.' She looked down and began pulling at a loose thread from the hem of her T-shirt. 'He was pissed off was all. When he saw I didn't have a bag he told me to turn out my pockets. I said no and that's when he grabbed me. I'm okay, don't worry.' Her gaze strayed across the lake to where a pair of black swans were gliding and spoke as if from the distance of a dream. 'Bianca hated those swans. One pecked her hand when she was feeding it some stale bread. I told her it was just the bird's nature, that it didn't make it a bad bird. The man who killed Bianca was bad though, he must have been. He was bad to the bone to do what he done.'

'You need a cup of tea. Or something stronger.' Stevie looked up to see Gail watching them from the balcony and gave her a reassuring wave. 'Come on, Stella, let's go home.'

'You are absolutely certain you haven't seen that man before?' Stevie asked again as they sat on the squeaking couch in Stella's lounge room. She wondered why Stella would lie to her. She was almost certain the man in the park was the same man who'd bumped into her on the stairwell the other night. She recalled the hoppy reek as he'd barged past and associated it with the beer can she'd seen lying on Stella's coffee table.

Stella waved her hand impatiently. She seemed tired out. 'Positive, I told you that. Can we just forget it?'

'You'll let me know if you do see him again?' Stevie asked, allowing just the right amount of suspicion to shade her words. This wasn't the right time or place to push, but she hoped her tone of voice was enough to let Stella know this was only a temporary reprieve.

'Yes, of course I'll tell you if I see him again.' Stella reached for her cigarettes and offered Stevie one. Stevie shook her head; after the sprint her lungs still felt filled with molten lead. It must be time for another go at quitting.

'You wanted to talk to me about something?' Stella said.

'I wanted another look in Bianca's room to see if there's anything I missed the first time around.'

'The crime's solved, they told me the guy's dead, why bother?' Stella replied in a voice laced with despair. 'Why bother about the man at the lake? Why bother about anything now?'

'Do you want some lunch?' Gail called from the kitchen. It was a timely interruption to Stella's rising hysteria.

Stella shook her head. Stevie reached into her bag, producing the print Clarissa had extracted from Kusak's computer, a head and shoulder shot of a slightly younger, slightly slimmer Bianca. Her bare shoulders were hunched and swathed in a ribbon of floating muslin and the painted lips did nothing to disguise the tension of a tight little smile. While it could hardly be considered pornography, the photo was a tasteless attempt at turning a child into a sexualised, alluring adult. The look on the face alone would have screamed out vulnerability to any predator with the wiring to receive it.

Miro Kusak.

Stella balled her fist and bit into her wrist. Shuddered. 'Oh, that, I'd forgotten about that.'

'Where was it taken?' Stevie asked.

'Bianca was desperate to do some modelling. I let her audition for a modelling agency a year or so ago, had seven hundred bucks worth of photos taken. But she was turned down, told to come back when she'd lost some weight.' Stella's face crumpled and her voice broke. 'She was nine years old and that stuck up bitch told her to lose some weight — can you imagine what that can do to a young girl? She wasn't fat at all, just a bit of puppy fat, but after that she felt like a real freak.'

Yes, Stevie could imagine what something like that could do to a child and felt the rage flare. She wondered what had induced Stella to let Bianca go to a photo shoot in the first place and put it down to mother's guilt again. Let the kid do more or less what she wants to make up for all the hours she'd been left alone.

The other pictures on Mason's computer may have come from the same modelling school, downloaded by someone with access to the collection — the photographer perhaps? It fitted with Clarissa's theory anyway. The modelling agency was the key, she was sure of it.

'Can you remember the name of the agency?' Stevie asked, sitting on the edge of her seat, trying her best to make the question sound routine. She crossed her fingers, hoping she'd get the information she wanted without having to confuse Stella with too many questions.

Stella shrugged. 'I don't know. It must've gone in one ear and out the other.'

'It's really important that you try to remember, Stella. I think the man who killed Bianca might have had access to the agency's files. The photo we found on Kusak's computer came with personal details of Bianca, including her email address. We think these files may have been distributed to a paedophile ring operating around Perth, which in turn sold them to private individuals. They've sold other pictures too, meaning that other children might be in danger. Please, Stella, try and remember.'

Stella shook her head in the manner of one who doesn't

expect success, but stopped as some memory slowly dawned. She wiped her nose with the back of her hand. 'I might have a receipt or something, I'm not sure where but, it was over a year ago.'

'Would you mind having a search while I have another look in Bianca's room?' Stevie asked.

Stella seemed to deflate, as if the task were too much for her, as if the last mental exercise had dried up all her reserves. She glanced at the couch. Stevie could tell that all she wanted to do was curl up into a ball and try to forget. She understood that, but she also understood how important it was to keep Stella busy, to put a stop to the despondency that threatened to overwhelm her. The woman needed to feel that in some small way she was helping to find justice for her daughter.

She took Stella's hand and gently pulled her from the couch. 'I think the kitchen drawers might be a good place to start. I have a drawer at home where I dump all my odds and ends of paperwork, maybe you do too?'

Gail needed no prompting. She moved into the lounge from the kitchen area and took her sister's arm. 'We used to keep our stuff in an old shoe box when we were kids, remember?'

Stella sniffed, gave a strained smile. 'Yeah, old habits die hard, it's on top of the pantry cupboard.'

The sisters moved arm in arm into the kitchen and Stevie took herself off to Bianca's bedroom.

'Enter on pain of death,' the sign on the door read. Izzy had scrawled something similar on her bedroom door — a less sophisticated 'Keep Out!' with a wobbly skull and crossbones.

There were other stickers and signs in Bianca's room that she didn't remember seeing before. 'Fuck, I think I'm turning into my mother.' How did Stella feel about that? And, 'Jim Beam lives here' slapped onto the wardrobe. Both seemed strangely precocious for a ten year old and Stevie wondered if she was still trying to play the part of the muslin-swathed woman-child in the photo.

Her mind wandered to Emma Breightling. Like Bianca, she also seemed to be in a hurry to grow up, but Emma had made much more of a success of it. She remembered Emma's emotional reaction to the newspaper headline about the death of what presumably was a stranger — it had left Stevie wondering if the girls might have known one another. Now there was a modelling agency, and Emma's mother ran a modelling agency. Somehow it would not surprise her if it was the very one that Bianca had auditioned for.

Stevie twirled the hair in her ponytail through her fingers as she thought. There had to be something else in this room. If she could find a way to free up her thinking, she might find it. There was a thread, she was sure of it, a connection between the two girls floating about in this room, something she'd overlooked the first time. She released her hair from the confining ponytail, as if her thoughts too might be unleashed.

The room was arranged exactly as before, Stella would probably keep it as a shrine to her daughter, never rearranging it or cleaning it again. Every night she would come in here and lie upon the bed, absorb memories from the scent on the pillow, try to ready herself for the day when they would disappear into the air like smoke.

Mindful of this, Stevie didn't touch the pillow. Sitting on the bed she leaned her back against the wall and faced the desk, allowing her gaze to trace the contents of the bookshelves. Left to right, left to right she trawled while the fluorescent pink iPod stared down at her like the eye of God. She blinked and tried to ignore the distraction of its glowing image, tried to focus on whatever was prodding at her subconscious.

'I want more stories!' It was something she'd heard Izzy say. No, it wasn't that, but she was getting close, it was something similar. She closed her eyes: *Because they don't have magic powers like Katy Enigma.*

Katy Enigma, the story Emma had been telling Izzy during that first babysitting session. Stevie snapped up straight on the bed and slammed her fist into her hand, 'Yesssssss!'

Springing from the bed she moved over to Bianca's desk and the jumble of half written stories she'd dismissed during her earlier search.

One title immediately caught her eye: 'Katy Enigma and the case of the missing puppy.' There were other Katy Enigma downloads, sandwiched amongst the mess of papers. Katy Enigma must be some new kind of new kids' fad, perhaps a series like Harry Potter, she thought. The stories were important, Stevie was sure of it. Perhaps both girls had belonged to an Internet message board or chat room devoted to the character, they might have written fan fiction together.

The eye continued to stare down at her as she leafed through the sheaf of stories. Ridiculous that a gimmicky music machine could make her feel so uncomfortable. Perhaps it was because it reminded her of a strange little poem her Gran used to recite, about the green eye of the little yellow god. Was this white-eyed pink iPod god trying to tell her something? Giving in to its implacable stare, she picked it up from the shelf and took it with the pile of stories into the kitchen.

'Stella, do you know anything about these Katy Enigma stories on Bianca's desk?'

Stella shook her head. She had not heard of Katy Enigma, she had no idea about Katy Enigma, and she didn't care if Stevie took the stories with her, or the iPod, she just wanted to go to bed.

It was the sister, Gail, who proffered the piece of paper, a receipt from Tall Poppies, signed by the owner, Miranda Breightling.

22

The sound of tea pouring into the cup reminded Wayne how badly he needed to use the bathroom. But he'd only just got the boy calm enough to sit at the table in the back room and he knew now wouldn't be the time to excuse himself. The bolted front door might not keep the kid from running a bunk, or something even crazier. He took comfort in the feel of the machete lying by his feet under the table. Although the boy had handed it over without too much persuasion, the flitting dark eyes told Wayne he was still about as predictable as a spark in a fireworks factory.

Angela finished pouring the tea then removed a plate of steaming dim sims from the microwave, keeping up a steady prattle to which Sammy responded with the occasional grunt or monosyllable. Charming and as polite as ever, she translated some of their conversation for Wayne, interspersing it with a brief account of Sammy's life up to now.

The boy's story was typical of many of the street kids Wayne had come across. Their parents were dead and they'd migrated from Vietnam with their uncle when Sammy was a baby. He'd run away from home last year just before he was due in children's court on a shoplifting charge. When he returned a few weeks later, the locks on his uncle's house had been changed and his tearful sister had been left with the job of telling him their uncle had disowned him.

Wayne reached for a paper napkin and tucked it down the front of his shirt before sinking his teeth into the yielding marshmallow softness of a dim sim. Not bad, not bad at all, he thought as he dipped the remaining half in the dish of soy sauce. He glanced up and smiled when he saw the girl looking at him. The boy hadn't looked up from his bowl since the start of the meal. He was obviously starving.

Wayne gestured to the empty chair beside him.

Angela shook her head, 'I have to serve the food. Also, there might be customers for the shop …'

'You don't need to serve the food, we can serve ourselves. We need to talk,' he said, keeping his tone firm but kind.

'If Mr Cheng finds out the shop is closed even ten minutes early, he'll get mad …'

Wayne reached into his jacket pocket and removed his ID card from his wallet. 'This card says he won't, understand?'

He slid the plate of dim sims towards her. When she did nothing but stare at it, he picked one up and put it in the bowl in front of her. 'I don't like eating alone.' He shot Sammy a disapproving glance. 'He doesn't count.' The kid continued to eat like there was no tomorrow.

'Are you going to tell Mr Cheng about Sammy trying to steal from the till?' Angela asked, lowering herself into the chair at last. Wayne dabbed at his mouth with his napkin, leaned back and took his time to regard the brother and sister.

'I might.'

Angela put her hand to her mouth. The boy pushed his chair out from the table and jumped up.

Wayne jabbed his finger at him. 'You, lad. Sit down, and listen to what I have to say. I said I *might* tell Mr Cheng, but that depends on you.' To the girl he said, 'And you Angela, for God's sake eat something. Just watching you stress out is giving me indigestion.'

The girl gave in and took a nibble. The boy remained standing. He folded his arms and glared.

'I said sit!' Wayne said as if to a wilful puppy.

Sammy glared at Wayne for a moment longer before finally lowering himself back into his chair.

'That's better,' Wayne said. 'Let's just play happy families for a while, okay? I need to get some things straight before we decide on a plan of action — like what to do with young Sammy here. Firstly, Angela, do you want to press robbery and assault charges against your brother?'

Her eyes widened and she shook her head violently.

'Has he ever done this before?'

She glanced at her brother who mouthed something guttural back at her.

'None of that now,' Wayne said. He didn't have to speak Vietnamese to know the gist of what that was about.

Angela fiddled with her plate, not meeting Wayne's eye. 'No, he never stole from the till before, I gave him money.'

'Your money?'

'Yes, usually I give him my money, but my uncle, he knows how much pay I get from Mr Cheng. I had to tell him I'd spent the money.'

Wayne sighed. 'And then you were the one who copped it from the old man?' He shot Sammy a look. 'What a tangled web, eh? And as your habit grew, your sister couldn't give you enough cash so you had to go elsewhere and take it for yourself.'

Sammy sniffed, wiped his nose across the sleeve of his jacket, and resumed his angry glare.

'This was the first time,' Angela said.

'The first time from here maybe, but what about other shops, or breaking and entering houses, bag snatching — you've done that before, yeah?'

The boy shrugged, took another mouthful of food. To his sister he said, 'Angela, get more dim sim.'

Wayne put his hand out to stop the girl from going anywhere. 'Now wait on mate, you're running your sister ragged. Sometimes you got to help yourself and I don't mean taking it either — know what I'm saying? Do you want to help yourself, Sammy, do you want a chance to go straight?'

'Not in fucking juvie, if that's what you mean.'

'I could charge you with attempted robbery with violence.'

The girl gasped.

'But if you cooperate, if you show some manners towards your sister, I might be able to get something else sorted.'

The boy eyed Wayne suspiciously. 'What, a foster home, an orphanage? You can't force my uncle to take me back, he hates my guts and I wouldn't stay there even if you did. He thinks I'm his punching bag. He put me in hospital when I was twelve, with a cracked rib.'

'Does your uncle hurt you too, Angela?' Wayne asked.

'No, he wouldn't dare.' She lifted her chin and he saw the return of some of the spark he'd seen in her the other day. 'I work hard, I do as I'm told, but I don't take shit, he knows that and so does Mr Cheng. If either of them laid a hand on me I'd leave.'

'But you let your little brother walk all over you,' Wayne reminded her.

'No, I don't.' Angela cast her eyes to the table.

Sure you don't, love, Wayne thought with an inner sigh. 'Angela, how old are you?'

'Sixteen,' she said.

He pondered the point for a moment; she was way too young to play the part of 'responsible adult'.

He said, 'There's a social worker I know, might be able to help you both out, providing Sammy agrees to undergo some kind of rehab. He'll need to attend a residential treatment program for a while, probably be placed in some kind of hostel as a ward of the state …'

Sammy let rip with a string of abuse aimed firstly at Wayne and then at his sister.

'If you want it that way, fine.' Wayne reached for his phone and called for a paddy wagon, his feet still planted firmly on the machete.

'No, wait, wait!' Sammy sprang from the table.

And promptly burst into tears.

23

In the hallway Stevie handed over a bottle of red. 'Take the top off for a while, let it breathe,' she said.

Tash unscrewed the cap, had a sniff and looked dubious. 'Think we should try CPR first?' Her hair was wet and slicked back. She'd not long returned from a trip with Terry to the public pool, she explained. A seventies cheesecloth skirt swished around her ankles, its drooping hem accentuating an aura of vulnerability that Tash usually went to great lengths to hide. Tash in a skirt was even more rare a sight than Stevie in a skirt.

'Dagging around home gear,' she said in answer to Stevie's quizzical look.

'I was thinking more like a perfect match for Wayne,' Stevie said, ducking away from the predictable swipe.

Stevie followed Tash into the kitchen where Terry, who didn't give her a second glance, was playing with his slot cars on the kitchen table.

Then disaster struck. Tash's hip nudged a jutting piece of track head just as the red car was about to reach the chequered flag. The delicate road system swept from the table to the floor and clattered in a mangled heap.

Purple with rage, Terry screamed at his sister. Before Stevie's eyes he transformed from a gentle child to a violent, booming-voiced man.

'It's okay Terry, it's not broken,' Stevie tried to placate him. 'It just needs to be put back on the table and slotted together again.'

Tash dropped to her haunches and began gathering up the strips of track. Stevie bent to help.

'I'll be right with this, Stevie,' Tash's voice caught. 'Take the wine and glasses into the lounge. I'll be there in a minute.'

Stevie pointed a finger at Terry as she passed. 'You behave now,' she warned. 'If I ever hear you talking to your sister like that again, you'll have to answer to me, right?'

Terry's rage had burnt itself out. He nodded his submission, looked sheepishly at Stevie then dropped to his knees to help Tash with the track.

Stevie left them to make up in private. In the lounge she put the bottle and glasses on a small table and sank into Tash's circular cane chair. Her heart went out to her friend — she'd always thought that as a single mother *she'd* had it tough.

At the academy, Tash had had few friends. People were put off by her brash, I-can-do-anything-any-man-can-do attitude; it was Stevie who'd been the popular party girl. How times had changed, she reflected as she folded herself deeper into the huge cane chair. Not many parties these days, thank God. Her idea of a good night now involved curling up on the sofa with Monty watching a movie from her vintage collection.

Tash was one of the few who'd stuck around after she'd had Izzy. She'd turn up on the doorstep with a bottle of brandy, pour Stevie a stiff one and take the screaming baby out for walks that would sometimes last hours. When Stevie and Izzy both had gastro, Tash was there with the mop and bucket, and when Stevie was having problems with her ex, Tash had given her a key to her house.

The tables had turned when Tash's parents were killed and she'd been the one left caring for Terry. Stevie had been there for her when she could, though she'd always wished she could have done more.

Tash came out of the kitchen with her characteristic self-satisfied smile. Peace and order reigned once more. She reached for the wine and poured a generous amount into each fat bellied glass. They clinked.

'I can see that it's more than a fixed Scalextrics that's got you excited,' Stevie said. 'Go on. You first.'

Tash made herself comfortable in the chair opposite. 'Did Clarissa tell you my photographer news?' she asked.

'That a dodgy photographer's been using the Internet cafe? Yeah, she did — tell me more.'

'The staff at the cafe described a regular client who says he's a photographer,' Tash explained. 'His session times correspond closely to the times the porn photos were upped.'

'Did you get a physical description?'

'Better than that, we have a name — Julian Holdsworth.'

'Might be an alias.' Despite her cautious response, Stevie found herself leaning as far forward as the cane chair would allow her. This was the closest lead they'd had so far.

'Don't you think it's a bit strange that a professional photographer should need the services of an Internet cafe? You'd think he'd have all the necessary high-tech computer equipment himself,' she mused aloud.

'It is weird. That's what I thought too, but the woman at the cafe said he complained of having a recurring virus,' Tash said. 'That's what made her remember him. She said she's never known anyone have such bad luck with computers. She'll contact us the moment he comes in again. Meanwhile, I've given a couple of the team the task of tracking him down.'

Stevie lit a cigarette, took a drag and queried the likelihood of a man giving out his real name and profession when uploading porn on the Internet, especially one who had gone to such lengths to hide his Internet ID.

Tash shrugged. 'It's a start. He could be overconfident — many a clever villain's downfall.'

'True,' Stevie conceded, raising her glass. 'Here's to the stupidity of criminals. Let us never overestimate them.' She took a good swig of her wine. It was time she got Mason's assault allegations out of the way. Here goes nothing.

'I, err, had a meeting with Dolly today.'

'Yeah, I know, we had to cancel our lunch date.'

'Robert Mason put in a complaint about you.'

Tash casually blew smoke towards the ceiling. 'Bullshit, I hardly touched him. You know that.'

'Dolly wanted me to give you a bollocking for it.'

Tash shrugged. 'Bollocking accepted. I suppose he mentioned the water pistol too?'

'Afraid so.'

Tash laughed. 'Now there's a story.' She explained how she'd secreted the water pistol out of the armoury from under the nose of the uniformed sergeant who'd been too busy inspecting her cleavage to see what she was doing with her hands. Tash told the story without guile, as if she had no idea of its implications. When she finished, though, she did take a moment to narrow her eyes and stare at Stevie through a smoky veil.

'You going to tell Dolly that?' she asked.

Stevie hesitated. 'No.'

'Good.' Tash blew away the cloud. 'I can take a few black marks against my name, but stealing from the armoury might be pushing it.'

Stevie took a sip of her wine and thought about the best approach. Straightforward honesty, she decided. 'I don't think you realise how close you got to the edge with that stunt, Tash. Kusak was killed with an automatic pistol. Monty had the guns in the armoury checked because of a notion he had that you might have snitched one when you took the water pistol.'

Tash paled. 'Jesus, shit. How the hell did he know about that?'

'He's mates with Sergeant Jenkins in the armoury.'

'Fuck, I should have guessed.'

'It's okay, that's been cleared up, the guns in the armoury have been tested and they're all clean.' She hesitated. 'But there's still the question of where you went after you'd seen Mrs Kusak.' She held Tash's eyes unwaveringly in her own and softened her voice. 'Tash, Monty and I both know she told you where Kusak was hiding out. And I know you didn't go straight home after you saw Mrs Kusak, because I called around and you weren't here. Where did you go?'

Tash's fingers dug into the sides of her chair and she stared back at Stevie with disbelief. 'What are you saying? You're saying you think I killed Miro Kusak?'

'No, no, of course I'm not. I'm warning you, that's all. Lucky for both of us Monty seems to have dropped the subject. But if it does rear its ugly head again, I think you should be ready to give an explanation of your movements that night.'

'He's jealous.'

'What?'

'Monty's jealous of our friendship, he's trying to shaft me.'

Stevie shook her head. 'I really don't think so.'

'He thinks I'm trying to steal you away from him.'

'Don't talk crap.' Her reaction was automatic, but Stevie had to admit to herself this was an angle she hadn't contemplated. Might this be a plausible explanation for Monty's recent moody behaviour? It did seem to coincide with her transfer to the Cyber Predator Team and her close working proximity with Tash.

Tash cursed Monty's name as she picked up her bag and

rummaged through it. She removed a crumpled receipt and all but threw it at Stevie.

'Tash, it's not me that needs convincing. I just wanted you to be prepared in case any more questions were asked …'

'Read it,' Tash said.

Stevie glanced down at the hurled ball of paper, unfolded it and smoothed down the creases. It was a receipt from a pharmacy for a purchase at six o'clock on the evening of Kusak's death.

'That's my local chemist where I stopped to get my migraine medication. I left Mrs K's at about five thirty and if you stick to the speed limit it takes about thirty-five minutes to get back to Inglewood from Mundaring — satisfied?'

'So where were you at six thirty when I called in here?'

'Oh, for Christ's sake,' Tash exclaimed. 'After the chemist I stopped at a friend's house. I took my migraine medication there and then zonked out, I wasn't safe to drive.' She held up a finger to stop Stevie from asking the next question. 'And don't bother asking for a name because you won't get one.'

'I'll have to ask for it if the shit hits.'

'Well it hasn't, has it? I mean, for fuck's sake, what does it matter? I couldn't have got back to Mundaring to shoot the guy. Hell, Stevie, I don't like driving that much at the best of times, never mind when I'm keeling over with a bloody migraine.'

Stevie knew she'd done the right thing in pushing the issue, but Tash's reluctance to co-operate left her with an unpleasant taste. She took another sip of wine and made an effort to rinse it away. They'd been friends for years; she couldn't see why the identity of a new lover had to be kept so secret.

'Put the receipt somewhere safe,' she said. 'Just in case. But if it looks like your career might end up on the line, you'd better be prepared to name names.'

'It's my career that's the problem,' Tash mumbled.

'What did you say?'

Tash opened her mouth as if about to say something else, then seemed to think better of it. She drew her knees up like a petulant child, shooting Stevie a dark look.

'Am I forgiven?' Stevie asked after several seconds of awkward silence.

Tash looked up to the ceiling. 'I suppose so.' Her stormy look began to clear, and when she met Stevie's eye a slow smile broke through. 'Monty's such a dickhead, isn't he?'

Stevie smiled back. *Yes, he can be sometimes, and so can you. But enough has been said, I've done my duty to both of you.*

She guided the conversation back to their case. She explained the connections she'd discovered between Emma and Bianca, that the modelling agency that had taken Bianca's photo was Tall Poppies — owned and managed by Emma Breightling's mother, Miranda.

Tash was forking her hair, making it stand up in short spikes. 'Hang on,' she said, 'this is ringing a bell.'

Taking her mobile phone from the coffee table, she rang someone at Central police records. Stevie strained to catch the conversation. From what she could gather it sounded like they had another lead. Her pulse quickened.

'Hey!' she raised her glass in a toast when Tash put the phone down. 'You're a genius, fill me in.'

Tash's eyes sparkled with excitement. 'I thought Miranda Breightling's name sounded familiar when you first mentioned her. It was from a couple of years ago, long before you joined Sex Crimes. There was a scandal involving a modelling agency soliciting girls in the Hay Street Mall. Miranda Breightling, proprietor of Tall Poppies, was stroking these wretched girls' flimsy egos, telling them they had *The Look* and promising them a career in modelling if they put themselves on her books. The *only* cost to them was footing the bill for a photo shoot with the company photographer. We had several complaints about this. One girl had stolen from her mother to pay the fees; another said they'd never received the photos, which were supposed to be theirs to keep.

'After they'd paid up, big surprise, most of the girls were told they were unsuitable. There was an investigation, the photographer …' Tash made a drum roll on the coffee table, 'Julian Holdsworth, and the owner, Miranda Breightling, were cautioned but not charged.'

'No wonder she doesn't like cops.'

'We thought at first that something even more seedy was going on, but actually, the only thing they really did was soliciting — it's their prerogative to turn unsuitable girls down after all. We've had nothing more on them since.'

Stevie beamed. 'So anyway, Holdsworth is using his real name? That should make him a snap to find.'

'He must've been pissed as all hell when their scam ended. So maybe he's found another outlet, and maybe that's selling kiddie porn on the net. Christ,' Tash shook her head, 'a paedophile photographer in a modelling school would be like putting a rabbit in a vegie patch.'

Stevie grimaced. She opened her over-stuffed briefcase and pulled out a wedge of paper. 'Now here's another angle I think might be interesting. These are stories Bianca had on her desk. Maybe she wrote them, maybe she downloaded them, I don't know. Either way, they star the same character that was in a story Emma was telling Izzy when she babysat for me. Have you ever come across a character in kids' books called Katy Enigma?'

'I don't think so. What's the story?'

'Not sure yet, except Izzy loved the stories. I guess I'll know more when I've been through this lot. And I'm hoping they'll give me a better picture of the kid. I'm also wondering what kind of involvement she had with Emma Breightling, there's the modelling and the Katy Enigma connection …'

'Hang on a moment, Stevie. Why don't you save yourself a lot of work and just ask Emma if she knew Bianca?'

'I did ask her, when I saw her reaction to a newspaper story about Bianca's death, but she said she didn't. She's a strange kid.' She ran her ponytail through her fingers. 'I'm not sure I can totally trust her; I've caught her in a lie before. I'd like to get some concrete evidence before I ask her again.'

Stevie took the iPod from her briefcase. 'And then there's this …'

'Holy shit, Stevie, I never thought I'd see you with one of those.'

Stevie regarded the pink-cased gadget and shrugged. 'I thought Bianca's taste in music might also tell me more about her.'

'So you'll be carrying out your research to boy bands and Pink, maybe even some Pussycat Dolls. Lucky you.'

'Well yeah, don't know how much of a help it will be but it's worth a try. I've never even used an iPod before, not sure if I even know how to turn it on. Damn, I didn't pick up the ear plugs, do you have any?'

Tash extended her hand and clicked her fingers. 'Give us a look.'

Stevie handed over the slender latex covered contraption. Tash pressed the ON button, said 'shove up' to Stevie and settled next to her in the circular chair so they could both see the small screen. Tash touched the central eye and the screen lit up, showing a list of files.

She tapped one with her finger. 'Hey, what's this?'

Stevie squinted at the screen and read, 'Audio play list one.'

'No, duh — underneath it, the rich text files.'

'Documents? I didn't know you could store documents on an iPod. I thought it was just for music.'

'Get with the program, girl, they can be used as external hard drives too. And you won't need ear plugs for this.'

'But she was only ten. What would she want with something like this?'

'Nearly eleven,' Tash corrected. 'Kids grow up fast. And maybe it's something she didn't want her mother to see on her computer. Let's go into my study and print these out.' She punched Stevie on the arm. 'I think we might've just found the mother lode.'

24

Excerpt from chat transcript 141206
HARUM SCARUM: how do u want the story to start?
BETTYBO: ummm ... it was a dark and stormy nite
HARUM SCARUM: LOL ok
BETTYBO: and I want the princess to kill the evil count
HARUM SCARUM: and torture him first?
BETTYBO: yeahhhhhh!!!

Stevie fought her way through the heat, the noise and the crush of traffic to meet up with Izzy and Monty for their picnic tea on the beach. The sea was flat as wine and the sun still bit. It was nearly six o'clock but the sand was still dotted with people. She stopped when she reached the end of the wobbly steps, put down the picnic basket, prised off her shoes and rolled up her jeans. The sand was warm underfoot; she grabbed the basket and made a beeline to the firmer sand at the sea's edge.

Shading her eyes with her hand she scanned the multitudes for her family. Finally she spotted her daughter in her red bathers, collecting shells in a small yellow bucket.

Izzy ran over when Stevie called, hugged her around the waist and began burrowing about with sandy hands into the picnic basket.

'Wait on there Miss Greedy; you're getting sand in the chips. Find Dad for me so we can start our tea.'

'You won't be able to find him,' Izzy said as she lunged again for the picnic basket. This time Stevie was ready for her and swung it away. 'You won't be able to find him,' Izzy repeated, 'cos I buried him!'

Stevie walked a few steps and searched the surrounding sand. She really didn't have time for Izzy's games this evening. Not only were their fish and chips getting cold, she was desperate to get home and start wading through Bianca's stories plus the sheaves of emails she and Tash had printed from Bianca's iPod.

Izzy's hand stopped her in her tracks, preventing her just in time from tumbling over a mountain of sand. 'Careful, you'll step on him!' her daughter warned.

A few cracks knifed their way through the compressed sand and the mountain groaned. Only Monty's head was visible and it shone from one end of the mound like that of a red painted tortoise.

'Monty, you idiot, you're burnt to a crisp!' Stevie cried.

'I think I fell asleep.'

'No sunscreen? No hat? Izzy, go find your father's hat!'

'I used it to carry water for my sand castle,' Izzy said.

'Then go and get it. Now!'

'Don't let him get up, I haven't finished decorating him yet,' Izzy called over her shoulder, running off to find Monty's hat.

Compressed sand slid off his body in great slabs as Monty sat up. He climbed groggily to his feet and shook like a dog, reaching out for Stevie when he almost lost his balance. After planting a sandy kiss on her cheek, he headed to the water to sluice off.

Stevie spread out the picnic blanket and opened up the parcels of fish and chips, the mouth-watering smell reminding her that she hadn't eaten since breakfast. She managed to hold off until her family returned, Izzy with the hat and bucket of shells, Monty with the smell of the sea on his skin.

While they ate, Izzy regaled them with every second of her day spent playing with her friend Georgia. When they'd finished their meal, Stevie told Izzy that if she wanted to bring her shells home she'd have to first wash them; it was all she could think of to get some time alone with Monty.

'I had a word with Tash,' Stevie got in quickly when Izzy skipped off. Monty's shrug made her pause and she sat poised with the last chip halfway to her mouth. 'Well, it's what you wanted me to do, isn't it?'

'Forget it, it's over, let's drop the subject.' Monty turned to watch Izzy at the water's edge. The sea was pulling the sun down; pinks, oranges and mauves smeared the sky around it.

Stevie decided to file the matter of Monty's strange mood in the too hard basket, to be retrieved later when she had the mental energy for it.

She filled him in on what she and Tash had discovered and gave him the name of the photographer. 'We should be making an arrest tomorrow.' She added, 'I'm hoping the printed documents from the iPod might tell us a bit more about how men like Kusak operate, and maybe give us some details on the Dream Team. I also think that Emma and Bianca knew each other, it's a long shot but I'm going to follow it through.'

'Good one, sounds like you're in for a busy night. Ring me if you find anything more of interest. Oh and by the way, the mystery of Mrs K's large cash withdrawal has been solved. She was planning on a trip to Italy next month and used it for an airline ticket and other expenses.'

'Not to pay a contract killer?' Stevie was hardly surprised.

'Right, scratch that theory. It's all on the street kid now.'

He screwed up the fish and chip paper and headed to a bin with it. 'Hey, what about your mother, aren't you supposed to pick her up from the station tonight?' he turned and asked.

'Oh shit, yes, at eight o'clock.' Stevie looked at her watch, then pleadingly at Monty as he'd trudged back through the sand to her. 'Will you, please? You were going to be having Izzy tonight, anyway.'

'Sure,' he said, without enthusiasm.

She rummaged in the basket for some sunscreen. 'Here, put this on, better late than never and it might stop you from peeling.'

He rubbed the lotion into his face, took some time to massage the remainder into his arm. She looked at him for a moment. 'Are you sure you're okay?'

In reply he handed her back the tube and stooped to rearrange the items in the basket. Izzy returned with her washed shells and insisted they both examine her latest find, a shell with legs.

'It's a hermit crab Izz, you can't take it home, it'll die and stink the place out,' Monty said.

Izzy protested and Monty gave in with an unusual lack of conviction. Stevie caught his eye and signalled her concern to him.

'Just a touch of the sun,' he said, putting the crab in the bucket.

Stevie ignored the breakfast dishes in the sink and settled onto her sofa with the emails, chat transcripts and printed stories. She'd also left copies with Tash, so they could meet at Central in the morning to discuss them.

Tempted as she was to get started on them straightaway she forced herself to pause, leaned her head against the back of the sofa and closed her eyes, trying to conjure up a portrait of Bianca Webster. Criminal profilers stressed the importance of getting into the mind of the killer, but Stevie knew it was just as important to get into the mind of the victim. Soon the image of the child became so clear in her mind's eye she could have been watching her from a web cam.

She visualised Bianca dipping a greasy hand into a packet of chips split open upon her desk. She could almost smell salt and vinegar in the air, see the crumbs dropping on to the keyboard, salt sprinkling the strewn papers. With much sighing and brow furrowing, the girl struggled to write coherently, typing with two lead-heavy fingers. She could see her lose concentration and pause to doodle on a piece of scrap paper, or scratch the name Daniel with a compass into the veneer of her desk. When a new email appeared, she'd give it a quick skim and impatiently type back words before they had even formed properly in her brain. Sometimes she got angry, sometimes she cried, sometimes she swore and stabbed at the desk with the point of her compass.

Stevie shook her head to rid it of the images — imagination was a powerful thing and as a cop she should use it with extreme caution: evidence, that's what she was after. She picked up a bunch of printouts and started to read.

Then read it again.

She should have guessed. Daniel, the name she'd seen carved into Bianca's desk, was Miro Kusak, not some rock or movie star as she'd earlier assumed.

None of 'Daniel's' earlier emails had been saved to the iPod. Stevie could only guess that Kusak had made the first move, getting Bianca's email address and photo from the Dream Team webmaster, Lolita. With her email address and the necessary computer skills, it would have been no problem for Kusak to cyber stalk Bianca wherever she chose to travel on the web. She needed to confirm this with Clarissa, but she suspected Kusak had probably infected Bianca's computer with a Trojan virus disguised as some innocent-looking email attachment addressed from a friend. Once installed on her computer it would forward to Kusak the log files of all her Internet activities.

Stella had told Stevie that her daughter was a loner, often seen sitting in the school playground fiddling with her iPod. Bianca had probably been reading Daniel's messages over and over again, trying to boost her fragile self-esteem. Stevie closed her eyes and took a breath and waited a moment for the ache of sadness to become manageable again.

The contents of Daniel's saved emails were sickeningly predictable, flattery and talk about their common interests mostly. '*I only have one parent too, we have so much in common; we're soul mates ...*' It was what she told the school kids at her talks: the cyber predator closely examines the profile of his victim and makes himself into what they want him to be. Unlike the inexperienced Robert Mason, Kusak seemed to have been able to hold back on the dirty talk — though Stevie had a feeling the needy Bianca Webster would've played along regardless.

Shuffling through the papers on the coffee table she picked one up at random, surprised to discover that this correspondence was not from Miro Kusak at all.

> From: B. Webster [bbo2@hotmail.net.au]
> Sent: Thursday, 12 January 2007 7:35 AM
> To: admin@katyenigma.com
> Subject: hi
>
> I hat my life, sometimes I wanna die. He was round the
> otha da & giv mum a blak i . i had to go next door cos
> Mrs smith the naybor thumpd on the wall then took
> mum to the hopital. Her arms broke 2. I hate him. hop
> things r o k with u.
> rite S.O.O.N
>
> lots of Luv bettybo xxxxxxxxxx

This message posed more questions than it answered. Stevie recognised Bianca's email address and assumed Bettybo to be her Internet nickname. But who was this man who terrified her so and had broken her mother's arm? The man on the stairwell and by the lake? 'Bob' of the mysterious phone call? — or were these men one and the same? Stella had told her she hadn't seen Bianca's father since the conception. Was this a stepfather Bianca was referring to, or a boyfriend, and why hadn't he been mentioned before?

If it hadn't been so late, Stevie would have been pounding on Stella's door now, demanding answers.

The email from Bianca was addressed to someone at a Katy Enigma website. At least that was something she could check out now. She moved over to her PC tucked into a workstation in the corner of her lounge room, pushing Izzy's collection of 'My Little Ponies' from the seat before she could sit down.

When the computer was booted up she typed Katy Enigma into the search engine. A Katy Enigma fan site came up at the top of the list, the only complete entry for the name. This meant that Katy Enigma wasn't the commercial fad she'd first assumed it to be. And since Emma had been telling Izzy Katy Enigma stories, Emma must be a member of this fan site too.

She clicked on the website link and waited for the page to load.

A cartoon figure of Katy Enigma appeared on the screen. The manga style animation had exaggerated eyes, a dark bob and scarlet hotpants with the letters KE emblazoned in fire on the bib.

'*Welcome to the Katy Enigma fan site,*' the large script at the top of the page said. '*Here you will find original stories featuring super-girl hero, Katy Enigma. Follow the links to read other stories written by fans, the chat room, message board, writing competitions, prizes and lots more!*'

The cursor drifted over the web page and she found a link to a message board, then to a form a potential member had to fill out before joining. She filled in the form, gave herself the screen name of *bizzylizzy* and clicked to submit it. Within a few minutes she was a member of the Katy Enigma site. As her eyes ran down the list of member names she wondered which, if any, belonged to Emma — *poshgirl, squeaky, oddmouse, katyfan*?

She checked out her own new profile, which she discovered was accessible to all the board members. Her email address wasn't displayed because she'd ticked the box asking for it not to be. Members could still contact each other through an internal private mailing box without revealing their email addresses. Soon she found Bettybo's profile and saw her private email address displayed for the world to see. Kusak had already known Bianca's email address, but even if he hadn't, she might just as well have knocked on his door and presented herself to him.

'If that's how Kusak did it, it's too easy,' Stevie mumbled to herself. He must have cyber stalked her via the Trojan Virus to the KE site, joined up as Daniel, pretended to be a Katy Enigma fan and then befriended her through the message board and chat room.

She rubbed her eyes, yawned, scrolled down pages filled with stories by members. Some of the stories were quite long, too long for her to read now. She'd see if she could persuade Clarissa to give up her Sunday morning to look through them, while she questioned Emma about the site.

Stevie made herself a mug of strong coffee and returned to the email printouts on the table.

> FROM admin@katyenigma.com
> SENT 12 January 2007 8:48 AM
> TO bbo2@hotmail.net.au
> SUBJECT hi
>

> Don't say things like that Bettybo, life is good. U just
> have 2 think of ways of giving yourself powa. Think of
> Katy Enigma, she wouldn't kill herself, would she? U cn
> b like KE, clever and fast and cute if u wanna b. luv HS

[bbo2@hotmail.net.au] 6 Febuary 2007 7:35 wrote:
Danel thinks Im cool and sexy. Im gonna meet him.

admin@katyenigma.com 8 Febuary 2007 7:52 wrote:
Idiot. He could be any1.
> HS

On 9/2/07 8:49 AM, "Bianca Webster"
   < bbo2@hotmail.net.au > wrote:
> well Up yors2!? ur jelos!

As far as Stevie knew, this was one of Bianca's last notes. She was abducted on 12 February from the Shenton Park Lake and her body found on 14 February at a building site in Midland.

Stevie retrieved her notebook from under the piles of paper and scribbled down what she'd learned from the emails. Someone who called themselves Harum Scarum corresponded privately with Bianca via the Katy Enigma website. 'HS' seemed to be doing his or her best to boost Bianca's brittle self-esteem, playing at pop psychology and attempting to 'empower' Bianca through stories featuring Katy Enigma. The printed versions of these stories were now strewn before Stevie on the coffee table. She glanced through them; they ranged from missing puppy scenarios and magic castle hideaways, to princesses, evil counts, anger, blood and vengeance.

Unfortunately this empowerment strategy hadn't worked. Bianca had needed or wanted further affirmation and she'd found it in the form of Miro Kusak posing as a boy called Daniel. Harum Scarum had tried to warn Bianca off the meeting, an email fight had followed which left Bianca still determined to go ahead.

Stevie didn't need to replay the remaining events in her head; the picture of the abduction, the abuse, the pump house and the duct tape were still livid in her mind.

She looked back at a chat transcript she'd noticed earlier. In it they were talking about running away: *betta 2 get even than run,* Harum Scarum had said.

Weariness began to creep in. Stevie yawned and swallowed her last gulp of coffee. Just one final look at the website then she'd call it a night and hand the problems over to the experts in the morning.

Back at her PC she clicked on the stories page and found something short, a poem with no title and no author listed.

Living nightmare, darkest fears, he comes at night.
His gain, my pain, I cry in vain and no one hears.
He is the monster from under my bed.

She thought for a moment, pondering the lines. As realisation dawned she covered her mouth with her hand. Oh God, is this what the site was really all about?

25

Excerpt from chat room transcript 151206
BETTYBO: he did it again 2me 2day
HARUM SCARUM: u ok?
BETTYBO: I wanna run away
HARUM SCARUM: me2 but we can't
BETTYBO: ynot?
HARUM SCARUM: betta 2 get even than run
BETTYBO: lik u?

Aidan Stoppard's Porsche was parked in the Breightlings' driveway. Stevie laid her hand flat on the bonnet as she hurried past it. Cold.

The black lacquer door opened before she had a chance to knock. Miranda stood before her with panda eyes, pillow hair and pale blotchy skin. When she saw Stevie standing there, she pulled her silk robe tight over her generous breasts, strikingly out of proportion with the rest of her small frame. 'Oh, it's you,' she said in puzzled recognition. 'That was very quick.'

'I only live around the corner from you Mrs Breightling. Central contacted me at home and I came right away.'

'Who is it?' Stevie heard a deep male voice from somewhere down the sepulchred hallway.

'The police, Aidan,' Miranda called over a porcelain shoulder.

From the distant family area Stevie recognised Aidan Stoppard. 'Already?' he queried.

'They told me you'd reported Emma missing,' Stevie said. Miranda took a deep breath, the ribs in her chest visibly straining. 'Yes, yes, you'd better come in. I think she's been kidnapped!'

With ballerina grace she turned on her bare heels and fled down the passageway into the waiting arms of Aidan Stoppard.

He looked gravely at Stevie as she approached, pushed Miranda gently to the side and handed her his business card. Stevie barely glanced at it, put it in her jeans pocket.

He cleared his throat and explained, 'I'm a friend of the family, popped in for breakfast. Miranda's just told me the news.' He spoke with a slightly flat intonation, the residue of some kind of faded London accent Stevie suspected. *The Bill* flashed briefly to mind.

She cut him no slack. 'No you didn't just pop in for breakfast, you stayed here overnight.'

The tight expression and the straightening of his shoulders told Stevie this was a man not used to being challenged.

'Emma and I get nervous when Christopher's away,' Miranda cut in, as if anticipating an unfavourable reaction from Stoppard. 'And Emma's prone to nightmares. She feels more secure with her Uncle Aidan around.'

Stoppard relaxed, spoke with a flash of white teeth, 'There you go then, sorry about the white lie, officer. People will talk and Miranda has a reputation to maintain. Christopher knows I stay here — the spare room's a home away from home for me.'

'Of course it is.' Stevie didn't bother to hide her sarcasm. Emma had told Stevie the other night that she *didn't* have problems with nightmares, that she was usually able to control her bad dreams. So which one of them was lying and why?

Emma had also told her that her mother and Aidan Stoppard were lovers.

She regarded Stoppard closely; he wore white pants and a lightweight dark polo neck. When she'd seen him the other day from the car, she'd assumed his hair had been wet from the shower, now she realised it must have been slicked down with gel. In contrast to Miranda's dying swan look, Stoppard looked clean, neat and pressed, as if he'd at least had the time to shower and change while Miranda was making her frantic calls to the police.

He fingered a longish curl behind his ear where a single diamond stud gleamed. 'Err, don't you want to hear the details?' he asked.

Stevie glanced at Miranda. She wasn't looking at either of them, but was busy rolling the hem of her robe back and forth between her fingers.

'Go on,' Stevie said.

'I heard screaming from Emma's room. I rushed in and turned the light on. She woke up, seemed very embarrassed, said she had a nightmare and apologised for disturbing me.'

'She often gets night terrors,' Miranda stammered. 'When she was younger it was always the monster from under her bed. I would've gone if I'd heard her, but I'd taken a sleeping pill and was out for the count.'

A hollow feeling grew in the pit of Stevie's stomach.

'And what time was it that you went into Emma's room, Mr Stoppard?' Stevie asked, the hollow feeling turning to dread.

'About one o'clock, I'd say.'

Stevie kept her voice level. 'Did she say anything else?'

'She said there was a man in her room. I searched it, looked in the wardrobe, under the bed, out the window — just to humour her, yeah? She seemed reassured by this and went back to sleep. I feel like a right prat now of course, I should have believed her.'

'Stupid, Aidan, stupid,' Miranda spat, the air around her crackling as if with static. She reached for a glass half filled with orange juice, and downed it in a couple of swallows. Aidan looked at her, his eyes narrow with anger. But when Miranda returned his glare, Stevie was sure she saw something else flash in them.

Stevie asked Miranda to take her up to Emma's room. Stoppard followed them up the stone staircase.

The room wasn't the orderly high tech sanctuary Stevie had imagined. The single bed was a mess of twisted sheets and the chair near it upturned with one of the curtains draped over it as if yanked from the track. Hot air and flies poured in through the open window.

'Was the room like this when you first checked on Emma, Mr Stoppard?' she asked as she looked around the room. A pile of magazines seemed to have been tipped from the desk and fanned across the floor. She glanced at the titles, mostly computer mags but also copies of *New Scientist* and *Psychology Today*. A softball bat lay at an angle next to them.

'No, it was a lot tidier than this,' Stoppard replied. 'But the window was open and I closed it.' He hesitated, the silence sounded contrived, as if he was willing himself to at least sound repentant. 'It does look like she was telling the truth after all, doesn't it? It wasn't a dream, the man was real and he must have come back later and taken her.'

A World Vision poster on the pin board above Emma's desk had a picture of a small African boy pinned onto it. There was also a snap of a khaki-clad man on the board, crouching down as if to examine a ragged line of African children. The picture seemed old and the colours faded.

'Who's that?' Stevie said, pointing.

'Her father, years ago, before we were married,' Miranda replied with a dismissive wave of her hand.

A comfy armchair next to Emma's desk was covered with a Mexican throw rug and a well-worn teddy bear was sitting on it. It hadn't occurred to Stevie that Emma would be the kind to hang on to an old teddy — her grandmother's encyclopaedia maybe, but not a teddy. A postcard was propped upon the Teddy's arms, showing a rolling scenic view with a European castle in the foreground. She swallowed down the growing ache in her throat. *You're all right Emma, you're safe; I know you are and I'll find you.*

Stoppard followed her movements intently, joining her at the bedroom window when she moved over to examine it. 'Did you lock this after closing it?' she asked him.

'No, I'm afraid not,' Stoppard said. 'It didn't cross my mind; it's on the second floor, isn't it. It would be pretty hard for someone to get in.'

'Stupid, Aidan, stupid,' Miranda spat again.

Stoppard briefly closed his eyes and rubbed the back of his head as if it ached.

Stevie peered down through the open window. Emma's room was at the front of the house, the view of the road blocked only by a line of skinny pine trees. She could see the flyscreen lying in the garden bed next to the wall on which a rose trellis was tacked. Part of the trellis looked as if it had been prised away from the wall, the young rose left to waver in the breeze.

'Is this damage new, Mrs Breightling?' Stevie pointed to the trellis.

Miranda moved next to her and peered down. 'Yes, I think so. The gardener only put it up last year.'

'Do you think that's what the man climbed up to get through the window?' Stoppard asked.

'Possibly,' she said curtly, mentally noting the vacuousness of the question. A car pulled up and she saw Monty step out of an unmarked police car and behind him a blue and white with a couple of uniformed officers.

'My colleagues have arrived, they'll need to talk to you,' she addressed the hovering couple. 'Scene of crime officers will be searching this room and the rest of the house.' She cocked her head to Emma's PC. 'We'll need to take this too. Has Doctor Breightling been notified of Emma's disappearance, ma'am?'

'Mr Breightling, not Doctor Breightling,' Miranda corrected. 'He's a surgeon. Yes, he's due home today, any minute in fact. Aidan rang him and he was already driving home from the airport.' She looked down at her attire and let out a dramatic sigh. 'I suppose I'd better go and get dressed.'

Stevie met Monty in the hall and filled him in on Emma's disappearance. She also took the opportunity to mention some of her discoveries from the previous night.

'So, who is this Harum Scarum character?' Monty asked when she'd finished. 'Adult, kid, male, female?'

'I've no idea, I'm handing the problem over to Clarissa as soon as I get away from here.'

'But you think this Katy Enigma site, this Harum Scarum, supports abused kids — it's not just another way of gaining their trust and conning them?' he queried, rubbing his chin.

'I'm not sure of anything yet. It's just that some of the stories and poems are very suggestive. And no, I don't think it's a scam. I think any actual counselling support that goes on probably happens in private emails, like those between Harum Scarum and Bianca. But the thing is, I think Emma's involved with this website too. Not only did she tell Izzy Katy Enigma stories, but there's an anonymous poem on the site that sounds like something she may have written. It implies abuse.'

Monty cocked an eyebrow; a website helping abused children becomes undermined by paedophiles — the irony wasn't lost on Stevie either.

'So this site might have been discovered by another paedophile who's now taken Emma?' Monty asked.

Stevie sighed. 'I don't know what to think. I can't believe Emma would be conned as easily as Bianca.'

'It's a stretch, Stevie.'

'It's all we have.'

They heard the sound of an approaching car. Through the open front door they watched a silver Mercedes turn into the driveway and pass into the garage through an automatic roller door.

Monty tipped his head toward the closing garage door. 'The father?'

'I guess so, I've never met him.'

'Is the mother still getting changed?'

'She doesn't change,' Stevie said. 'She sheds.'

A tallish man in a well-made suit, Christopher Breightling had quick blue eyes which spent more time flitting between his friend and his wife than on Monty who was speaking to him.

'We'll need to put a recording device on your home and mobile phones,' Monty continued with his brief. 'If she's been kidnapped for money, you'll probably be getting some kind of a ransom message soon.'

'But what if she's been taken by a pervert,' Miranda said. 'What if we hear nothing until she's found like that last girl, dumped in a garbage bin?'

Christopher's shoulders slumped as he sat at the breakfast bar. His hand slid across the granite surface to clasp his wife's, which lay unresponsive under his. He slowly released it as if he was well aware of the futility of his gesture, his features taking on a stamp of defeated weariness.

There was constant coming and going as police officers photographed and dusted for prints, searched the house. The garden bed below Emma's bedroom window had already been examined, the SOCO officer reporting the discovery of several similar bare footprints, approximately women's size five.

'Has Emma ever run away from home, Mrs Breightling?' Stevie asked.

'No, why should she?' Miranda replied with a prickly look.

'I don't claim to know Emma particularly well, but I did get the impression from talking to her the other day that she wasn't happy at the moment.'

'Then I don't think you know her at all,' said Christopher Breightling. 'She is a perfectly happy child.'

'There was only one set of footprints under the window, Mr Breightling,' Monty said. 'And we think they might be Emma's. We found no evidence of prints belonging to any one else. We think Emma might have climbed out of the window herself.'

'The man might have gone down the stairs and grabbed her from the front of the house when she was trying to escape him,' Stoppard persisted with his theory.

Stevie ignored him and spoke to Christopher. 'When I was chatting with her the other day, she told me she didn't want to go east to boarding school.'

Christopher lifted his head in surprise. 'What? She told you that?' He glanced at his wife.

Miranda shrugged.

A physical and emotional wreck when she'd first admitted Stevie to her home, Miranda was now a different woman. Made up, hair coiffed and wearing an elegant fuchsia sundress, she could have been on her way to a garden party rather than being questioned over her daughter's possible abduction. Did she care at all? While there was no prescribed script for this kind of emotional trauma, Stevie couldn't help comparing Miranda's appearance to the empty shell that was Stella Webster.

Stevie excused herself from the group in the family room and made her way to the front of the house where she found the SOCO sergeant in the hall. She asked him to accompany her to the master bedroom, which had yet to be searched.

The gown Miranda had been wearing lay crumpled in the middle of the floor, one discarded slipper, then another, followed by some knotted panties, formed a trail to the en-suite bathroom. She skirted the puddles on the floor, took in the dripping mirror, flapped her hands at the steam still hanging in the air. Lipsticks and lotions, bottles and tubes of make-up lay strewn across the vanity top.

Stevie slipped on a pair of latex gloves and prised the lid off a bottle of natural health pills near the sink, tipping a few into her hand.

'Do these look like echinacea tablets to you?' she asked the sergeant. He bent to examine the small white pills in her palm. Without answering, he picked up a pestle and mortar from the bench top and ran his fingers along the marble surfaces, showing Stevie the fine white powder on his fingertips.

'Silly bitch,' he said.

Stevie agreed. 'This explains her transformation.' The sergeant recorded the details of the find and Stevie returned to the family room and pulled Monty aside.

When he'd heard what she had to say, he held up the bottle of pills and rattled them in front of others. 'Compressed cocaine,' he said, 'found in your bathroom, Mrs Breightling.'

Miranda's mouth formed an 'O', which she covered delicately with one finger in a 1950's ingenue gesture. Was she sending herself up?

Christopher Breightling looked angrily at his wife. 'Miranda ...' he began and stopped. He loosened the knot of his tie, 'Inspector, surely this is not the time or the place ...'

'Have some compassion, man,' Stoppard interjected, large

chin thrust forward with belligerence. Stevie made as if to look away, but continued to observe him through her peripheral vision. She might have been mistaken, but she could've sworn she saw a twinkle of amusement in those deep-set eyes.

Breightling clenched his fists.

Monty said nothing, merely slipped the pills into his pocket and began to pace the room. He stopped at the abstract *objet d'art* and touched one of the sharp points, his face briefly showing the same surprised look Stevie had seen — was it only yesterday? — on Izzy's.

'It's an original Sienna-Pastor sculpture.' Miranda swivelled around on the barstool to face Monty, her tanned legs crossed, one high-heeled sandal hanging from her foot and dangling seductively towards him. Already working hard at getting the possession charges dropped, Stevie thought. 'It's worth a lot of money,' Miranda added.

Breightling palmed his forehead with exasperation. 'Can we please return to the subject of my daughter's disappearance, Inspector?'

'Certainly, Mr Breightling, where were we?' Monty knew very well where they were. 'Ah yes, we were trying to ascertain your daughter's frame of mind, wondering if she might have run away. Sergeant Hooper was under the impression that Emma was unhappy, that she didn't want to go east to boarding school.'

'I'm sorry, but that's simply ridiculous. Emma is an extremely gifted child,' Christopher Breightling told them. 'She really finds it natural to want to learn, to achieve. The boarding school she'll be going to has an extensive gifted program.'

Miranda said, 'She couldn't wait to go, she never shut up about it — that's true isn't it, Aidan?' To Stoppard again, not the husband, Stevie noted.

Stoppard nodded. Stevie looked at Christopher Breightling. His knuckles were white, and a complex mixture of emotions played across his face.

'Then is there something else she might have been unhappy about?' Stevie's look burned into Stoppard. He turned his palms to each parent and shrugged, as if to say, why's she got it in for me?

They needed to separate Stoppard from Emma's parents. It was creepy, it was downright unhealthy the way they sat together like that, three little dickie birds sitting on a wall. What was it between them? And just what were the ties that seemed to be binding them so uncomfortably together?

Monty must have been thinking along similar lines. 'Mr Stoppard,' he said, 'I'd like you to come up to Emma's room with me now and we'll go over again what you told Sergeant Hooper.'

Stoppard let out an impatient sigh, looked at his watch, and told them he had things to do.

Before they could leave, a uniformed constable approached Monty and whispered something in his ear. Monty listened for a moment then addressed Breightling. 'You have a gun safe in your garage?'

Breightling slid off the barstool. 'What of it?'

'We'd like to have a look inside it. We need the key.'

'I've nothing to hide,' Christopher said, moving towards a tall pantry cupboard. 'I would have told you if you'd asked that I'm the owner of a licensed hand gun and a couple of shotguns.' He positioned a small kitchen ladder next to the pantry and stood on it to reach the highest shelf, taking a set of keys from a hook.

'Nothing to be alarmed about, sir,' Monty said. 'My officer has already confirmed with the database that you have a number of registered firearms. We just need to check them out.'

Stevie and Monty followed Christopher through a kitchen door leading into a three-car garage. Bolted to the floor next to Breightling's Mercedes SLX they saw a heavy steel gun cabinet as tall as a change room locker.

Monty asked Breightling to open the cabinet. His hands shook; he was clearly upset over his daughter's disappearance. He made a couple of unsuccessful attempts at slotting the key into the lock before the door swung open, showing the body of the locker. He passed Monty two Purdy over-and-under shotguns in wooden cases, explaining that they once belonged to his father and he used them for clay pigeon shooting. While Monty examined the guns, Breightling continued to grope around in the cabinet, struggling to reach something on the top shelf.

Monty handed the shotguns to a watching constable. 'Allow me.' He gently pushed Breightling aside and removed the bundles.

'My wife's jewels,' Christopher said as Monty handed the two velvet bags to Stevie. 'The handgun must be further back.'

Monty stuck his hand in, his fingers clanging on the metal at the back of the cabinet and came out with nothing.

'This is ridiculous,' Christopher exclaimed. He felt blindly towards the back of the cabinet, his panic mounting. 'I can't believe it, it's gone!'

He spun around wildly, as if expecting to see the gun lying around in the garage somewhere.

'When did you last see it, sir?' Stevie asked as she replaced the rings and necklaces she'd been examining into their respective velvet pouches.

A muscle in Breightling's cheek twitched. He drew his hands over his face as if trying to wipe it away. 'A few weeks ago? Maybe a month; I haven't had much time for the firing range recently.'

'The data base has it listed as a Glock 22,' Monty said.

'That's right. I've been meaning to get into some competition shooting.'

'Your keys weren't in a particularly safe place, it wouldn't be very hard for someone to get to the gun,' Stevie said.

'Well, I could hardly keep them with me, could I? Miranda needs easy access to her jewellery. Besides, no one else knows where they're kept.' Breightling took a breath, rubbed his cheek again. 'Actually, there's something else you should know, something else that's missing from the safe. Frankly, I find this loss more disturbing than the gun's.' He paused.

'Go on,' Stevie said.

'A set of antique scalpels, my great-grandfather's from the Boer War.' He paused for thought. 'Come to think of it, I think I remember seeing the gun in the safe when I last cleaned them about three weeks ago. The scalpels need cleaning every month, you see. They're made of high-carbonised steel and would rust if not regularly maintained. They haven't been used for years, but they're still as sharp as razors. They have a lot of sentimental value to me as well as being worth a small fortune.'

Monty and Stevie exchanged glances. 'Why would someone take a handgun and scalpels, but leave the jewels and the shotguns?' Monty thought aloud. 'Make sure the cabinet gets dusted for prints,' he told the uniformed officer as he strode back to the kitchen. Out of the corner of his mouth he said softly to Stevie. 'He may be a surgeon, but did you see his hands shake when he was opening the safe? I wouldn't trust him cutting a cake.'

Monty spoke again when they were once more congregated in the family room. 'Now, I need Mr Stoppard to go over last night's events in Emma's bedroom with me.'

'Is that necessary Inspector? I've already been over it with Sergeant Hooper and I do have business in the city.'

'I'll let you know when you can leave, sir. Besides, I'm sure the Breightlings could use the support of an old family friend such as yourself.'

Stevie watched Miranda swivel on her stool, her gaze never leaving Stoppard as he climbed the stairs behind Monty. Breightling's eyes dropped to the breakfast bar, engrossed it seemed with the sparkles in the granite, the twitch in his cheek now a fully realised facial tic. Not only had Emma been telling her the truth about Stoppard and Miranda being lovers, Stevie thought, but Christopher Breightling knew it too. Why the hell, then, did he put up with it?

26

Stevie had still not recovered from the shock of Emma's disappearance; she stood numbly waiting for Stella to answer the door. There had to be something Stella could tell her about Emma Breightling, she thought, something that could lead them to the girl's whereabouts. It was impossible to believe that Stella had been as ignorant about Bianca's Internet activities as she'd maintained. The emails saved on the iPod had already revealed that Stella had withheld information about an abusive relationship. Stevie couldn't help but wonder what else she was covering up.

She gave one last desperate thump at the heavy door and was turning to leave when Stella's sister opened it.

'Oh hi Gail. Sorry to disturb you. Could I have a word with Stella?'

'Stella's still asleep love, I'd hate to wake her just now, she's that washed out. Would you like a cuppa?' Gail waved her in, covering a yawn with her other hand.

Stevie declined the offer of tea, but accepted the invitation to pull up a chair at the kitchen table. 'Has Stella said anything more to you about the man who was harassing her in the park?' she asked as Gail moved around the kitchen area, preparing her breakfast.

Gail shrugged. 'Not a peep.'

'And you've never seen him hanging around the flats before?'

A shake of the head.

Without mentioning the contents of Bianca's emails, Stevie asked if she had any knowledge of her sister being involved in an abusive relationship.

'I'm afraid I don't know much about her at all. Stella left home about fifteen years ago and since then none of us really heard from her, she wasn't very close to the family. As horrible as it sounds, this terrible business has drawn us together again.'

'Do you believe her about how she broke her arm?'

'That she fell down the stairs? Well, those stairs are pretty dangerous, especially when rain gets down the stairwell.' Gail's toast popped and she spread it with margarine and Vegemite. Stevie hadn't had time for breakfast and the savoury aroma made her stomach rumble.

Gail smiled and put the plate of toast on the table in front of her. 'Go on, be a devil, with a figure like yours I bet you can eat what you want.'

'Thanks.' Stevie took a slice, asking between mouthfuls, 'Has she received any strange phone calls since you've been here with her, had any men call around?'

'No. Look, you may as well have a cuppa with that.' Gail handed Stevie the tea she'd made for herself.

The bedroom door creaked open and Stella appeared in a rumpled nightie. The plaster cast had been removed since Stevie had last seen her and her left arm looked frail as a plucked chicken wing. 'Oh, it's you,' she said as she leaned wearily against the doorframe.

'She thinks you knew that man who bothered you in the park, that he's been beating you up,' Gail said to her sister.

Shit. Stevie nearly choked on her toast. This wasn't the approach she'd had in mind. She climbed to her feet and put a calming hand out to Stella, 'Why don't you come and sit down?'

'I've had just about enough of you!' Stella cried, shaking Stevie's hand off. 'Just get the fuck out of here and leave me alone!'

'Stella, another girl has gone missing. This is important, I think Bianca knew her from the Internet …'

Stella spun back into her bedroom and slammed the door in her face.

Stevie counted to ten in her head before turning to the stunned sister. 'Well, that went well didn't it?'

What a day. Later that afternoon at Central, the team sat around a table in one of the conference rooms to swap notes and brainstorm. The air conditioning had conked out for the third time that week, faces glowed and tempers flared.

Stevie kicked off her trainers and pulled at her short-sleeved top, trying to invoke a non-existent breeze. Monty's face was as red as it had been at the beach, his tie hung at his neck like a noose, and his white shirt was patterned with threads of sweat. He looked at his watch and scowled.

The door flung open and Tash hurried in, the banging and crashing from the air conditioning mechanics in the corridor trailing in behind her.

'Sorry I'm late,' she gasped and thumped into the chair next to Stevie.

Monty made a point of getting up and closing the door. 'Stevie, a brief summary for Constable Hayward, please,' he ground out. While Stevie filled Tash in on Emma Breightling's disappearance, he struggled to open a window, cursing under his breath when he discovered that no amount of heaving and thumping could break the seal.

'No ransom note, no telephone message?' Tash asked when Stevie had finished her rundown.

Stevie was almost certain they were dealing with a runaway

and told Tash so. After pleas for information were broadcast on the radio a woman had reported picking up a girl matching Emma's description and dropping her off in Mundaring in the early hours of the morning.

Despite this lead, Monty suggested it was best to humour the parents for the time being and continue to pursue the investigation as a possible kidnap — the kid on the highway might not have been Emma. Better to err on the side of caution, he told the team, than find themselves with a pile of litigation in their laps. For now they just had to suck it and see, hoping their questions would be answered when Clarissa had finished the post mortem on Emma's PC.

Stevie asked Tash if she'd got hold of the photographer.

'Yeah, that's why I was late.' From under dark brows Tash shot Monty a withering look. 'Mr Holdsworth is waiting in the interview room downstairs.' To the rest of the team she said, 'We suspect him of supplying a paedophile ring with the photos he took for the modelling agency.'

'Good one, let's keep him sweating, we can talk to him later.' Stevie returned to the topic of Emma Breightling. 'I've discovered some interesting connections between Emma Breightling and Bianca Webster. Not only was Bianca turned down by Miranda Breightling's modelling agency, but both girls were members of the same Internet message board / fan site that seems to be about supporting abused kids.'

'So you think Bianca and Emma knew each other?' Wayne asked.

'Internet pals, I think so, but I don't know if they ever met. Miranda said she couldn't remember any Bianca Webster, but when I showed her the pic we got from Kusak's computer, she admitted that the child looked vaguely familiar. I went to see Stella this morning, but before I could ask her about it, the meeting went south, she practically threw me out of the flat.

I'll call around later when she's calmed down.'

'Would you like me to come too?'

She threw Monty an appreciative smile; there was a chance his presence might make Stella more cooperative. Over the years she'd learned never to underestimate the effect of a sympathetic, attractive member of the opposite sex on a distraught witness.

'Wait one,' Wayne raised a finger. 'Are you suggesting Emma's disappearance and Bianca's murder are related?'

Stevie let out a heavy sigh. 'I really don't know.'

'So now you're telling us that Emma might also have been snatched by Lolita and the Dream Team?' Barry's flippant tone made the group sound like a fifties rock band. 'But you just said she was a runaway.'

Stevie poked at the papers in front of her with her pen, determined not to give him the satisfaction of a reaction. And he'd wondered why his application for the Cyber Predator Team had been turned down.

'If I hadn't met Emma before, I'd say yes, it's a possibility, but the girl I know seems too clever to allow herself to be trapped by someone like that. I think she's run away because of abuse, most probably by "old family friend" Aidan Stoppard.'

'Have you checked him out on the National Child Sex offender Register?' Wayne asked.

'Yes, and he's not on it. I've made an appointment to see Emma's school counsellor at her home this afternoon, she may be able to tell me something. The more I can find out about her, the more likely I can figure out what's happened to her, why and where she might have gone.'

'Angus, find out as much as you can about this Aidan Stoppard,' Monty said.

Angus nodded and wrote himself a note. 'How do you spell Aidan?'

Stevie reached into the pocket of her jeans and slid across the business card Stoppard had given her.

'Thanks,' Angus glanced at the scenic view on the front of the card and flipped to the business details on the back. 'Importer of Mexican art with a hills showroom called Chateau-by-the-Lake, and an accountant too, with his own company and a St Georges Terrace office,' he paraphrased. 'Want me to check out Breightling as well, boss?'

Monty nodded.

'Hang on a minute Angus.' She held out her hand to him. 'Let's have another look at that card.' After examining it for a moment she frowned and said to Monty. 'This is the same picture as on the postcard in Emma's room. I thought it must have been from Europe.'

Monty frowned. 'I didn't notice any postcard when I was in there with Stoppard. But hang on a minute.' He delved into his briefcase, took out SOCO's inventory of Emma's room and shook his head. 'Not listed.'

'I don't understand, what's the big deal?' Tash asked.

'It was there, I saw it — I'm sure it was the same scene.' Stevie looked to Monty to see if he could make sense of it. 'The postcard was balanced on her teddy bear's arms. I wonder if she'd done it deliberately, so it would be seen? At the time it didn't occur to me that it was significant. But the picture is of Stoppard's showroom, some kind of a European style castle in the hills. He must have taken it, don't you see?'

'Sure he could have — but it sounds a bit cloak and dagger.'

Stevie glanced at Barry, noticed the beginnings of a smirk. She was too tired to deal with this.

'Look, can I get a word in, guys. I need to get out again,' said Wayne. Stevie decided to keep her thoughts to herself for the moment, and responded to Monty's raised eyebrows with a shrug.

Monty sighed and pointed his pen at Wayne. 'Tell everyone what you're up to at the moment.'

'I've found the kid who'd been hanging around with Zhang Li. It seems he *was* with Li at the time he was killed. He told me he saw it happen, but then clammed up when I asked him for details. I'm waiting on a social worker now for the interview.'

'So if we find Zhang Li's killer, we'll more than likely find Kusak's killer. Some coup, eh?' Barry beamed at the serious faces surrounding him.

'Things are never as easy as they can look,' Wayne cautioned.

27

With his curly blond hair, porn-star moustache and fish belly complexion, Julian Holdsworth was everything Stevie imagined a paedophile webmaster to be. Although he seemed genuinely shocked to hear of Emma's disappearance, and Stevie felt inclined to believe him, she made no effort to hide the contempt in her voice.

'You've been identified by staff at the Mt Lawley Internet cafe as a frequent visitor and your signature is scrawled all over the logs. You always choose to sit in the booth furthest away from the counter where no one can see your screen.'

'Would you like a lawyer, Mr Holdsworth?' Tash cut in.

Sweat gleamed on Holdsworth's brow. He fidgeted with the collar of his open neck shirt and undid another button to reveal a glint of a gold chain through a tangle of dark chest hair.

'Innocent men don't need lawyers,' he said.

Christ, how often had Stevie heard them say that? She reached for the file and opened it on the table, fanning the glossy hardcore photos before him. Tapping her pen on one of the photos, she said 'For the benefit of the tape I am showing Mr Holdsworth exhibit C7.'

'Oh God, that's disgusting.' Holdsworth turned away.

She pointed to another. 'Look at this please sir. For the benefit of the tape I am showing Mr Holdsworth exhibit C3.'

He gave the photo a timid, sideways glance. 'Christ,' he put his hand over his mouth. 'How can you even imagine I could be responsible for distributing these?'

He was a good actor; the man really did look as if he was about to puke, he'd turned as green as the interview room walls. Stevie scanned the room, wondering if there was a suitable receptacle available, but all she found was an empty coffee cup. She hoped it wouldn't be needed.

She said, 'These photos were sent from the Internet cafe you were logged in at, from your account, on two consecutive days last December.'

Holdsworth marshalled his strength, folded his arms and looked her in the eye. 'I didn't send them.'

'What about these, these and these.' Tash pointed out several more, reading out their identification numbers for the tape. 'Coincidences don't happen that often,' she added.

'They're nothing to do with me.'

'What about these photos, Mr Holdsworth, surely you don't deny taking these?' Stevie showed him the 'art' photos from Tall Poppies.

He glanced at them, gave a start then looked more closely. 'Oh yeah, they're mine, my God, where the hell did you get them from?'

'These were sent from the same Internet cafe, the same account, on the very days you were logged in.'

'I took them, yes, but I never distributed them on the Internet.'

'Lolita,' Tash said.

Holdsworth looked at her blankly, swallowed. 'Wasn't that a movie?'

'All right Mr Holdsworth,' Stevie said. 'Let's try something a bit easier. Tell me why someone like you, with a whole studio of computer equipment, needs to use the services of an Internet cafe?'

Holdsworth bit his lip and said nothing. He picked up the empty cup before him as if he were trying to read the tea leaves at the bottom.

'Our experts are pulling your computer apart now,' Stevie went on. 'You may as well just save us all a great deal of bother. I'm afraid our techs aren't always as gentle with impounded equipment as they could be.'

Holdsworth crumpled the cup in his hand. 'Shit, okay, I'll tell you, but you won't find anything illegal on my computer, and certainly no porn.'

Tash who had been prowling around the room pulled up a chair next to him.

He took a breath. 'Online gambling. I visit a US site that's illegal in Australia. I use the cafe so no record is left on my computer. The gambling site is also riddled with viruses which I don't want on my equipment.'

The detectives took their time to digest this, exchanging arch glances as they did so.

Tash straightened in her chair. 'That's not good enough, Mr Holdsworth, you'll have to do better than that.'

'I couldn't go to prison for that, surely? A fine? Maybe I should call my lawyer after all?'

Neither detective responded.

He looked from one to the other of them, brow furrowed with thought as he undid another shirt button. 'Christ it's hot in here. Okay, there's something else too.' His eyes settled on Tash. 'These kinds of pics are of no interest to me at all, not that they ever would be, even if I wasn't ... gay.'

Tash slumped back in her chair.

Stevie slid a pen and paper toward him to write down names of people who could corroborate what he'd just said. What a waste of bloody time, she thought. The Dream Team site was devoted solely to the exploitation of underage girls, so it was highly unlikely that Lolita would be gay, or even bisexual. He might, of course, be running it as a purely business concern, but it was rare that people were into this kind of abuse just for the money.

Holdsworth scratched away with the pen for a while. 'These guys will back me up.'

'You'd have saved yourself a lot of bother if you'd told us that straight away,' Stevie said,

Tash's expression hadn't lost any of its early contempt. 'Ashamed of being gay are you, Mr Holdsworth?'

Holdsworth placed a full stop after the last name and put the pen down. 'No, but I work with children. It could easily be assumed by the ignorant masses that because I'm gay I'm into little boys, which I'm not. I keep my orientation to myself for the sake of my job.'

Stevie pushed the button of the tape recorder. 'Stopping for a break at 12:45.'

Stevie and Tash pushed their way through the swinging doors into the operations room and made their way to Clarissa's desk. 'Is it possible to access someone's Internet connection through a local area network in say an Internet cafe, and send stuff through it without the knowledge of the person who's logged in?' Stevie asked.

Clarissa squeezed her dimpled chin as she thought. 'LAN sniff you mean? These cafes don't tend to have the best security. Does it have a wireless connection?'

Stevie had no idea what LAN sniff might mean. She looked to Tash who'd been somewhat thoughtful and subdued since Holdsworth's revelation. Tash nodded 'yes'.

'Then all it needs is someone in the know to be sitting in a car outside with a laptop to pick up signals from the cafe,' Clarissa said. 'He — or she — can log in from his own computer then log into a computer in the cafe to control it. If he deletes his system logs as he goes, it's virtually untraceable.'

'We think that might be what's happened to Julian Holdsworth,' Stevie said. 'He visits the cafe several nights a week and logs in for a set time, regular as clockwork.'

'Then it would be someone who knows his routine, knows him well enough to guess his password,' Clarissa said.

'But not well enough to know he's gay,' Tash said quietly.

Tash and Stevie split up, Tash to find out how the Emma Breightling search was going and follow up on Holdsworth's friends, Stevie returning to Julian Holdsworth. If they were in an old movie, she thought as she stepped back into the interview room, the interrogatory spotlight would be dimmed, the swinging bulb now stilled.

Once he'd learned he was no longer under arrest, Holdsworth accepted her profuse apologies with as much alacrity as he did the free lunch she sent out for.

'It was Miranda's idea, that little scam in the Mall,' he said through a mouthful of lamb kebab. Stevie's serving still lay wrapped on the table in front of her. She picked away at the paper. If worry for Emma had diminished her appetite, revulsion at the sight of the gravy dripping from the side of Holdsworth's butter yellow moustache killed it altogether.

'To tell you the truth I'm glad you guys put a stop to it before too much harm was done,' Holdsworth said, eager it seemed to restore some lost points.

Stevie thought back to the photo of the muslin-clad Bianca Webster and bit her lip. From where she stood, Bianca's modelling session had kick-started the events that had ultimately led to her death.

'I've never known such a greedy bitch as Miranda,' Holdsworth went on. 'Want, want, want, more, more, more.'

He drained his coffee and held out the cup, raised eyebrows indicating he'd like another.

Stevie took the cup and handed it to a uniformed constable passing by the open door and returned to her seat. She decided to capitalise on the distance Holdsworth seemed to want to put between himself and Miranda Breightling. Clasping her hands on the table in front of her she affected a tone of gossippy interest. 'What about Miranda's husband, Christopher?'

Julian Holdsworth finished chewing his kebab and dabbed at his mouth with the corner of a paper serviette, leaving small traces of gravy on his moustache. He licked his fingers and leaned conspiratorially towards her. With the metaphorical spotlight no longer shining in his eyes, she could see he was enjoying the drama.

'Quite a bit older than she is, ten, fifteen years maybe. He's a plastic surgeon, but dabbles in cosmetic surgery on the side — probably experiments on his wife, I mean have you seen her …' he circled his hands around his chest area. 'I think he used to be a bit of a philanthropist, one of those surgeons who was always flitting off to war zones to treat the unfortunate, correct deformities, patch up landmine victims — you know, the saintly type. His good deeds died somewhat of a death when he married Miranda — then the cosmetic side of things began to take over.'

'More money in cosmetic surgery I suppose,' Stevie commented, remembering Emma saying something similar. It was, after all, a lot easier to be a philanthropist when you were rich. 'Do you think they might be having financial difficulties?'

'You'd have to ask the accountant that, I wouldn't know. She can be a bit slow settling her invoices, but that's generally the way these days, isn't it?'

'Her accountant — would that be Aidan Stoppard?'

'Yup.'

'What do you know of him?'

'Not much. He and Miranda were at school together, some high school or other on the wrong side of town. That's part of Miranda's problem, a huge chip on the shoulder. She told me once, after one bottle of bubbly too many, that when she first left school and started making new friends, she'd tell taxi drivers in a big loud voice to take her to an address in Claremont. Once she'd left the friends behind, she'd get the taxi to drop her off at a bus stop so she could bus it home to the outer suburbs with no one the wiser.'

'A social climber.'

'You can say that again, it's obvious she only married Christopher for his money and social position. And he's *still* besotted with her, I can't see why, the silly bugger. He's no dumb arse; he has to see through her — I suppose there's no accounting for taste.'

'And what do you think of Aidan Stoppard?' she asked.

Holdsworth shrugged. 'Okay, I suppose.'

'You don't sound very enthusiastic. Do you know him well?'

'Not really, only in passing. Enough to say hi when he drops in at the agency, sometimes work talk. Why the interest?'

'With Emma missing, everything about the family and the agency is of interest.' She explained the minimal details of the circumstances surrounding Bianca's death, the paedophile ring that had somehow acquired copies of his photos, and why they had suspected him of supplying them.

He rubbed his moustache. 'You think someone deliberately singled me out for this?'

'Yes, someone who didn't know you were a homosexual, I suspect.'

'I told you I don't advertise.'

'But you do have a very predictable routine at the cafe.' Stevie allowed a slight smile, which Holdsworth returned somewhat sheepishly.

'I was trying to shake the gambling habit,' he said. 'I think maybe I have now, but I wish it hadn't had to be like this.'

A constable shuffled in with fresh coffee.

Stevie went on. 'Have you ever lost or suspected your photos stolen? Has someone ever tampered with your computer, you think?'

Holdsworth paused for thought. 'No, but it wouldn't be hard to scan the pics and put them back on my desk — my office door doesn't have a lock, anyone could take them …'

'They're the kind of photos that would appeal to a paedophile—'

'Oh come on, you're not harping back to that again. I photograph what I'm told, nothing more, nothing less. And I don't do porn. If you have a beef with anyone, take it out on Miranda Breightling, not me.'

'What about the snaps of the girls getting dressed in the change room?'

'No way!'

Stevie took from the file before her a photo of a young girl wearing nothing but underwear, bending down to pick up an item of clothing from the floor. She slid it across the table to him. Aware that he was under the light again, Holdsworth flushed and jumped to his feet. 'That's not mine, Jesus, I swear it! Maybe someone used my equipment. Maybe there's a hidden camera, that's it …'

'Then I suggest you do all you can to help us find the guy who did it. Your reputation's at stake in this.'

'Help you? What do you think I'm doing?'

'Have you seen anyone hanging around the modelling agency recently who shouldn't have been there?'

Holdsworth sat down again and folded his arms. 'There's always creeps hanging around, hoping to get a glimpse of the girls. To her credit, Miranda insists that parents arrive on time for pick-up, that the girls aren't expected to make their own way home.

'They need to get a bouncer for the place. Christopher tells them to clear off when he's there, but he's not the kind to get his hands dirty. Christ, he was almost flattened by some bruiser the other night. I nearly called the cops when I saw them in the street, it looked like things were about to get violent.'

'But you didn't call the police?'

'Well, they seemed to sort things out, ended up walking off arm in arm.'

'Arm in arm? That's sounds a bit strange.'

'I thought so too, especially as earlier they looked like they wanted to tear each other's throat out.'

'Where did they walk to?'

'A pub, a parked car, I dunno.'

'Did you get a glimpse of this man?'

'Not really, it was pretty dark.'

'Short, tall?'

'Smaller than Christopher I think, but powerfully built. And you know, I think there was a kid too, lurking around.'

A kid? The phone interrupted Stevie's thoughts. She left Holdsworth and moved to the corridor outside the interview room to talk to Monty.

'Thought you'd want to know that the final forensic report is in on Kusak's van,' he said.

'Go ahead.'

'The long dark strand of hair found in Kusak's van has been identified as belonging to Emma Breightling. It was matched with hair from the brush in her bathroom.'

She told Monty she needed to talk to him, pocketed her phone and thanked Holdsworth for his help and sent him on his way.

But on her way to Monty's office she received an urgent

page from Clarissa. *Shit*, everything seemed to happen at once in this place.

'Make it quick Clarissa, something's come up,' she said as she pushed through the swing doors of the ops room.

'Yeah, well this is important too. I've done some more digging on the Katy Enigma site and some of the stuff is pretty shocking when you look closely. A lot of stories by kids obviously trying to deal with issues of abuse. The poem you found was just a start.'

'Yeah, ok, ok, go on.' Stevie was itching to get upstairs and see Monty.

Clarissa clicked her mouse and opened a link. 'This is a new one, it only came in this morning.'

Stevie stooped to peer at the screen.

Katy Enigma knew that she was the only one up to the task of eliminating the monster. She devised a cunning plan, which involved the staging of her own abduction. The plan was very risky, but she knew she had to attempt it or die trying.

She left a series of clever clues in her bedroom. She wasn't sure if the police would get them or not, but that didn't matter. What mattered was that the monster would understand and the monster would follow her to her secret hiding place. Once across the drawbridge and into the castle there would be no escape, and no one to hear his cries. He would be as helpless as any of his victims and Katy would make sure he suffered even more.

To kill a vampire you use a wooden stake, to kill a werewolf you use a silver bullet, but to kill the monster from under the bed you work slowly, using an ancient set of silver blades ...

28

Stevie didn't have time to wait for the lifts and took the stairs up to Monty's office two at a time. 'I think I know where Emma is; she's at Stoppard's showroom. The postcard on the teddy was obviously a clue, and Stoppard knew it too, that's why he took it,' she said as she burst into the office. 'I'm going there now, only I need Tash …'

Monty gave little reaction to her words preoccupied it seemed with trying to reach into the pocket of his jacket hanging on the back of his chair.

'Just a minute, Stevie, let me just get this. Hell …' He put his hand to his chest. Sweat glistened in a pool at the base of his throat. His face had turned quite grey.

'Monty, what's the matter?' she said, her own throat tightening in panic.

'Just get my thing for me, I'll be okay.' He seemed to be having trouble pushing out his words.

'What thing?' Stevie desperately groped in his jacket pocket — coins, car keys — finally pulling out a small orange canister. 'This?'

Monty nodded and took the Nitrolingual pump from her and administered a couple of quick sprays under his tongue in a way that told her he'd done it before.

'Just a bit of chest pain,' he murmured. 'It'll go soon.'

Stevie clutched his shoulders, the whereabouts of Emma

Breightling now the furthest thing from her mind.

The medication began to kick in. Monty rubbed his hands over his face, slowly straightened in his chair and looked at her blearily. She put her cheek against his and ran her fingers through his hair. 'You scared me. Thank god, thank God,' she murmured over again.

He took her hand and kissed it. 'Get going,' he said. 'Go and find Emma.'

'Not until I know you're on your way to hospital.'

'I've had my spray, I'll be okay now.'

Stevie shook her head, reached for the phone and called an ambulance, despite his protests.

'How long have you had this?' she asked after she'd put the phone down, trying to keep her tone free of recrimination.

'Not long, the doctor said it's just a bit of angina. It started in my jaw, I thought it was toothache —'

'The toothache, of course.'

'I'm booked in for tests next week.'

'A bit of angina and you didn't tell me …' she stopped as she noticed his colour change and knelt again at his side and stroked his face. 'It's okay, I know now, but I wish I hadn't had to find out like this.'

The light from the window shone on his hair and made it glow like the slanting rays of autumn. It was an observation she'd often made before, but not for some time she realised, with dismay.

'Emma,' he said.

'I'll go as soon as I know you're okay.'

'What made you think …?'

'Everything's beginning to fall into place,' she interrupted, deciding it was better for her to do the talking and save him the effort of asking the questions. 'I think Emma's been suffering long-term abuse from Aidan Stoppard. The message board she and Bianca belonged to was mainly for kids with these kinds of problems. She's run away to Stoppard's place in the hills and is planning some kind of ambush there. The scalpels — remember how they were missing from Breightling's safe?'

Monty shook his head. 'You've got to be kidding. The kid's got them? How did you—'

'Sorry Mont, but we don't have time for this right now. You just have to trust me.'

'Always in a hurry, there's never any time …'

'Listen,' Stevie cut him off. 'Any idea where Stoppard is now?'

'No idea. Maybe still with the Breightlings.' He reached for the phone. 'I'll check with the officer who's waiting with them.'

Stevie stopped him with her hand before he could punch in the numbers. 'Don't worry, I'll get someone onto him.'

Just then, Wayne knocked and entered the office.

Stevie climbed to her feet, still holding Monty's hand. 'He's not well, I've called an ambulance.'

Wayne took in Monty's pale face, the sweat beading on his forehead, and his jaw dropped. 'Fuck, shouldn't he be lying down?'

'No, he bloody well shouldn't be lying down,' Monty snapped.

'Well, he should at least calm down then,' Stevie said.

Wayne was shuffling his feet, she could tell he was searching for something positive to report.

At last he said, 'I've got Sammy Nguyen and a social worker in the interview room downstairs, boss.'

'Good. Before you start though, we need to bring in Aidan Stoppard. Get some people onto that pronto. See if you can organise a full scale search of his country place, Chateau-by-the-Lake'

'On what grounds? I can't just pluck a search warrant from the air, Mont, I need some sort of evidence.'

'Then leave it to me for the time being,' Stevie said. 'Tash and I will conduct the preliminaries, see what we can find.'

Monty washed his hands over his face. 'You'd better go now. If you think you know where Emma is, go and find her. Take whoever you need. And be bloody careful, Stoppard could easily slip through the net, and God knows how he might react if he finds himself cornered. In fact, you'd better sign out for some side arms.'

'But the ambulance …' Stevie hesitated.

'Go,' Monty urged. 'I'm all right.' He gave her a smile that made her throat ache. Fighting back tears she kissed him, squeezed Wayne's arm and left the room.

29

Excerpt from chat transcript 210107
   HARUM SCARUM: I know some1 who does gross things 2
   BETTYBO: do u want 2 kill him 2?
   HARUM SCARUM: oh yeah that would b sooooo sweet

Emma Breightling no longer heard the frogs croaking in the lake or the night-time warbling of the magpies in the trees. To her, the only sound was the gravel crackling under the Porsche's tyres and her own heart thumping in her ears. She held her breath as she stood behind the Chateau door, peeping through the crack. The purr of the engine ceased and the car door slammed.

A key turned in its lock and the Judas door creaked open. She heard the slap of footsteps on the front path, the whistle of a jaunty tune.

When he came into her line of vision, the whistling stopped. He shot a smile in her direction, as if he had X-ray vision, as if he could see her jammed there behind the front door. Oh God, he knew she was there! She wanted him to think that she was waiting for him, but she hadn't planned on getting herself trapped here behind the door — *stupid, Emma, stupid!*

Before she could even attempt an escape, his foot hit the door with a crash, slamming her into the wall. He ducked from the falling pot as it shattered to the floor sending a shower of muddy water splashing across the quarry tiles. By the time he'd grabbed her arm and spun her around he was laughing out loud.

'You silly little girl! Did you really think I'd fall for that? We read the story together, don't you remember — the Famous Five wasn't it?'

Emma tried to yank her arm from his grasp but his fingers sank deeper into her flesh. She screamed, 'Let me go! The police will be here soon — they know all about you!'

'They know nothing about me, darlin', nothing at all; they didn't even see your post card. A little cryptic for a simple plod I'd have thought. I guess you wanted me to think you'd changed your mind, that a little tumble in the hay with good old Uncle Aidan wasn't quite as bad as you'd first thought.'

He chucked her under the chin and studied her face. 'You really are an intriguing little thing, so different from your mother.' He burrowed his face in her hair. 'The lovely smell of a brand new dolly, straight from the box ...'

She tried to recoil but he held on to her tight, pushing her against the wall with one hand as his other worked its way down her body until he reached the packet of scalpels and removed them from her pocket.

'Well well, what do we have here — looks like daddy's missing heirlooms.' He examined the felt-wrapped packet and laughed. 'Oh I see now. The idea was to lure me here, overpower me and carve me up with these.' He clicked his tongue. 'And your parents think you're so bright. Well it seems you're not so bright about everything, eh Emma? Underneath it all you're just a silly little brat with an over-active imagination.'

She braced herself as he pinned her arms to her sides and pulled her against his body. Pressing his open lips to hers, he rammed his tongue into her mouth. She gagged as she attempted to tear her mouth away, struggling at the same time to drive her knee into his groin.

When he finally drew back he smiled and said, 'Oh yeah, and a fighter too. We are certainly going to have fun with you.'

Her lips stung. She choked down a sob and wiped her mouth on the shoulder of her T-shirt and forced herself to look at him. What was he talking about — we?

She noticed a ripe bruise on his cheek. Maybe the pot had nicked him after all; she hoped it had. Maybe the wallop on the head she'd given him last night would finally take effect. Maybe any minute now he'd keel over and drop dead at her feet.

'Your father,' he put his finger to the bruise. 'It seems the great ice man, your precious, talented, silver-spoon-in-the-mouth father is starting to melt.'

'He'll tell the police. He'll tell them what you're really like!'

'But he doesn't know what I'm really like, darlin'. As far as he knows, I'm just the guy who screws his wife and screws him out of his money. He doesn't know I'm going for the trifecta — his little girl too. And even if he did, he wouldn't dare. Your father is a coward. He won't be helping you, even if he could.'

Emma swallowed and filled her voice with false bravado. 'But I know about all the gross things you do up here, and it's not just the things you try and do with me. I've already told the police. They know everything. I told you, they're coming.'

Stoppard paled, squeezing her arm so hard now she thought it would break. She shouldn't have said that. Oh God, he really was going to kill her now, he was. Stupid stupid stupid. He stared at her so hard she could almost hear the cogs turning in his brain.

One side of his lip curled and finally he spoke. 'You little bitch, true or not, you'll live just long enough to regret this.'

Taking her hand, he yanked her down the front passageway

of the Chateau, kicking at the broken shards of pottery and negotiating his way around the puddles of water. 'Don't slip,' he said, 'there's a good girl. My mates don't do damaged goods.'

'So, just what were these clues that Emma was supposed to have left for us in her bedroom?' Tash asked as they sped towards the blue haze of the hills, lights flashing and siren wailing.

'I can only think it was the postcard of Stoppard's chateau. The Mexican throw rug might have been a clue too I suppose, the guy imports Mexican art. But if it hadn't been for the appearance of that story on the web page, I don't think I'd have put two and two together.'

'Has Stoppard been picked up yet?'

'No, he left the Breightlings at midday, said he was going to his office in the city, but he wasn't there when the uniforms went to fetch him. He wasn't at his Terrace apartment either.'

'Do you think he's out there already?'

Stevie shook her head and shrugged. If he was, she didn't know who was in the greater danger, Stoppard or Emma.

Tash creased her brows as she thought. 'Is she really capable of murder you think?'

Damn! It was uncanny how they'd share a line of thinking. It took a moment for Stevie to answer. She was thinking about the long dark hair found in Kusak's car. When at last she did speak, she had trouble finding her voice, as if her own ears did not wish to hear the truth. 'Yeah, y'know, I think she might be. She's not your average kid.'

They drove a short way in silence, both lost in their own thoughts. Stevie tried to remind herself not to make pre-emptive judgements until they'd gathered more facts; the presence of one hair did not make Emma a murderer.

She had Tash ring around until she came up with an after

hours number for Donna French, the counsellor at Emma's school. It was a frustrating conversation, the psychologist reluctant to tell Stevie anything about Emma's history other than what she already knew: that she was a gifted child and kept down for a year at school because of poor hearing at an early age.

'Shit, Donna,' Stevie found herself losing patience. 'This kid could be in real danger. Isn't there anything else you can tell me?'

'If she's in danger, then you need to find her. You don't need her psychological profile. Patient confidentiality, Stevie.'

'Then give me a generic run-down of a gifted child,' she snapped.

She heard Donna sigh. 'Okay, but this isn't necessarily Emma Breightling, right?'

'Go on.'

'You'd be amazed at how many gifted children get misdiagnosed because often their behaviour is thought to be ADHD.'

'Emma was kept down because of glue ear, was she also thought to be ADHD?'

Donna ignored her. 'Impatience, restlessness, easily bored, you can see how sometimes giftedness can be confused with ADHD. Certain personality factors also often accompany high intellect and creativity that can be very difficult for both parents and teachers alike. Power struggles between the child with parents and teachers are not uncommon.'

'I can see that with the mother,' Stevie interrupted.

'The gifted child was once only assessed within the very narrow framework of academic achievement, meaning that the personality problems afflicting such children were often disregarded. Things are changing, thank goodness, and the psychology of such children is now getting more research. They can end up as very disturbed kids if not handled correctly, on rare occasions even multiple personality disorders develop.'

'Multiple personalities — you have to be joking!' Tash exclaimed.

There was a pause while Donna attempted to identify the voice.

'Detective Constable Hayward,' Stevie told her, a finger on her lips to Tash.

Donna regained her stride. 'Yes, but as I said, MPD is very rare. Gifted children tend to feel emotions intensely, they are sensitive and idealistic, the downside being that they are susceptible to feelings of anxiety and helplessness, and in turn, depression. They get intensely frustrated with those who don't feel as deeply as themselves.'

'Does Emma have many friends?' Stevie asked.

'They are often ostracised by their peers, seen by them as know-it-alls, nerds or even freaks.'

'Emma seems to prefer to hang out with younger kids.'

'I can't comment.'

'She seems to have an intense desire to help vulnerable children.'

'It goes with the territory.'

'What about committing a crime? Would a child like this see the ends as justifying the means?'

'Stevie, it's all just speculation, I really can't say ...'

'Thanks, Donna. Thanks a lot.'

Stevie hung up, put her foot to the floor and joined Tash in a medley of curses aimed at the blur of scenery speeding by the car window. It wasn't Donna's fault, Stevie said when they'd both calmed down, Donna had said all she could within the constraints of the job. She told Tash she'd ring Donna back later when the shit had stopped hitting the fan, when they'd found Emma.

Next she tried to call Monty at the hospital, but they wouldn't let her speak to him while he was still being examined. The nurse assured Stevie that his condition was stable. Perhaps it was just as well they couldn't talk, she thought with a sigh, it would've been impossible with Tash in the car too. There was much she needed to tell him, and it wasn't all about Emma and the case.

Tash turned the siren off as they left the city and the traffic behind. They were silent again. Stevie didn't know what she was most afraid of finding.

30

A steep driveway, about a kilometre long, was the only way to reach Aidan Stoppard's country showroom. Stevie and Tash bumped their way down the poorly maintained bitumen as they headed towards a valley hemmed in by hills of dense jarrah. It was twilight, but they could still make out the shine of the lake and the faux-turreted Chateau spooning around the curve of its southern edge. Full-grown deciduous trees dotted the lawns and beneath them sprouted the silhouettes of squat figures with bulging eyes, protruding ears and swollen tongues. Stoppard's Mexican artwork Stevie presumed, and shivered.

From a good distance she could see Stoppard's Porsche parked in a carport next to a high wall surrounding the shore side of the building. There were no windows overlooking them, so she switched off the engine and coasted in silently, rolling to a stop behind his car, blocking it off should there be any attempt at a getaway.

Neither of them spoke. Tash reached under her jacket and checked her gun. An iron-studded Judas door in a larger wooden door in the surrounding brick wall seemed to be the only way in.

'*It was a magic, fairy tale kind of a place,*' Stevie remembered Emma telling Izzy. '*Part castle and part luxury villa, and it was built over a lake where a billion waterlilies grew.*'

And here it was, just as she had said, and just as pictured on

Stoppard's business card and the postcard. Stevie slipped on her shoulder holster, covered it with her denim jacket, and grabbed a torch from the glove box. In the twilight, objects had begun to take on a grainy texture.

She indicated for Tash to check the lakeside of the Chateau, while she explored the garden side. She found no other doors or windows, though halfway along the wall was a small opening with a heavy iron door, much like an old-fashioned coal chute. The door remained rigid when she pushed against it. She rubbed the rust from her palms onto the seat of her jeans.

Tash was waiting for her back at the Judas door. 'There's no getting around the side of the Chateau, unless you want to swim for it,' she whispered.

Stevie explained that the garden side was similarly inaccessible while she pushed against the Judas door, then the larger door in which it was situated, finding both locked. She tipped her head toward the wall, cupping her hands as a step for Tash. Then with a couple of heaves and a jump she was on the other side of the wall herself, standing in the courtyard next to her.

The dying light caught the shine of waterfalls and ornamental ponds, birdbaths and the umbrella shapes of palms. An eccentric set of stone steps spiralled their way up a tower almost as tall as a lighthouse, looming on her right hand side. Through its small windows she saw the shadowy shapes of more Mexican gargoyles.

Light shone from under the front door; two small windows on either side of it were heavily curtained. They moved silently across the moss covered paving, following a small, unfenced path along the side of the building, the only margin between the rough walled chateau and the lake.

A floating jetty fingered its way from the path. Stevie could just make out the shape of a diving board at its end and a tethered rowboat. A fish jumped and broke the stillness of the dark water, sending out ripples of silver bangles. From across the lake, she heard the low muttering of roosting chooks. Perhaps the boat was used to row to the island to gather eggs. This place would be a paradise for kids. No wonder Emma used it as her home base for Katy Enigma.

They crept towards the back of the Chateau and came across a small paved barbecue area accessed by some partially closed French doors through which a sheet of light flooded. Water lapped at some semi-submerged steps leading from the paving into the lake. Under the surface, the shadows of great fish glided like submarines.

The detectives stood on either side of the French doors and watched Stoppard move about the room, walking between a stereo system and a large oak table on which several cardboard boxes had been placed. The delicate strains of Pachelbel's Canon floated past them, tripping over the golden light before disappearing into the darkness of the lake beyond, while the deep bass steps of the cello lingered on.

The ceilings of the room were as high as a medieval banquet hall, but instead of shields and weapons, the walls were covered with hanging masks: gargoyle heads with horns and pointy beards, bared fangs and mouths shaped in silent screams. Price tags dangled from the masks. A huge carved wooden throne with a red and white 'special' sign sat in a corner.

Stevie shivered.

Tash gripped her arm. 'You ready?' she mouthed.

Stevie straightened from her crouch, counted to ten, then opened the French doors with a flourish.

'Bloody hell!' Stoppard dropped the box he'd just lifted from the table.

'Good evening Mr Stoppard,' she said, shutting the doors behind them.

Tash moved to the stereo and turned the music off. She took

a moment to gaze around the room, her eyes settling on the table covered in boxes. 'What've you got here, thinking about moving house?' Tash delved into a box and pulled out a fistful of CDs and DVDs. Another box clearly contained photographic equipment, a tripod leaning against the table next to it.

Stoppard's eyes widened. 'Hey, wait, what the hell do you think you're doing?'

'We have reason to believe Emma Breightling's here somewhere in this house,' Stevie said.

'Well I can assure you she's not. I'd appreciate it if you took your sticky paws off of my things; some of my equipment is very delicate. You can't just barge into a man's house like this and start rummaging around with his things.' His mother tongue became more emphasised as his diction sped up, Stevie noticed; he was saying *wiv*, not with, and *fings*.

'We can if we have reason to believe a life might be in danger.'

'Crap!'

Stevie pointed to the table. 'What's all this stuff for, anyway?'

Stoppard managed to call back some of his composure, reverting once more to an Australian rhythm of speech. He dismissed her question with a casual wave. 'It's a corporate video I'm having filmed here. Some footage has already been taken. The crew are coming back next weekend to finish it off.'

'For the showroom? Interesting.' Stevie looked at the numbered covers of the DVDs. 'Not much on the labels, but I guess you must have some kind of an index of what's what.' She gazed around the room, seeing no sign of a TV. It would have been interesting to see what was on those DVDs.

'There's an index somewhere around. Maybe one of the crew has it.' He smiled, fingered the curl behind his ear and looked her in the eyes. 'You still haven't told me what this is all about.'

Stevie tilted her head to Tash. 'Carry on.'

Tash climbed some wooden stairs leading up out of the hall. They heard a thump on the floor above their heads, the sound of a door creaking open.

'Sit down, Mr Stoppard,' Stevie pointed to a heavy backed chair at the table. 'We need to question you further about the disappearance of Emma Breightling.'

Stoppard dropped into the chair, folded his arms and crossed his legs. His white pants were streaked with what appeared to be mud.

'What's that from?' Stevie indicated the dirt.

'Burying bodies, what do you think?' When Stevie didn't return his smile, he sighed. 'A bit of impromptu gardening — c'mon officer, I've already told you what I know.'

'You were told by the officers that we might need to contact you again. You gave them a mobile phone number that you have not been answering. You said you would either be at your city office or your apartment, but you weren't at either of those places when they called around.'

'I asked if I could go home, they said yes. This is my home too.'

'You gave me your card, but you never mentioned this place to anyone else. I'll bet you're kicking yourself now about giving it to me. A bit over confident, weren't you?'

Stoppard pursed his lips. 'I've nothing to hide.'

'Yes you do. You've been abusing Emma Breightling.'

He threw his eyes to the ceiling. 'For God's sake, where did you get that from, her father? Nothing but the ranting of a desperate man whose child is missing. I've never touched Emma and I'll sue anyone for slander who says I did. You've no bloody proof.'

He was right: other than the mysterious circumstances surrounding Emma's disappearance, all Stevie had was an ambiguous poem on a web page which she couldn't even prove was written by Emma.

'The officer at the Breightlings' house said you and Mr Breightling had words, that he hit you.' Stevie indicated the bruise on Stoppard's cheek.

'And I told your officer that Breightling's action was of no concern to me. I told him to put the outburst down to anxiety over his missing daughter. I won't press charges.'

'How very compassionate of you. But I understood it had more to do with the affair you've been having with his wife, to whom you've also been supplying cocaine.'

Stoppard moistened his lips. 'He's not the first man to have been cuckolded. Maybe if he'd given her a bit more attention it wouldn't have happened. He's no one but himself to blame. As for the coke, well …' he spread his palms to indicate its insignificance.

'Did Emma come here, Stoppard, is she hidden somewhere in the Chateau?'

'Why the hell would she want to come here?'

'I understand the chateau means a lot to her; she knows the place well and has been visiting it all her life. She even writes stories about it.' Stevie made a show of spinning around to admire her surroundings. 'It's a wonderful place, a fantasy place. You must have invested a lot of time and money in it.'

'With the help of a very talented architect and an artist friend of mine,' Stoppard said with false modesty. 'An escape from the city, but less than an hour's drive away. A place for people to bring their families, picnic and enjoy the art in a relaxing environment — and hopefully leave with lighter cheque books.' A thin-lipped smile worthy of the *St Trinian's* spiv flickered across his mouth.

'I'll bet the kids love it.' Stevie didn't bother to restrain her sarcasm.

Stoppard looked at her and tented his fingers. 'You don't give up do you?'

'Emma has an active imagination. She might see this place as some kind of sanctuary.'

'Well yes, that's true, but please listen, officer. One, she's never been here without Miranda or Chris. Two, she's just a kid — how would she get up here? Three, if she was here I would have told her parents or the police immediately.'

'You were in a hurry to get up here yourself.' Stevie indicated to the boxes.

'I told you I needed to get things ready for the film crew.'

Just then there was a shout as Tash came crashing down the stairs and triumphantly thumped a felt-wrapped bundle on the table in front of Stoppard.

Stoppard sucked in a breath.

'Scalpels, Stevie, Breightling's missing scalpels. In a bedside cabinet in one of the upstairs bedrooms,' Tash said in an excited rush.

Stevie opened the bundle and the silver blades tumbled into her hands.

'I've never seen those things before in my life,' Stoppard said. 'They must have been left there by a guest …'

Something inside Stevie snapped. 'You're a fucking perverted bastard, Stoppard, who preys on the weak and vulnerable, on kids who can't fight back.' Slamming her hands on the table she rammed her face into his. 'Where is she, Stoppard, God damnit!'

Tash pulled her away from the table. 'Easy, Stevie, easy. Why don't I have a word with him while you continue the search? I've done upstairs, you can look downstairs and in the yard.'

Stevie nodded, wiped the sweat from her forehead, took a breath and tried to calm herself. 'I'll phone Central, tell Angus about the scalpels. That will get the whole team up here.'

31

Wayne sat in an interview room waiting for the arrival of Sammy Nguyen and the social worker. He drained his cup of coffee, leaned back in the chair and yawned.

Barry poked his head around the door. 'What are you still doing here?'

'I'm waiting for the Asian kid. I was supposed to see him earlier, but had to put him off when I went with Monty to the hospital.'

'Don't get me wrong mate, but that's not part of the job description is it?'

'Listen you wanker, I did it for Stevie. She wouldn't have left otherwise.'

Barry ran his hand across his shaved scalp and straddled a chair. 'Is Mont going to be okay?'

'They think so.'

'Has Stevie called in?'

'Yep. She's located Stoppard and thinks Emma's somewhere at his place. They've found Dr Breightling's scalpels and think Emma must have taken them from the safe. Angus is organising a warrant and the local cops should be on their way there.'

A constable showed Sammy and the social worker into the interview room. Sammy's face lit up when he saw Wayne.

'This is my colleague DS Barry Pickering,' Wayne said to

the new arrivals. 'He was just leaving.' Wayne nodded to the door and told Barry he'd see him in the morning.

The social worker, Mrs Jenkins, fussed over Sammy, pulled his chair out for him and asked if he wanted something from the vending machine in the corridor, to which he shook his head. She emphasised the lateness of the hour to Wayne and told them she had to have Sammy back at the hostel by nine thirty.

The boy glanced at Wayne and rolled his eyes. Kids like Sammy Nguyen were creatures of the night. He'd just be waking up now.

Wayne shot Sammy a wink before turning to the tape. 'Interview with Sammy Nguyen, 18 February, 20:35 hours, those present …' They stated their names for the tape. Wayne told Sam he wasn't under arrest, explained his rights to him and thanked him for his cooperation. Then he folded his hands on the table in front of him and began.

'Sam, we had a little chat yesterday and you started to tell me things but then you stopped, worried I think, that you might get into trouble?'

'Yeah, but then you said I wouldn't, that I was too young. You said if I helped you, you'd help me.'

'That's right. But in order for you to help us properly, I need to tape this talk in front of a witness, so we can use what you have to say in court, do you understand?'

Sammy nodded.

'You have to speak for the tape,' Wayne said.

'Yeah, I'm cool with it.'

'And no one is forcing you to talk are they, Sammy?' Mrs Jenkins said.

'Nah,' said Sam.

'Okay, tell us what you started to tell me yesterday.' Wayne lifted encouraging eyebrows.

The boy scratched his thin arm. 'I was living on the street, dossing with mates under the Narrows Bridge, when I heard someone say that some rich Chinese guy had just landed and was looking for someone to interpret for him. I speak Mandarin, Cantonese and my own Vietnamese dialect as well as bloody good English, right? I knew I was the man for the job. I got in touch with the dude, and he seemed fine, treated me good and I got to interpret his business dealings for him.'

'What did this man do, Sam?' Wayne asked.

'He was a moneylender, name of Zhang Li. He was rolling in it, you should have seen all the bling, the posh hotels he stayed at. I started giving him English lessons too, and he picked it up fine. I was worried if I taught him too well he wouldn't need me any more, so I slowed the lessons down a bit. Gave him wrong words every now and then.' Sam sniggered at the memory. Wayne and the social worker exchanged smiles.

'Tell us some more about this man Zhang Li,' Wayne said.

'He could be one rough bastard. He wasn't well; I learned to stay clear of him when he was in one of his moods. Sometimes he'd get real aggro when people were late with their repayments. He carried a knife, once I saw him cut a bloke's finger off with it.' Sam made a scissor shape with his fingers. Mrs Jenkins winced and Sam capitalised on the effect by making geyser-like motions with his hands.

'Tell us what happened on the night of the 27th of January,' Wayne said.

'Ummm … when?'

Wayne pulled out a pocket diary and pointed to the date. 'The day after Australia Day. You were at the river in Maylands.'

'Oh yeah, then. We were out collecting a debt. Li said he was getting fed up with this prick who was way behind with his payments. Said that after we'd seen him, we'd visit the fella who put him onto us, because it looked like he'd given us a bum steer.'

'Can you remember the names of either of these men?'

'Nah, mate.'

'Anything about them at all?'

Sammy scratched his head.

'Never mind, continue with your story, maybe something else will come to you.'

'Li said he'd had enough of this guy's bullshit, the guy who recommended the other guy as a good catch, I mean. Oh yeah, that guy, the one who gave us the bum steer, had poncy white shoes, that's right.'

'Good boy.'

'White shoes told us this guy was a soft touch, and filthy rich. Don't know why he was borrowing money if he was so rich, but that wasn't my problem. Anyway, he wasn't paying back, and it turned out he wasn't soft at all.' He stopped for a moment.

'Go on, Sam,' Wayne said.

'So we go to meet this guy in the city. Li poked him in the ribs with his knife, told him to find his car so they could go for a little drive. Li make him drive us to the river in Maylands, near all the bamboo. He told the guy he was going to cut his finger off for not paying his debts, and the guy begged him not to. He was crying and carrying on, said he wouldn't be able to work without a finger, said it was all a mistake, he'd get the money blah blah blah. Li got him on the ground. He wanted me to help hold him down, but I seen him do it before and it was gross, blood everywhere.' He shot Mrs Jenkins a cheeky look. 'Li yelled at me, said I was fired. Then the doc reached into his …'

Wayne straightened in his seat, 'Wait a minute, kid, you said the doc — was this rich guy a doctor?'

'Umm yeah, guess he was, guess I only just remembered,' Sam rubbed his nose and glanced away.

Sure you did kid, and you've known both of the men's names all along, but under all the cocky bluster, you're too terrified to admit it. 'Go on,' Wayne prompted.

'Yeah, he reached into his coat with his other hand, pulled out a gun and shot Li in the head — can you believe that? I mean just about no one in Perth carries handguns. If the bullet hadn't killed him, poor old Li would've died of shock anyway I reckon.

'I ran away then, and he shouted at me, said I was going to get it too, said he knew where to find me. I nearly pissed myself, man.'

'Did you see what the doc did with the gun?'

'No, I guess he chucked it in the river.'

He can't have chucked it in the river, Wayne thought, because it was used just over two weeks later to kill Miro Kusak.

The kid's hand shook on the plastic cup of water and he almost missed his lips. He seemed to have suffered quite a considerable drop in confidence since he'd made the mistake of mentioning the 'doc'.

'Sam, would you mind having a look at some photos with me?' It wouldn't be too hard to find a photo of the once philanthropic plastic surgeon. The pathologist's report on the body from the river had mentioned how the face had been removed with surgical skill. It had to be him.

'If you'll just come with me, Sam …'

Sam shook his head.

'I think he's had enough, Detective Pickering,' Mrs Jenkins said. 'The boy's had a horrific experience. My job is to ensure that this interview is conducted in a proper and non-exploitive way and that's what I intend to do.'

Wayne blew out a breath but had to agree. The strain was beginning to show on Sam's pale face, despite the earlier bravado. He turned off the tape. 'Okay, I suppose we have enough to get started.' He'd be making no arrests tonight, he thought, feeling tired and defeated, and yet he was so close. He could only hope that Stevie was having more luck at the Chateau.

He moulded his mouth into a smile and patted Sammy on the back. 'How's the hostel going?'

'It sucks and the food tastes like shit,' Sam said.

'But don't forget, if you continue with the program, they'll see if they can find you an apprenticeship,' the social worker said.

'Whoopee doo,' Sammy said. 'They keep crapping on to me about taking one day at a time — that's what I'm gonna do.'

And that, Wayne decided, was what he was going to have to do too. 'I want you to go back to the hostel now, Sam, have a good sleep and try to remember some more about that night, like the men's names, or anything else about them.' He turned to the social worker, 'I'll need to see him again in the morning. I'll dig up some photos that might jog his memory.'

32

The Chateau itself was much smaller than it appeared from the outside. Upstairs there were two bedrooms and a bathroom, which Tash had already searched. A galley kitchen, another bathroom and the main bedroom were located downstairs. The bed here was a four-poster, carved with elaborate geometric designs. A curtain covered a small in built wardrobe where Stevie found some men's casual clothes and a pair of work-boots. A small bookcase filled with yellowing paperbacks leaned against one of the walls.

In the bathroom Stevie found compressed cocaine hidden amongst echinacea tablets. She returned to the great hall and placed the bottle on the table before Stoppard.

He shrugged, 'I get it from Mexico, for personal use. I wouldn't be stupid enough to sell it.'

Stevie glanced at Tash. It seemed she had got no further with their suspect. If anything he appeared more relaxed. In some strange way his casual acknowledgement to the cocaine possession, the way he was trying to deflect from the major issue, was more disturbing to Stevie than his denial of seeing Emma.

'I'm going outside to check out the tower,' she told Tash.

The spiral stairs on the outside of the tower had no railing and she wound her way up carefully. On her way she examined three floors of circular rooms, all with dimly lit grottoes displaying a variety of exotic statues and carvings; creatures with strange hooked beaks and wings that were never meant to fly.

The topmost level was reached by a ladder from a trapdoor in the ceiling. Here she found a small office with shelves of files. She picked a CD from a neat pile. Unlike those in the boxes downstairs, this was clearly labelled: 'Accounts 2005–2006.'

A sleeping PC sat on a small desk. She snapped on latex gloves from her pocket and touched a key, finding herself on the Katy Enigma site. She knew what this meant; either Stoppard had been lurking on the site, or Emma had posted her story from here.

Stevie racked through her shaky knowledge of computers and websites. As she thought she gazed through a porthole window at the inky water below. A floodlit fountain came to life in the middle of the lake. Must be controlled by a timer, she thought idly. The glowing orbs of protea blossoms caught her eye on the far side as the lake burst with prisms of colour.

But she wasn't here to admire the view. Her eyes slipped back to the computer screen, noticing the various commands and codes in its margin. She realised then that she was in the administration panel, a page only accessible to the site owner.

Which meant Emma had posted her story from here. They had him.

Having not yet explored the entrance to the Chateau, Stevie opted to return through the front door. Evidence of a struggle greeted her as soon as she stepped into the entrance. Clearly, someone had attempted a clean up, but shards of broken pottery and lumps of soil and streaks of mud were stll visible. Two sets of footprints, one large, one small, tracked down the passageway. Treading carefully, Stevie followed them, a grim smile upon her face. No way could that slimy bastard wriggle out of it now, no matter how much money he had.

Stoppard's scream made her pull up short. She hugged the walls as she made her way down the passageway towards the light from the great hall. Gingerly, she peered around the doorframe.

She saw Stoppard bound to a chair with a curtain tie, struggling to break free. Tash stood over him brandishing one of the scalpels.

'You can't do this to me, you wouldn't dare!' Stoppard yelled.

'I've done it before, mate and got away with it too,' Tash said. 'The last guy, one of your little crawling pals, got a bullet to the head. He was lucky, a helluva lot luckier than you're gonna be.'

Christ, Tash. Stevie's hand went to the gun under her denim jacket. She held it loosely by her side and stepped into the room.

'Put that down Hayward,' she said, surprised at her own cool. She glanced at Stoppard and saw immediately that his fly was undone and gaping, but he was apparently unhurt.

Tash tossed the scalpel on to the table. 'Stevie we haven't got time for this. He's actually admitted that she's here somewhere in the Chateau, but not where. If she's not dead already, she might soon well be.'

Stevie grabbed Tash by the arm and pulled her out of Stoppard's earshot into the master bedroom. Then she didn't hold back. 'Jesus Christ Tash! Didn't anything sink through your thick skull the last time — much as you might feel like it, you can't do that to suspects!'

'He said she's here,' Tash repeated. 'If you'd given me just a bit longer, I'd have found out where.'

'And how would you have done that?'

'Gone for his balls.'

'You're bluffing.'

Tash washed her hands over her face, paused for a moment then looked into Stevie's eyes. 'Am I?'

Stevie's gut twisted. This was not what she wanted to hear.

Suddenly Tash leapt up from the bed. 'Shhh, Stevie, did you hear that?'

They both froze. Through the sounds of the cicadas and frogs from the lake a vague muffled thump reached their ears.

Stevie spun on her heels, looking around the room. 'Where's that coming from?'

'You searched in here?'

She nodded.

Tash dropped to her knees and slithered under the bed, her cowboy boots scuffing on the tiles. Stevie tapped at the plaster wall behind the curtained wardrobe.

In a muffled voice Tash called out, 'The wall feels hollow around here.'

Stevie continued to scan the room until her eyes settled on the bookcase with the faded paperbacks. Then they heard it again, a faint cry, a thump. It sounded close, and it was coming from behind the bedroom wall. Stevie called out louder, 'Emma, Emma?' Then she remembered.

If by some bad luck, one of them was to get into the castle, she could escape by the secret passageway hidden behind the bookcase in her bedroom.

Tash slid back out from under the bed.

'She's behind there!' Stevie pointed to a bookcase on the wall. There was a decorated knob at the top; she pulled on it and the bookcase swung open like a door. Behind the bookcase they found another door, similar in design to the coal chute she'd seen outside. She drew the bolt and heaved the door open.

Tash found a light switch and Stevie felt an immediate flood of relief. The L-shaped room was lined with bench seats and colourful cushions, the walls filled with delicate pieces of Mexican art. And in the smaller part of the L, Emma lay on a rough wooden bed, hands and feet tied, mouth gagged with duct tape. She blinked back at them in the harsh light, eyes filling when she saw Stevie. Within seconds Stevie had her untied, back in the bedroom, crying and shaking in her arms.

Over the child's shoulder, Stevie told Tash to take Stoppard out to the car and cuff him inside it.

She didn't know how long she sat on the bed with Emma, clasping her until the sobs finally eased. Scraping the hair off the little damp face, she murmured, 'Did he hurt you, Emma?'

The girl shook her head and spoke through hiccupping breaths. 'He said he was saving me for someone, he said he had to get rid of me … I told him the police were coming. He gave me something to drink which made me sleepy and then he made some phone calls, but I can't remember much about them because I was half asleep. I think someone was going to come and get me. Stevie,' the girl's voice became very high. 'He said the man was going to put me in the movies and then he was going to kill me!'

Stevie pulled the child close, felt the tears pricking her eyes. 'Hush now, it's okay, you're safe.'

As she held Emma tight, her eyes travelled around the small room. Above the bed, tacked to the rough plaster wall, she saw the same crucifix as in the hardcore photographs seized from Mason and Kusak's computers. The thin line she'd seen at the bottom of the cross turned out to be a price tag.

It seemed everything in this place had a price.

Stevie took the mobile from her pocket and called Angus. He told her they were about twenty minutes away. She explained that Stoppard might be expecting a visitor and suggested they remained out of sight near the entrance to the driveway to apprehend anyone turning into it.

'Coffee's ready!' Tash called out from the kitchen.

Emma clung to Stevie's hand and said in a breathless rush, 'I hitched all the way here. I was so scared I didn't even have time to grab my shoes.' She pointed to a small cut on her toe and padded barefoot with Stevie into the great hall.

They sat around the table. Tash had found a tin of fruitcake and was hungrily eating a slice. Stevie couldn't face even the thought of food.

'Emma,' she said gently, 'I need you to tell us exactly what things are like between you and Aidan Stoppard, and I need to know what happened in your room last night.'

Emma picked at cake crumbs while she spoke. 'I've known Uncle Aidan all my life. He used to watch me in the bath when I was little, scrub my back, that sort of thing, I thought it was normal. Miranda said that because he had no kids of his own, he just liked to play at being a dad. Then when I got older I realised it wasn't normal, I didn't need to be washed when I was seven or eight, but he kept on coming in, so I started locking the bathroom door.

'Dad used to read me bedtime stories but when he was home late, Uncle Aidan read to me. He used to make a big thing of tucking me up and saying goodnight. At first it was okay, but as I got older it started to get, well, he seemed to want to get even more touchy feely.'

'Did you ever mention this to either of your parents?'

'I tried but they never listened. Miranda thinks the sun shines from his bum. And Christopher, I don't know. Miranda says he's going through some kind of mid-life male menopause crisis thing — I used to be able to talk to him,' she shrugged. 'But now it's really hard, he's always in a bad mood.

'Anyway, I told Uncle Aidan I was too old for stories, but he still insisted on coming in to tuck me up. Then about a year ago he touched me, you know, down there, and I screamed like mad and Mum came in. Uncle Aidan told her I was having night terrors and she believed him. I knew then that I'd never be getting any help from her and I started locking the bedroom door after that. Whenever he stayed over after that, he'd turn the handle and try to come in. I always kept it locked but he never gave up ...' Her voice trailed off and she took a sip of coffee as if to steady her nerves. 'Last night I decided not to lock it.'

'Because you wanted him to follow you to the Chateau?'

Emma looked down at the table. 'I guess so,' she whispered. 'I wanted to trap him.'

'You wanted to hurt him?'

Emma couldn't meet Stevie's eyes. 'Yes,' she whispered. 'That's why I took the scalpels.' She started to fidget and twist in her seat.

'Are you okay?' Stevie asked.

'Can I go to the toilet? I'm busting.'

When she was out of earshot Tash shook her head. 'She thought she could take on a grown man?'

'She might not have been able to manage it, but her alter ego could have.'

'You mean Katy Enigma?'

'I haven't questioned her about the site yet, but I'm pretty sure she's Harum Scarum.'

'Then she might be able to tell us more about Bianca Webster ...'

'I'll talk to her about that later, let's take one thing at a time.' The toilet flushed. 'Shhhhh ...'

Emma reappeared. 'Actually,' she said as she wiped her

hands on her tracksuit pants. 'You were a bit slower at finding me than I thought you would. I left clues all over the place. Didn't you notice the postcard and the Mexican blanket in my room?'

'Oh, sure,' Stevie couldn't help smiling. 'And the footprints in the flower beds pointing to the hills, silly me.'

Emma continued with her story. 'I was ready for Uncle Aidan this time. I was lying under the bedclothes fully dressed with my softball bat. When he tried to touch me I whacked him over the head with it. I didn't knock him out but I reckon he got a terrible shock. Then I climbed out of my bedroom window while he was rolling around on the floor and swearing.

'A nice woman picked me up from the main road and I told her my mum and me had had a row in the car earlier in the day and I'd jumped out at the traffic lights. I told her I was really sorry I'd done that and that I wanted to go home. She took me to a house in Mundaring where I said I lived and dropped me off outside it. There was a bike on the back verandah and I took it and cycled here. It took ages and my legs were killing me by the time I arrived. I chucked the bike in the lake.' She looked through her circular glasses, her large magnified eyes darting from one to the other of them. 'But I'll pay the owner back for it, I swear I will …'

'Why didn't you just beat him to death while he was lying on your floor?' Tash asked, subtle as ever.

Emma squashed cake crumbs with her finger. 'Well, I, err, I don't really know …'

Stevie filled in the blanks. *Because Katy Enigma wouldn't have done anything quite so banal.*

'I guess I wanted you to come to the Chateau too,' Emma said. 'Then you could see for yourself what else he was up to.'

'Was Stoppard already here when you arrived?' Tash asked.

'No, but I was pretty sure he would come, so I prepared my …' she hesitated. 'My trap for him.'

Tash ruffled her hair with her hands, but said nothing, as if she still hadn't come to terms with the idea of a thirteen year old girl taking on a grown man.

'Well, you gave me the idea Stevie. You spoke about entrapment when you came to my school,' Emma said defensively.

Shit, Stevie wouldn't be using that word again in a hurry. 'You balanced a pot on the top of the door, hoping it would fall on his head,' she said.

'Yes, it was really heavy, I had to tip the soil out before I could put it on top of the door. Then I filled a bucket with water and put that in the pot to make it heavy again. Well anyway,' she sighed. 'The best laid plans … it missed. He was ready for it.'

'Then what happened?' Stevie asked.

'Then he took me to that secret room where you found me. He gave me something to drink that made me sleepy and then he started taking stuff out of the room and packing it up, to take away and hide I guess.' She indicated the boxes on the table. 'These boxes I think. Once when I stayed here I caught him watching one of his DVDs in the secret room when everyone was asleep, it was so gross I was nearly sick.'

'I think the room where Emma was imprisoned was used for filming the hardcore porn,' Stevie told Trash.

Emma nodded. 'I reckon some of the people who came here with their families to buy his art were only pretending. They were actually hiring their own kids out for him to film.'

Tash cupped a hand over her mouth. Like Stevie, she was having difficulty coming to terms with the horror that had been going on in the Chateau. Tash met Stevie's eye and mouthed, 'Lolita.'

'Anyway,' Emma went on, 'if you want to see, the TV's over here.' She sprang eagerly to her feet and went to the wood panelled wall next to the Mexican throne. Pushing on a discreet knob she opened up hidden wooden doors to reveal a flat screen TV.

Stevie glanced at Tash and cleared her throat. 'It's okay, Emma, we'll watch them later when we try to identify the kids involved.'

33

A short, balding man turned his car into Stoppard's driveway. When Angus and his team apprehended him, Andrew Bishop claimed he'd made a wrong turn and denied knowing anyone called Aidan Stoppard.

Angus led the man towards the unmarked police car in which Stoppard was still cuffed. The windows had steamed up, Stoppard only a vague blur behind the glass.

Tash and Stevie came out to meet them. Tash leaned over and said to Stevie through the side of her mouth, 'Oh dear, looks like I forgot to leave a window open for him.'

A gush of extremities exploded from the car when Angus opened the door.

'I've been unlawfully detained in here for over an hour; I'm hot and I'm thirsty and I need a piss; you can't do this to me; I demand to see my lawyer ...' Stoppard swallowed the rest of his sentence when he saw Bishop's soft shiny face staring at him through the car door. 'Who's this?'

'We were hoping you could tell us,' Angus said.

'Never seen him before in my life,' Stoppard said. No surprises there.

When both men had been driven away, Stevie stood in the carport and rang Central to see that Emma's parents were notified that she was safe and would be brought home soon. Then she phoned Monty at the hospital and told him the good news. The blipping and beeping of the heart monitor underscored their telephone conversation. He sounded groggy and ready for sleep. She told him she loved him and would be seeing him soon. The old ache returned and she found herself blinking away tears.

Tash had accompanied Angus with the suspects, leaving a forensics team to search the Chateau for any further incriminating evidence. Emma and Stevie stood in the driveway until the frogs in the lake swallowed the sound of the disappearing cars.

Stevie held her hand out to the girl. 'C'mon hon, time to get you back to the city. We need to record an official interview with one of your parents present.'

The girl wiped her mouth with her hand. 'I don't feel very well,' she whispered. 'I need the toilet again.'

Stevie waited for Emma in the great hall. The child looked paler than ever when she returned.

'Tummy trouble?' Stevie asked

Emma nodded and rubbed her stomach. 'Can we just wait here for a bit longer? If I go in the car now I think I might be sick.' She sank into one of the chairs.

'I thought you'd be wanting to get away from this place as soon as possible.' Stevie sat down next to her.

'No, I like it here.'

She'd rather be here than with her parents, Stevie thought. Sad. The forensics team had erected lights in the courtyard, and brilliant artificial light shone through the window. Every now and then lenses of Emma's glasses flickered silver.

Stevie reached for her hand and gave it a squeeze.

'If Mr McGuire's in hospital, who's looking after Izzy?' Emma asked, her soft brown eyes filled with concern.

'She's staying with my mum, Izzy's grandma. Her place is like a second home.'

'Izzy must be worried sick about her dad.'

'She's okay; my mother's explained everything to her. I'll take her to the hospital to see him in the morning.'

'That might be scary for her.' Emma opened her mouth as if to say something else, then closed it again. It was obvious that there was a lot more on her mind than worry for Izzy.

'Look, Emma, I know you've had a hard time, but I think you've left out quite a bit — when I interview you at Central, you'll have to tell me everything.'

The girl took off her glasses and pressed her hands into her eyes. 'In front of my parents? Do I have to, can't I just tell you now?'

'I might be able to find someone else to sit in with you if it would make you feel more comfortable.'

Emma hesitated, let out a sigh. 'No it's okay. I suppose they'd have to find out eventually.'

'You can talk to me now if you like, but you don't have to.' Stevie had a sudden feeling that the girl might clam up during the official interview. Surely a few off the record questions while she seemed willing to talk wouldn't do any harm? It might help the official questioning run more smoothly and that would mean less trauma for Emma in the long run.

'You seem to understand a lot about paedophiles, how they work and what they do,' she said.

Emma shrugged, 'I read a lot.'

'Tell me then, how you got to know Bianca Webster.'

The girl looked to the high ceiling, her voice shook. 'How, how do you know that?'

'I've read the emails and chat transcripts Bianca stored on her iPod.'

Emma's hands twisted before her on the table. 'I taught Bianca how to save stuff to her iPod. She didn't want her mum finding them on her computer.'

There was a long silence.

'Emma?'

When the child finally spoke, it was through both hands covering her mouth, as if she was trying to separate herself from what was being said.

'I met her at the agency; sometimes I have to wait for Miranda there after school. Bianca was crying, I felt sorry for her and we began to talk. I told her about a kids' website which had some great stories on it and I said I thought it might cheer her up.'

Stevie gently removed Emma's hands from her mouth. 'And then you began writing Katy Enigma stories for her?' She paused. 'Look at me Emma.'

'Ummm …' Emma turned her head away again. 'Not exactly.'

'Yes you did, I found them. It's your website, Emma, you call yourself Harum Scarum.'

'Oh …' Silence stretched between them. Stevie said nothing, hoping to let it work for her.

Finally Emma gave a resigned sigh. 'Mainly she just read mine, but she had a go at writing the stories too sometimes. They got better each time, I think I really helped her and she seemed to get happier. But then, then she turned to that fraud Daniel. She was so unhappy and she needed some kind of escape. I don't think my stories were helping her anymore. She kept asking me to meet her face to face, but I didn't think it was such a good idea. Sometimes it's best to retain a bit of distance from the people you're trying to help, don't you think?

'But I stuffed up, I handled it wrong and now she's dead. Maybe if I'd agreed to meet and talk to her she would be alive now. But I've got to know so many kids on the website and I can't meet them all, can I?'

Emma lost the battle with her tears. 'There's so much else, I just don't know how to say it. You're going to think I'm a really really bad person.'

'I'd never think that, Emma,' Stevie said, weighing in her mind just how much she could push the child without causing her too much distress. 'Tell me what you know about Miro Kusak's death.'

The child gulped down air. 'They'll send me to prison. I did a bad thing.'

'Emma?' Stevie gently encouraged.

Emma shook her head violently. 'No, no, I can't tell you.'

34

Emma barely spoke on the journey back to the city. Earlier she'd admitted to having something to do with Kusak's death, but she back-tracked on the drive home, telling Stevie she didn't know anything. She'd only said what she'd said earlier because she wished it was true, wished that she really had killed him. This is one disturbed kid, Stevie thought as she glanced at the miserable figure curled in the front seat of the car.

'How do you think one of your hairs got onto the dashboard of Kusak's car, Emma?' she asked, keeping her tone soft.

Emma sniffed. 'Did it? Ummmm, I don't know.' Her face contorted as she battled to retrieve the memory — or invent the lie, Stevie wasn't sure. 'Hang on, I think I know; I sent Bianca some of my old clothes, I posted them a few months ago — maybe she was wearing something of mine when she was kidnapped and it had my hair on it?'

She was sure the girl was lying, but Stevie tried to keep her voice free from the suspicion she felt. 'Can you describe the clothes you gave to her?'

'It was a while ago, I'm not really sure, T-shirts, shorts,' Emma said with a vague wave of her hand.

Stevie's resolve slipped as exasperation moved in. 'Emma, who are you trying to protect, yourself or someone else?'

Emma slapped both hands upon the dashboard, the sudden noise making Stevie swerve the car in surprise. 'I'm not protecting anyone and you can't say I am, you can't prove anything!' she cried.

Stevie remained silent, gripped the steering wheel and wished she had been more patient. Emma was right; she couldn't prove anything. She still didn't know exactly what happened that night at the lookout with Miro Kusak. Whatever it was, she knew Emma hadn't acted alone. The only thing she could think to do now was set up a meeting with Donna French. She might be able to give Emma some kind of counselling, persuade her to tell the authorities what she knew.

They drove on in silence for several more minutes. At last the tension began to ease. The girl leaned forward and began to fiddle with the radio, trying to find a station she liked. After a while she gave up and resigned herself to Stevie's oldies station. Soon the unmistakable dissonance of a Hendrix riff filled the car.

Stevie judged the time to be right to ask a question that had been niggling in the back of her mind for some time now.

'Emma,' she asked, 'just one more thing; your Internet nickname, Harum Scarum, what does it mean?'

The small white face turned from the radio and faced hers. Stevie had to strain to catch the words, whispered to the backdrop of *Purple Haze*.

'It means confusion,' she said.

At Central they met up with Emma's father. He'd turned into an old man since Stevie had last seen him, with hunched shoulders and trembling hands. Tears glistened in his eyes as he pulled his daughter close. They recorded an interview in which she explained everything that had happened to her over the last twenty-four hours. As he learned about the true nature of Aidan Stoppard he covered his face with his hands, then slammed a fist on the table and cried, 'I'll kill him!' Emma flinched at the explosion and Stevie warned Breightling to control himself.

His eyes softened as he met his daughter's. 'I'm sorry darling, so sorry for everything,' he whispered and clasped her hand upon the table. Stevie noticed Emma squeeze it back.

When the interview was over, Stevie escorted father and daughter back to their house. With eyes red and puffy, the strain of the last twenty-four hours seemed also to be finally showing on Miranda's face. She held Emma tight and sobbed with genuine relief when she met them at the door. But she might as well have been something reptilian if the look on Emma's face was anything to go by. For one fleeting moment, Stevie felt sorry for Miranda.

'Have they've locked Aidan up?' Miranda asked when she finally let her daughter go.

Stevie nodded; there was little else she could say in front of the child.

Christopher placed an arm around Emma's shoulder. 'Why don't you go and have a shower and get ready for bed?'

'Will you come and see me later?' Emma asked him.

Miranda looked at her watch and frowned.

'Of course,' Breightling said.

'It's nearly one o'clock,' Miranda said.

'I'd go and see her if it was five o'clock, Miranda.'

'Yes, of course and I will too, she's had a terrible time,' Miranda conceded with a deep sigh.

Emma disappeared upstairs and Christopher offered Stevie a seat on an uncomfortable wooden bench near the window. The sound of trickling water from the garden pond and the croaking of the frogs reminded Stevie of the sound effects at Stoppard's Chateau-by-the-Lake. Christopher suggested a drink. When she declined he poured a double measure of scotch into a crystal glass for himself, topped up Miranda's orange juice with vodka.

'You must believe us, we had no idea that Aidan was like this, no idea at all,' Miranda said, agitating the ice in her glass.

'The pornography in that secret room ... all those visitors he gets to the Chateau ...' Breightling forked slim fingers through his sparse hair. 'Everything is beginning to make sense.'

'I can't believe that he tried to hurt her. He's her godfather for God's sake!' Miranda's voice was shrill, only a couple of notches below hysteria.

'Last time we went up to the Chateau, she didn't want to go, remember how she was, Miranda?' Breightling didn't look at his wife, just stared into his glass, swirling the liquid.

'Well, she only said that to you. I wasn't privileged to the information.'

'I thought it was because of the hideous statues on the lawn,' Christopher looked at Stevie. 'I told her to stop being silly.' His voice shook. He pulled out a bar stool and slumped next to his wife. Stevie wondered why they never seemed to opt for the more comfortable sofa — too intimate perhaps?

'You've known Stoppard for a long time?' Stevie asked him.

'I was involved in a land development with him years ago. I was cutting down my practice hours, sick of the long hours and my frequent trips abroad. Aidan had been at school with Miranda.'

'We met when we were both in year ten,' Miranda said. 'He'd just come over from England with his mother. He was so much more interesting than the other children, bright, worldly.' Her sigh was almost dreamy. *Jesus*, woman, Stevie thought, do you have no regrets at all?

'Worldly all right,' Breightling laughed bitterly. 'He's got money now of course. He's a self-made man who never tires of reminding me of it.'

Miranda stiffened on her stool. 'It's all very well to be clever after the event, Christopher. No one forced you to do business with him. You haven't always thought this way about him.'

Stevie held her palms up to the couple.

Breightling took a breath and his eyes dropped once more to his scotch. 'Yes well, he introduced us, actually.' Stevie got the idea he would have been more than happy to erase that part of his life. Had it really been love at first sight? Maybe as far as Breightling was concerned — but did he have an inkling of what a prize he would have been for a woman like Miranda? And one tall poppy Aidan Stoppard must have relished shooting down.

Stevie wondered what else had been in it for Stoppard. A soft touch surgeon with little business acumen, perhaps? An attractive wife who produced an even more attractive daughter? The thought was so sickening, it had to be true.

'Are you still involved in business with Stoppard, Mr Breightling?' Stevie asked.

'Of course, he was our accountant,' Miranda put in.

Christopher gave a vague wave of his hand. 'Still a few things here and there — more's the pity.'

'And how are they going?' Stevie asked.

'Terribly,' said Miranda.

Breightling put his empty glass down. His face was twitching. 'Nothing we can't extract ourselves from. Just don't, don't be so melodramatic, Miranda.'

'I'd like to warn you, Mr Breightling, that it won't be hard for us to get access to your financial records,' Stevie said.

Christopher Breightling dropped his head into his hands.

Monday morning

35

Excerpt from chat room transcript 141106
HARUM SCARUM: things beta with u now?
BETTYBO: no. scary
HARUM SCARUM did u c him again?
BETTYBO: mum did. he hit her. I wan 2 meet u F2F
HARUM SCARUM: sme and tell me about it
BETTYBO: ok

Wayne picked up Stevie on his way to the Breightling house. She'd already taken Izzy to see Monty in hospital, and told him how much better Monty looked — well enough even to complain about the food and speculate that there might really be such a place as the Rosa Klebb School of Nursing.

Wayne told her about his second interview with Sammy Nguyen. The kid had confirmed his suspicions that Aidan Stoppard was the man who'd introduced them to Zhang Li's killer — identified him from his recent mugshot. And identified Christopher Breightling as the murdering doctor from a photograph Wayne found on a cosmetic surgery site.

'I think he knew the doc's name all along. Looks like Sammy was thinking of going into the blackmail business — get the doctor to pay for his silence. He's been casing out Breightling's joint and Miranda's business.'

Stevie grunted. 'Just as well he didn't get any further. One manipulative kid on the loose is enough.'

'Interesting thing, one night he was about to jump the wall at the Breightlings' house when he saw a girl fishing around in the garden pond and chickened out. The girl had to be Emma. What do you reckon she was doing?'

'Somehow I doubt she was catching tadpoles,' Stevie murmured.

She was still pondering what Emma might have been up to in the pond when Angus rang. She listened to his report while Wayne continued to weave his way through the traffic to the Breightling's home.

'We've got him,' she said to Wayne when she punched the off button. 'We now have a convincing motive for Li's murder and it backs up everything Sammy's told you.'

'Financial pressure from Stoppard?'

'Financial thumbscrews more like. According to Angus, Stoppard and Breightling have been involved in a series of small developments since they first met, all instigated by Stoppard and all yielding modest returns. Then a few years ago the investment opportunity of a lifetime pops up. They invest in a large property in Wanneroo with plans of developing it into some kind of golfing estate. Stoppard provides the security for the loan with both parties responsible for repayments. But once the development starts, Stoppard calls on Breightling to repay the lot, which of course he doesn't have, having just poured thousands into his wife's business — which suddenly happens to be failing — upon the advice of his accountant.'

'Who happens to be Stoppard — and, let me guess, Tall Poppies is far from failing?' Wayne asked.

'Right. Angus thinks Stoppard's been cooking the books, getting together a tasty nest egg for himself, with or without Miranda, we're not yet sure. Anyway, Breightling can't get the money in the required time frame, so Stoppard puts the partnership into receivership and they are forced to sell the property for a song.'

'Don't tell me, to another company owned by Stoppard ...'

'Yes, which Breightling had no idea about. So in the end, Breightling is teetering on the verge of bankruptcy, when his old pal Stoppard says, hey, I know a guy who might be able to help you with a loan.'

'And the rest is history. Jeez, with friends like Stoppard ...'

'You don't just get screwed for your money, you lose your wife and daughter too.'

'I wonder which was the most important to Stoppard?' Wayne mused. 'Do you think he hoped Li would knock Breightling off?'

'Maybe, but not necessarily. I think Stoppard just wanted to see Breightling suffer.'

'That's something I just don't get. How long has Breightling known about him and his wife? I can't understand why the hell he's been putting up with it.'

'Yeah well, relationships — who knows? But as far as Stoppard was concerned, Miranda and Breightling staying together would be worth much more financially to him. I doubt he was ready to let Breightling go until he'd sucked him totally dry.'

'The guy's a mongrel.'

'And at the moment he's exercising his right to remain silent. But we'll get him. Clarissa's pulling apart his laptop as we speak; it's just a matter of time. She's already accessed the Dream Team chat room, it's full of creeps setting up deals, swapping and sharing their material.' She worried her thumbnail for a moment. 'There's a link where you can order video footage of any kind of abuse you want to see, rape on demand, even snuff movies.'

Wayne shook his head.

'There are members in the US, the UK and Germany — it's going to be of interest to police on several continents. We might even be setting up a worldwide sting.'

'How would you do that?'

'By highjacking Stoppard's online identity. But we have to act quickly, while we still have a media blackout — we don't want word getting out that Lolita's been arrested.'

'I can see you'll be having your hands full for a while.'

'Yeah, plus identifying the kids in Stoppard's films, and their parents or so-called carers.'

Traffic was lighter now. They whizzed down Guildford Road in silence for a while before Wayne spoke again.

'Okay, so we've worked out the Zhang Li angle, but what about Kusak? They were both killed by the gun that belonged to Emma's father.'

Stevie shrugged. 'Maybe Emma and her father did it together? All along I've had the feeling she's trying to protect someone.'

'But do you really think he'd use his own daughter as bait to catch a paedophile?'

She shook her head. 'No, for all his faults, Breightling loves his daughter. He would never put her in harm's way like that.'

'But so far that's what the evidence is telling us.' Wayne pulled the car to a stop outside the Breightlings' house. 'Here we are.'

Christopher Breightling opened the black lacquer door and squinted at them through the bright sunlight. He was in need of a shave and his pale T-shirt was stained with what appeared to be red wine.

'What do you want? Can't you just leave us alone for a while?' he said.

Stevie was getting used to the effect she'd been having on

people lately. She edged her foot into the crack in the door to prevent him from slamming it in their faces. 'We need another word, sir.'

He rubbed his hands over his face. 'When is this ghastly business going to end?'

'I'm afraid it's only just warming up,' Wayne said as they pushed past him into the house. The curtains were still drawn, the kitchen strewn with evidence of a long night and the air sour with old wine. Music thundered down from Emma's room on the mezzanine, a particularly loud heavy metal riff that made Christopher clamp his hands over his ears and groan.

Wayne flicked his head in the direction of the music and Stevie climbed the twisted staircase to Emma's room. The girl was still in her pyjamas, lying on her bed propped up on her elbows and engrossed in sketching something. She wasn't aware of Stevie's presence until the stereo was switched off.

'Oh, hi,' Emma said, looking up from her drawing.

'I didn't know you were into heavy metal,' Stevie said.

The girl shrugged. 'Sometimes, in some moods.'

'Then it sounds like you must be very angry.'

Emma returned to her sketching. 'What are you doing here?' she said, keeping her eyes on her work.

Stevie sank onto the edge of the bed. 'I'm afraid we've come to arrest your father.'

At last she seemed to have the girl's attention. The pale face flushed, the pencil snapped on the paper. 'Why?' she demanded.

'We think he's responsible for two fatal shootings.' Somehow, a shooting sounded so much softer than murder.

Emma spun herself into a sitting position. Light from the window glinted on her glasses, making them look like windows with the shutters down.

Stevie looked at the drawings; images of gargoyles and pointy-tongued dragons. When Emma saw she was looking at them, she scraped them up, screwed them into a ball and threw them at her.

'You're wrong, you're wrong!' Emma shouted. Then she sprang to her feet, grabbed a photo from the desk and held it out to Stevie with both hands. It was the much younger Breightling with the African children. 'Look at this, my father's a doctor, he doesn't kill people, he helps people!' Then she burst into tears.

Stevie took the photo and put it back on the desk and attempted to comfort the girl. She clasped her thin shoulders and searched the small anguished face. 'Emma, take some deep breaths. You are going to have to tell someone what you know about the death of Miro Kusak. It's the only thing that might help your father now.'

Wayne peered around the door. 'You ready?' He was clearly bursting with something he wanted to tell her.

'No, not yet,' she said. She went out into the passageway with him.

'He's broken down,' Wayne whispered. 'Said he killed Zhang Li in self defence. He's coming with me to Central to make a full confession. He's just getting changed.'

Stevie cocked a surprised eyebrow. 'That didn't take long.'

'Well, he's no Aidan Stoppard, is he?'

'What about Kusak?'

'Said he's never heard of him.'

'Where's the mother?'

'Not here.'

Stevie felt her anger flare. 'For God's sake, that woman is too much. Is she just oblivious to everything that's going on around her? I'm looking forward to a word with her ... wilful neglect, what do you reckon? Can we charge her with that?'

Wayne raised an eyebrow. 'Save it Stevie, ranting at her isn't going to do any good. Breightling took her to the hospital first thing this morning; apparently she OD'd on sedatives last night. She's done it before, he says, when he brought up the D word with her. Seems she knows just the right amount of pills to take to avoid the nasty side effects.'

Maybe this was part of the reason Breightling stayed around, Stevie thought, the old leave-me-and-I'll-kill-myself-trick. She put her head back through the bedroom door and told Emma to get dressed as Wayne headed off to hurry up Breightling.

Wayne was right, Stevie thought as she slumped against the wall of the mezzanine landing. Maybe it was just as well Miranda wasn't here right now. Dishing it up to Miranda might make her feel better, but in the long term it would only make communication with the woman more difficult than it was already. And wilful neglect on top of the possession charges might make the authorities question Miranda's suitability to keep her child. While the woman was no paradigm of motherhood, she was probably better than no mother at all.

She went back into Emma's room. 'Wash your face Emma, you're coming with me to Central.' It was time for some answers.

'Are you okay?' she asked as they headed to the front counter at Central.

Emma shrugged. 'When are they letting Mum out of hospital?'

'Later this afternoon, hopefully.'

'Can I stay at your place tonight, just in case she can't come home?'

Good God no, Stevie thought, and fill Izzy's head with those weird stories? She shook her head and squeezed the girl's arm. 'I'm sorry, hon, it wouldn't be appropriate. You have an aunt in

Westminster, don't you? I can give her a ring, just in case. Do you have her number?

Emma heaved a heavy sigh. 'No, we hardly ever see her.'

Stevie was leaning across to ask the desk sergeant for the phone book when she overheard a well-dressed middle-aged woman ask for Sammy Nguyen's paperwork which had been left there for her to collect. Stevie gathered from the conversation that this woman with the kind, grandmotherly face was Mrs Jenkins, Sammy's case officer from child welfare.

Seizing the opportunity to get the interview with Emma started as quickly as possible, Stevie introduced herself to Mrs Jenkins. The social worker said she would be pleased to sit in on Emma's interview.

'I seem to be getting quite good at this,' she said, smiling at Emma as she pulled up a chair at the interview room table. She placed the manila file on the table in front of her and removed some unused pages, writing Emma's name at the head of the top sheet. Emma slumped next to the woman, her chin in her hands, her dark hair spilling like a veil over her face.

'Come on now dear, get your hair from your eyes and sit up straight,' Mrs Jenkins said.

Emma did as instructed. Stevie decided she liked this woman. She switched the tape on, stated the time and the names of those present.

'Emma,' she said. 'Last night you told me you'd done a bad thing, but you wouldn't tell me anything else about it. Was it something to do with Miro Kusak, the man who killed your friend Bianca? You see, your father has admitted to killing a man with his gun and it turns out that it was the same gun that was used to kill Mr Kusak. Did you tell your father about him, Emma? Did you tell him what Miro Kusak had done to your friend? Did you and your father go to the lookout and kill him together?'

Emma took her glasses off and shook her head wildly, her hair once more falling over her face. But when she spoke it was in an even and unemotional tone. 'My dad had nothing to do with Miro Kusak's murder. I took my dad's gun from the safe and I gave it to someone else. You're right, I planned it, but not with my father.'

Stevie glanced at the social worker. The woman had her eyes fixed on Sammy Nguyen's file in front of her. Perhaps she was beginning to regret volunteering for the job. It wasn't every day one became involved with a child accused of murder.

'Emma, who did you give the gun to?' she asked.

Emma bit at her bottom lip.

'Who did you give it to?'

'Bianca's dad, Mr Bennett. Nick Bennett.'

But Stella said she hadn't seen Bianca's father since the conception! Stevie's mind filled with questions, but she forced herself to let the girl continue without interruption.

'He was very angry about Bianca's death. He'd been having sex with her you know. In secret. He said he'd kill her if she told anyone, even her mum. But she told me. He saw her as his property, you see — he could have sex with her, but no one else could.'

The social worker squirmed in her seat. Stevie thought her discomfort was probably less about what was said, than *how* it was said. Emma's matter of fact tone even had Stevie suppressing a shiver.

'I wanted to kill Kusak when he killed Bianca, but I knew I couldn't do it on my own, so I got Mr Bennett to do it for me.'

'How did you manage to contact him?'

'Bianca told me. We were going to write a story about him, just pretend, you know, but I still like to get the details right. He lives in a scungy block of flats in Mosman Park. He's been to jail where he learned IT stuff and he's fully into computers.

He has the words love and hate tattooed on his knuckles, they look gross. Bianca gave me his email address and his phone number because we were going to write a story about stalking him and getting revenge — we called him Count Luvanhate.' The memory caused a brief smile to flick across Emma's face. 'I also had all Daniel's details — Daniel is Miro Kusak — because Bianca forwarded me his emails too, including one with his mobile number. I just called Kusak and arranged to meet him in Shenton Park, just like Bianca did. It was easy.'

It must have been when Kusak was on the run from the police, Stevie thought. Would the man have taken such a risk?

Emma seemed to sense Stevie's incredulity. 'I think he couldn't believe his luck, having another girl so soon after the last one.' She giggled, and the sound sent an icy tingle up Stevie's back. Mrs Jenkins looked across at her, wide eyed.

Emma seemed to have no idea of the effect she was having and went on. 'I said I was a friend of Bianca's and that we had something to discuss. He thought I was stupid enough to come alone and try and blackmail him, because that's what I told him. But you know about creeps like him, they can't control themselves once they get horny. I wore a short skirt and a tight top, not my usual stuff.

'I counted on him thinking he had nothing to lose. Neither did I, I knew Mr Bennett would look out for me.' She looked up at Stevie. 'Don't think I was stupid. I knew he probably wanted me for himself, anyway. But I decided I'd sort that problem out later. I just felt that I had to at least try and do something to avenge Bianca, I couldn't let that creep get away with it.' Emma flicked the hair from her face. 'I got into his car and he tied me up and put me in the back. I was a bit scared so it wasn't much of an act and I can cry on demand anyway —' Emma broke off abruptly, for the first time she looked uncomfortable, directing a sheepish look at Stevie from under her dark fringe.

'Go on,' Stevie prompted.

'It must have seemed quite realistic to him. He drove to Mundaring with Bianca's dad following behind. It was so easy; Mr Bennett shot him at the lookout with my dad's gun. He wanted to shoot the dog too, but I wouldn't let him. It was such a beautiful dog …'

On that unnerving note Stevie turned the tape off. She looked towards Mrs Jenkins, whose florid complexion had turned pasty white. They needed a break. Stevie also needed to organise an urgent APB for Nick Bennett and summon Stella Webster to Central — loath as she was, she'd charge her with obstruction if she had to.

'I'll be back soon,' Stevie said as she excused herself. As she was leaving the room she heard Mrs Jenkins ask Emma if she wanted anything from the vending machine.

'A coke please, if that's okay,' Emma replied politely.

'Stay where you are then dear, I'll get it,' Mrs Jenkins said. As she passed Stevie in the corridor she whispered, 'I think I'm getting too old for this job. I don't understand kids anymore.'

That makes two of us, Stevie thought.

Tuesday

36

Excerpt from chat transcript 271206
HARUM SCARUM: And what do you want to call the evil count who hurts the princess?
BETTYBO: Umm ... count luvanhate??
HARUM SCARUM: Katy Enigma will help the princess. The count will pay for what he did to her.

'What did they do with the gun?' Monty asked the next day as he sat up in the hospital bed, picking at one of his peeling ECG leads.

Stevie pulled his hand away and kept hold of it. 'She said Bennett threw it in the weir.'

'Do you believe that? The weir was dragged and nothing except Bianca's laptop was found.'

'No I don't believe her. Wayne's kid saw her the other night, fishing around in the garden pond. I've ordered another search at the Breightlings' — it's happening as we speak, concentrating on the pond this time.'

'And what's the story with Bianca's dad?'

'I think I finally got the truth out of Stella. She pretty much confirmed what Emma told us. Bennett has a history of violence and drug abuse. He's been in and out of jail over the years for assault and armed robbery. He's been back in Stella's life this last year or so, traced her through the Internet, and has been putting her through hell since. He's put her into hospital at least once. Bianca also mentioned it in one of her emails to Emma.'

'So he's the man we saw on the stairs, the same guy who hassled Stella in the park?'

'Apparently.'

'Then why did Stella tell us she hadn't seem him since Bianca's conception?'

'She said she was terrified of him and also ashamed of the situation she'd found herself stuck in. She didn't want to admit that she'd failed so badly in her duty of care to Bianca — she knew about the abuse apparently'

'But why the hell didn't she do something about it?' Monty exclaimed. 'I just don't understand people like this!'

'Oh, come on, she's a victim too ...' Stevie stopped herself before an argument developed, knowing it wouldn't do his blood pressure any good. She wondered how long she'd have to tiptoe around him like this. It wouldn't alter her feelings for him, but nor would it lessen the desire she sometimes had to nail him to the floor.

'You're turning into an insensitive, grumpy old man,' she said.

'I've always been an insensitive, grumpy old man.'

She leaned across the bed and kissed him on the lips. When she pulled back she said, 'We brought Nick Bennett in last night. He's denying everything, of course, says he's never heard of anyone called Emma Breightling.'

'Alibi?'

'He said he was visited at home by a mate the night Kusak was murdered, but we can't get hold of the guy. He's a cray fisherman and at sea at the moment. But the piece of torn fabric I found at the scene looks like a match to a shirt we found bundled up at the back of his wardrobe. It should be enough to hold him until we can get hold of his mate.'

'How's the Breightling girl?'

Stevie looked down at their entwined hands. 'I don't know, Donna's been talking to her but she won't tell me anything.'

'True victims feel remorse, guilt — does Emma?'

Stevie's eyes strayed to the heart monitor. Guilt; she was glad she didn't have a machine attached to her emotions at this moment.

'She's worried about going to prison.'

'A child under fourteen is deemed not to have committed an offence unless she was aware she was doing something wrong,' Monty said. 'In other words she needs to know it's an offence to kill someone. That she *didn't* know will be up to her defence lawyer to prove, but they shouldn't have much trouble. You can see where everyone's sympathies will lie.' Monty leaned back against the pillows; he looked exhausted. 'Her father locked up for manslaughter, mutilation of a corpse and conspiring to cover up a crime; her godfather with a myriad of paedophilia charges plus importation of cocaine —'

'For personal use only, of course,' Stevie interrupted.

'— secreted in his Mexican statues. And cooking the agency books — a nice pinch of white collar financial crime to throw into the pot.' Monty scratched his chin and gave a thin laugh. 'Imagine Breightling and Stoppard in the same cell, there'd be some fireworks.'

'I know whose corner I'd be in. But one thing I don't understand about all this is how a man like Breightling could change so much. He once had a deep social conscience and a terrific reputation. What happened to all that?'

Monty shrugged. 'Lust? Infatuation?'

'He was middle aged, lonely and rich when he met Miranda. He'd devoted his entire adult life to his career. He must have been smitten by her, so much that he was unable to detach even when he discovered what she was really like. I suppose when she had Emma, he found himself cemented in even more firmly. Miranda and Stoppard worked a pretty slick operation. They were milking Breightling for everything he had, then they were going to take off together. Or so Miranda believed — she's admitted that much by the way.'

'It sounds to me like Stoppard was using Miranda as much as he was Breightling. Dragging it out for fifteen years …'

'I think that's because Stoppard was insanely jealous of Breightling,' said Stevie. 'For him it was more than just a scam, it was personal. Breightling stood for everything Stoppard could never be — a respected citizen from an established, wealthy family. He played it out as long as he could to cause as much pain as possible. He's talking now by the way. Claims Emma tried to seduce him that night she ran away. He says she stood on the mezzanine after Miranda had gone to bed, wearing very little, and lured him into her room.'

Monty collapsed back on his pillows and groaned. 'That sounds like a familiar line — *She wanted it your honour, honest she did.*'

'Keep calm, your blood pressure will only shoot up again.' Both of them turned their eyes to the monitor by the bed. 'Try and have a sleep, I'll stay a bit longer,' Stevie said gently.

Monty closed his eyes and soon his chest was rising and falling in time with the bleeping machine. Stevie's mind went back to something Emma had said to her yesterday when they were finishing up the interview.

'I love my parents, even my mother; kind of, but you know, I really don't like them. I feel sorry for Christopher, he's weak and greedy for money. I don't think he'll cope very well in prison. I even feel sorry for Miranda, she's a mess, she'll never get over the social stigma; Tall Poppies will have to close. They'll probably divorce and when Christopher's released I'll end up being shuffled between

them like Izzy is between you and Mr McGuire.'

Stevie squeezed Monty's hand and whispered. 'No, it won't be like that, Monty, I promise.'

Her phone buzzed with a text. It woke Monty and he jerked awake.

Stevie fumbled for the off button and looked guiltily around for a nurse. She shouldn't have her mobile on in here.

'Better read it,' Monty said, his voice raspy with sleep. Stevie read the SMS from Tash aloud:

Cant get shit to stick. Bennett insists piece of shirt planted, cant hold him any longer, Emmas word against his. Released on police bail.

'I can't think, I can't eat, I can't read, and I definitely cannot face Tall Poppies this afternoon,' Emma's mother told her. 'I'm going out for some retail therapy before your father's credit card gets cancelled.'

The fusillade of Miranda's heels echoed around the empty marble hall long after the lacquer door was slammed.

Emma Breightling performed a little victory dance. Then she took the cordless phone from the kitchen bench and punched in the well-remembered number. The phone was picked up after only a few rings.

'It's me, Stella, guess what?' Emma said, unable to hold her excitement back. 'We did it. We got away with it!'

'They've got Nick?' Stella sounded incredulous. 'They believed you?'

'Yeah, they arrested him last night. I think what you told the cops really helped too. They're going to get him for all those things he did to you and Bianca, and for killing Miro Kusak.'

Stella let out a long sigh. 'They'll probably want to talk to me again.'

'It'll all work out, don't worry about it. You had your arm in a cast, remember — how could you possibly kill a man when you had a broken arm?'

'It was my left arm, love, I'm right-handed and I drive an automatic car.'

'They won't get past the broken arm Stella, honestly, they think you're incapable and pathetic.'

There was silence from the other end of the phone; Emma wondered if she'd overdone it.

'Maybe I am,' Stella said softly.

'We're weak on our own, but together we can do anything.' That was something she had written as Katy Enigma; it was funny, but sometimes she felt as if Katy Enigma was actually living inside her body, talking to her.

Emma could sense that Stella was sinking further into apathy and searched for something to buck her up again. 'They found that piece of shirt I put on the bush, the one you tore when you and Nick had that fight. There's no way he can get out of it. And he has no alibi. And Thursday was just so the right night to do it — Nick was always home then, watching his favourite crap reality show. The police just have to charge him.'

Stella made little a whimpering sound down the phone. 'Bianca and me always knew we were safe on Thursday nights.' Her voice sounded even weaker than usual, and distant, as if she was talking from overseas.

'Where are you?' Emma asked.

'I'm in the car, halfway to Geraldton, just going for a short break. I couldn't bear it in Perth any longer. I hate the idea of you facing all this alone, but I promise I'll call when I get back. Are you all right?'

'Yeah, well, they've been giving me the third degree; lot's of counselling and stuff. I think everyone just feels sorry for me. There's not much they can do. You see I'm too young to understand the seriousness of my offence.' Emma smiled so wide she could feel the pressure of her braces against her lips.

But her satisfaction was short lived. Someone was thumping on the front door. 'Hang on Stella, someone's here, I'd better check. It's probably just the police come to collect some of Dad's things,' she said as she walked down the hall to the door with the phone still clamped to her ear.

Through the phone, Stella heard the door creak open followed by the menacing rumble of an angry voice. Her heart almost stopped beating. It was Nick's voice.

'You bitch, you and Stella, bitches, the pair of you — YOU SET ME UP!'

Stella heard the smashing of glass then the crunch of the phone falling to the floor.

And then the screaming started.

Stella's frantic call came through on Stevie's mobile when she and Tash were in the operations room, bemoaning how Nick had slipped through the system.

Stevie ran with galloping heart to the car park, the phone clamped to her ear and Tash hurrying at her heels. Stella Webster was hysterical, her story garbled and confused. But there was no confusion about her description of what she'd heard going on in the Breightling house over the phone. The screams of Emma being mutilated and murdered by Nick Bennett. Stevie reassured Stella as best she could and told her to pull over on the roadside and wait for assistance. Then she hung up.

'How the hell did Bennett find Emma?' Tash asked, jumping into the Commodore.

'You and Barry questioned him, you tell me.'

Tash thought for a moment. 'Oh shit.'

'You mentioned her name, didn't you? All he needed to do was check the phone book.'

'We had to ask him if he knew her, didn't we? How were we to know he was going to be let out on a stupid technicality?'

There was no point in pursuing this further, what was done was done. Bickering between themselves was not going to get them any faster to Emma. Tash phoned for an ambulance and police back up to meet them at the Breightling house, then called the Geraldton police to meet up with Stella.

'We're never going to make it,' she said as Stevie ran a red light on Guildford Road.

The magnetic light on the car roof flashed, the siren wailed. Stevie's knuckles were white on the steering wheel. 'Never say never Tash, Emma's a resourceful kid.'

They screamed to a halt outside the house. Stevie took the front and Tash dashed around the back. The lacquer door hung open and Stevie stepped into the hallway, broken glass crunching under her feet. A picture had been pulled from the wall and used as a weapon it seemed, its frame smashed and dangling from the torn canvas. She followed a trail of blood to the family area, where she found yet more blood, sprayed across the kitchen bench tops and dripping down the walls.

The broken balustrade lay in a jumbled heap at the bottom of the stairs. Dust from the debris was still rising like smoke and wafted in the shafts of light from the skylight. Stevie saw Tash cautiously making her way through the French doors, leaving them open behind her. The smell of damp soil, and the sound of gurgling water, brought some much-needed freshness to the room.

Suddenly Tash stopped dead in her tracks; her hand flew to her mouth. Stevie edged closer and saw him too, heard the deep sucking sounds coming from the man's body. Nick Bennett gave one last writhe and went slack, becoming one with the hideous *objet d'art* on which he was impaled.

Stevie was the first to recover her senses. 'Tash, hurry that ambulance up,' she ordered, stepping over the tangle of balustrades to where Emma lay curled like an embryo with hands over her ears. Her eyes were wide and staring and she emitted a low-pitched keening when she saw Stevie.

'Emma, are you hurt?' Stevie gently patted the child down. Finding no sign of injury she eased her to her feet and guided her to the front lounge room, as far away from the carnage as she could get.

Emma shook her head as if coming out of a trance. Finding her voice she said, 'I hit him over the head with the picture when he came at me and then he chased me up the stairs. The banister, he fell through the banister when he was trying to catch me. Stevie, I was scared …'

Emma curled into her as far as she could go. Stevie held her tight and tried to calm the child's violent shivering.

She stroked her hair and patted her back as tears soaked through her shirt. My God, Emma, she thought, what on earth is going to become of you?

Some days later

37

Monty's flight was finally called: *QF 71 to London, boarding now.* Sitting around a table in the airport cafe, none of them made an effort to move. Izzy sat on her father's knee, burrowing into him. In her hand she clutched a box she'd made from ice cream sticks and decorated with shells; her present to her Scottish Grandma.

Stevie sat with her arm linked through Monty's, trying to absorb as much of him as she could, while she could.

'The queue's so long, there's no point joining it just yet,' he said.

Stevie watched a young couple kissing and hugging. A moment later the woman was sucked through the departure door. Stevie's eyes filled and she looked away.

'Boarding pass, passport, money, medication, nicotine gum?' she asked, battling to keep her voice steady.

He nodded. 'You got yours too?'

She put on a brave smile and produced a crumpled packet of Nicorettes from her jeans pocket. 'Bet you crack first,' she tried for some light heartedness.

He kicked the small holdall at his feet. 'I'd better see if I can fit this in too,' he said to Izzy. Still holding her to him, he took the decorative box with one hand and slid it into one of the bag's compartments.

Izzy's face crumpled, she stuck her thumb in her mouth and

buried her head in his chest. 'I don't want you to go, Dad!'

'It's not for long Izz, he'll soon be back.' Stevie regarded Monty in her peripheral vision; saw him briefly close his eyes, his throat moving as he swallowed.

'Dad's been sick: he just needs to go back to his mum for a while and have a rest. You like being with me when you're sick, don't you?'

'But when will you be back?' Izzy asked him.

'In about three weeks, the time will whiz by.'

Izzy seemed to take comfort from this. The thumb popped from her mouth. The toys in the window of one of the duty free shops seemed to beckon.

'Can I go over there?' she pointed.

'Just as long as you stay where I can see you,' Stevie said.

'How's Natasha?' Monty asked, his eyes fixed on their daughter as she rummaged through the items in a specials basket outside the shop.

'Still talking to me, which is a surprise seeing as I've recommended that she undertake some retraining at the academy — a course on questioning suspects.'

Monty raised his eyebrows — impressed that she was *finally* taking her seniority seriously perhaps? Whatever his thoughts, she was glad he didn't express them.

'And when she's done the course she's being transferred — at her own request I might add.'

Stevie didn't think his eyebrows could go any higher.

'Why would she do that, I wonder?' he asked.

Stevie hesitated, smiled. 'The same reason I transferred from the SCS. A relationship with the boss.'

It took a moment to sink in. He shook his head in disbelief. 'Dolly? Hayward? You've got to be kidding. Dolly was the …'

'Yes, the mystery pal she went to see after Mrs Kusak.'

'Jesus, no wonder she didn't want that name bandied around.'

The final call for Monty's flight was announced. Only a handful of people were left at the departure gate. Izzy and Stevie trailed behind him to the desk. The security guard examined his boarding pass then Monty stepped aside to cuddle Izzy. 'Be good and help Mum, she's going to be busier than ever now she's been promoted.'

It was Stevie's turn. Tears cooled her cheeks and burned her throat when he hugged her. 'We both need to do some serious thinking. It's for the best, you know it is,' he whispered in her ear.

He pulled back, wiped a tear from her cheek with his thumb and made his way down the long tunnel.

He didn't look back.

With Izzy a dead weight in her arms, the walk back to the car felt as if she was ploughing through waist deep mud. The pressure of Izzy's leg made the ring on Stevie's finger swivel, the stone dig into the flesh. She paused to readjust it, then gave a 'mother's hitch', hoisting Izzy further up her hip.

Mother and daughter.

Her thoughts strayed to Stella Webster.

When news came through to the ops room of Stella's confession, it was to the accompaniment of loud cheering. Everyone in the unit rejoiced, it seemed, that the underdog had bitten back.

In her statement Stella said after Bianca's body was found, Emma had telephoned her to tell her what she knew about Miro Kusak and 'Daniel'. It was then that she'd planned Kusak's murder. Stella maintained that Emma had been no more than her accomplice and the supplier of the gun.

It seemed very likely that once news broke about cracking the paedophile ring, public opinion would ensure a minimal sentence for the bereaved mother. And Emma's age meant that her identity could not be revealed — Stevie supposed she should be grateful for small mercies.

Her phone rang as she was searching for change for the ticket machine. Izzy was grizzling and she could hardly hear Tash's voice through the racket. Something about the pub and a celebration. She finally hushed Izzy up by getting her to search through her purse for change as Tash prattled on. 'Come on, you have to join us. Dolly's coming and we have a lot to celebrate. Even Barry's being bearable, probably knows I'd flatten him ... Stevie ... Did Monty get off okay? ... Stevie, are you there ... can you hear me? ... Are you all right?'

'Sorry Tash, reception's really bad, can't hear a thing, I'll ring you back.'

Stevie closed her eyes for a moment, then lifted Izzy up so she could put the coins in the slot and grab the ticket as it was spat out. She had finally stopped crying.

'What would you like to do now, Izz?' Stevie asked as she lowered her daughter to the ground.

Izzy sniffed. 'I want to go home and watch a movie with you. I need my favourite things.'

The Sound of Music? Jeez, must be about the twentieth time this month. 'That's the best idea I've heard all week,' Stevie said.

* * *

Hitler's bunker seemed strange and empty without Christopher, without Aidan Stoppard, without the banister rails. The police had taken away the gruesome artpiece which she'd always hated, and organised cleaners to mop up the blood. A stranger would never have known what had happened here. The real estate agent had hammered the sign outside the front and soon she would be starting school over east, paid for by a trust fund Christopher had set up years ago for her. It was the only money he hadn't lost to Aidan Stoppard.

Miranda was asleep. Again. Emma wondered when she'd run out of GPs to get tranquillisers from, wondered how she'd cope in the little unit in Kingsley that she'd soon be moving to.

Stevie hadn't believed what she'd said about throwing the gun in the weir. They'd found it in the garden pond. It was embarrassing to have been caught out in another lie.

But at least they hadn't closed down her website.

Emma sat at her desk, ran her fingers through her dark hair and sighed — so much to do and so many people to email before morning came.

Katy Enigma was always of the belief that when one door closed, another one opened. The Monster had taken away her magic powers and they had taken away her secret weapon. They had also closed down her HQ where the dragon lived and the water lilies bloomed.

But no one could take away her words.

She packed her father's abandoned laptop and a few belongings into her backpack — it could hold a lot more stuff now that it wasn't weighed down with the jet engine — and she stepped with it into the black night. She didn't know the answers she sought, she didn't yet know the questions, or even the exact nature of her quest. All she knew as she stood there on the highway with her thumb poking out, feeling the hot push of the trucks' exhaust fumes in her face, was that what she was doing felt so right ...

Acknowledgements

Many thanks to the following for their invaluable technical advice and support: Janet Blagg, my editor who knows all the right buttons to press; Constable Elliot Cottrill and Inspector Tom Clay for their help with police procedure; Kellie Potter, computer whiz extraordinaire; Christine Nagel, Trish O'Neil and Carole Sutton for tips and ideas.

First published 2008 by
FREMANTLE ARTS CENTRE PRESS
25 Quarry Street, Fremantle
(PO Box 158, North Fremantle 6159)
Western Australia.
www.fremantlepress.com.au

Copyright © Felicity Young, 2008.

This book is copyright. Apart from any fair dealing for the purpose of private study, research, criticism or review, as permitted under the Copyright Act, no part may be reproduced by any process without written permission. Enquiries should be made to the publisher.

Consultant Editor Janet Blagg
Cover Designer Tracey Gibbs
Printed by Everbest Printing Company, China.

National Library of Australia
Cataloguing-in-publication data

Young, Felicity.
Harum scarum.

ISBN 9781921361104 (pbk.).

1. Murder - Investigation — Western Australia — Perth — Fiction. 2. Women detectives — Western Australia — Perth — Fiction. I. Title.

A823.4